"We need to talk, Nick said.

"Not over the phone, though. Can you come into town? I don't feel right about leaving Trisha alone, but I have to see you."

"I'm sorry, Nick. I'm not ready to talk yet. There are too many things I have to figure out first."

"Like whether or not you're leaving Oak Ridge?" he asked, more sharply than he intended. "Crystal, you can't drop something like that in my lap and then walk out—it's not fair. This is something that affects both of us."

"No, it doesn't, Nick. It's my life and I have to decide what's best for me."

"And what about me? Don't I count for anything?"

Crystal sank onto the sofa, trying not to cry. "You mean everything to me, Nick," she said softly. "That's the problem."

ABOUT THE AUTHOR

Connie Bennett, who is unafraid of tackling
hard-hitting issues in her books—alcoholism in
Believe in Me—is fast becoming a Superromance
reader favorite. Connie lives in Missouri and also
writes historical romances.

Books by Connie Bennett

HARLEQUIN SUPERROMANCE

Don't miss any of our special offers. Write to us at the
following address for information on our newest releases.

Harlequin Reader Service
P.O. Box 1397, Buffalo, NY 14240
Canadian address: P.O. Box 603,
Fort Erie, Ont. L2A 5X3

Believe in Me

CONNIE BENNETT

Harlequin Books

TORONTO • NEW YORK • LONDON
AMSTERDAM • PARIS • SYDNEY • HAMBURG
STOCKHOLM • ATHENS • TOKYO • MILAN

Published January 1991

ISBN 0-373-70436-4

BELIEVE IN ME

CHAPTER ONE

"FOR HE'S a jolly good felloooow, that nobody can deny!" The singing was painfully off-key, and the hurrahs and catcalls that followed the final verse were deafening. People stomped and cheered, making the rafters of the Lakeside Bar and Grill tremble.

Standing at the back of the noisy room, Crystal Elliot was applauding and cheering with the rest of her friends, because Dan Gatlin, who was retiring from the Forest Service after forty years, deserved each and every hurrah. In fact, if Crystal had her way, Ranger Dan would be canonized. He was a loyal public servant, a crusading defender of the Osage National Forest, a wonderful boss, and—most importantly—the only real father Crystal had ever known. It was going to be difficult for her to watch Dan and his wife, Naomi, leave Oak Ridge when they headed for the warm, dry climate of Arizona in a few weeks.

"Speech! Speech! Give us a speech, Dan!" someone shouted.

"Yeah, you're good at speeches!" another reveler yelled, causing the crowd to laugh uproariously.

Someone dragged a chair away from a nearby table and urged the retiring forest ranger onto it so that he towered over the crowd. "All right, all right," he said, waving for everyone to quiet down. "If it's a speech you want, it's a speech you'll get."

"Keep it short!" Marty Mancusso shouted from the back of the room.

"I just can't please everybody, can I?" Dan asked over the resulting laughter. When it died away, Ranger Gatlin took a long, sentimental look at his friends and colleagues. His glance settled on Crystal for a moment, and he gave her a wink before moving his gaze on to the attractive middle-aged woman standing next to her.

"Some party, huh, Naomi?" he asked his wife.

She smiled at him, her pale blue eyes still twinkling with love and respect after forty-one years of marriage. "Enjoy it while you can," she called back. "There's a lot of packing to be done at home."

"How well I know," he muttered, turning his gaze to the crowd. "It's going to be hard to leave," he admitted sadly.

"Thirty years ago when the Service transferred me to this district of the Osage, you folks took Naomi and me in. You made us part of the community, made us feel at home. Some of us have had our differences over the years, but we've survived it all, and I think we're better for it. I *know* the Oak Ridge district of the Osage National Forest is better—all because you people took an active interest in protecting your most valuable resource."

That brought a round of applause and a few whistles as everyone patted themselves on the back for being such good citizens, but Crystal reflected wryly that if it hadn't been for Dan Gatlin, the people of Newton County wouldn't even have known the Osage existed. Almost single-handedly, Dan had raised the consciousness of the public so that every man, woman and child for fifty miles in any direction knew that there were a hundred thousand acres of magnificent forest land sitting virtually in their backyards. He'd shown them that the forest was theirs to use—and to take care of.

"You all know I'm pretty protective of the forest that's been entrusted to me all these years," Dan continued when the applause died down. "Being a district ranger is a job I've taken very seriously. The Osage has been my life. I guess the only thing that's going to make leaving it easier to bear is that I know that the forest, its wildlife, and its recreation facilities are passing into the hands of someone more than capable of handling the job."

He grinned and looked toward the back of the room. "I know she's capable, because I taught her just about everything she knows. And if it's okay with you, folks, I'd like to make this party more than just a commemoration of my retirement—I'd like to make it a celebration, too."

"Oh, no," Crystal murmured under her breath when she realized where Dan was leading. She resisted the urge to run for the door; the announcement he was about to make was premature, at best. Crystal shook her head vigorously, trying to get him to quit while he was ahead, but Dan Gatlin was unstoppable.

"This is as good a time as any to let everybody know that Crystal Elliot has been promoted—she's going to be your new district ranger once I'm gone!"

The crowd exploded again, and everyone turned, looking for the newly appointed district ranger. Someone shouted "Speech, speech," and Crystal wished the floor would open up and swallow her whole. She hated being in the spotlight, hated attention of any kind. There had been so much attention when she was a girl, and all of it negative. To compensate, she'd developed a tough, protective inner shell, and over that was layered a bright, breezy personality that seemed to put everyone at ease.

It was her way of blending in, of being one of the guys so that she wouldn't call undue attention to herself.

Sometimes that defense strategy backfired, though. Like now. Dan was shifting the focus of the crowd to her, and the worst part of it was, the attention was unwarranted because her official appointment hadn't come through. Dan had recommended her for the job and the district supervisor had said it was in the bag, but Crystal wasn't going to believe the promotion was for real until she had it on paper, in writing. Bitter experience had taught her that it didn't pay to get her hopes up.

But the crowd was calling for her to make a speech, and Dan was beckoning her toward him. Crystal smiled and shook her head, declining the invitation, but Naomi Gatlin laid a hand on her arm.

"Go on, honey, talk to them," the older woman insisted. "You deserve the limelight."

"But, Mom, the job's not mine yet," Crystal argued, bending low so that her foster mother could hear her.

Naomi favored her with a forbearing smile. "That's your problem, Crystal—you don't have enough faith in yourself."

Crystal laughed. "I've got plenty of faith in myself, Mom. It's the rest of the world I'm not too sure of."

"Don't be silly. Now, go on up there."

"Speech!"

"But—"

"Come on, Legs! Give us a speech!"

Crystal cringed inwardly at the nickname that had followed her since high school. At the embarrassing height of six feet, the name was deserved, but she still hated it. "Don't call me Legs, Sparky!" she shouted good-naturedly, and was rewarded by a blush from the former classmate who hated the nickname Sparky as much as she hated Legs. Everyone else laughed and continued calling for her to join Dan at the front of the room by the bar, and there was simply no escape. Marty Mancusso gave her a gentle nudge, and the crowd did the rest. On a wave of renewed cheering, Crystal was herded toward the retiring ranger. A chair was shoved next to Dan's, and Crystal's tall, slender body was all but lifted onto the makeshift dais.

The added height made her feel terribly awkward, but out of long practice, Crystal made sure no one sensed her discomfort. She grinned at the people, most of whom she'd known all her life, and pretended that she was enjoying herself. In truth, though, it didn't take a lot of pretending. "I'm not as good at talking as Dan is," she began, sending a bright smile to the man who'd gotten her into this mess. "And the only speech I know begins with 'Four score and seven years ago . . .'"

Everyone laughed, as she'd hoped they would. "But I would like to tell Dan that he's going to be missed. We have a lot to thank him for." Her smile turned wistful. "Me, in particular. He's left some pretty big footprints in the Osage, and no one will ever be able to fill them." A knot of emotion clogged her throat as she recalled all the wonderful hours she'd spent at Dan's side in the forest. She had to stop for a second before she could finish. "And no one will ever be able to fill the space he's made in our hearts, either."

That brought another fervent round of applause, and when Crystal turned to Dan she saw that he was surprised by the sentiment she'd expressed.

Of course, it didn't surprise Dan that she *felt* it, only that she'd said it aloud. Crystal had been twelve years old when he and Naomi had taken her into their home. She'd been only one of a succession of foster children they'd had a hand in raising, but they had made Crystal their own. They had guided her, loved her, cheered her triumphs, and softened the blows of her defeats. Most of all, they had done their best to teach the frightened, emotionally battered child that there were people in the world she could trust and depend on.

The first twelve years of her life had been a nightmare, but with Dan and Naomi's love and her own incredible inner strength, Crystal had grown into a beautiful, giving woman filled with life and love. The scars she bore were still there, for those who knew where to look for them, but Dan was inordinately proud of what she had done with her life—especially since she was following in his footsteps. She was his daughter in every sense of the word that mattered, and it touched him that she would so openly acknowledge their special bond. Taking her hand, he pulled her into his arms for a great bear hug.

"If you make me cry, I'll kick you in the shins," she whispered in his ear. Her voice was light and teasing, but Dan knew she was almost half serious. Crying in public would mortify Crystal.

Gently she finally pulled away, but kept her hand firmly in Dan's. He squeezed hard, then looked out at the sea of friends he'd soon be leaving behind. "I thought this was supposed to be a party! Let's have a little music, dancing, and merrymaking, folks!"

That brought the biggest cheer of all. Someone slipped a quarter into the jukebox, and as Crystal and Dan stepped down from their chairs, Willie Nelson began serenading them. The crowd dispersed, some returning to their tables, some to the postage-stamp-size dance floor, and a few accompanied Dan and Crystal back to the table Naomi was holding for them.

"That was a lovely speech, Crystal," Naomi complimented her as they all sat.

"Short, but *very* sweet," Dan said.

"I ought to shoot you for putting me on the spot like that," Crystal said without rancor. "If this promotion doesn't come through, I'm going to be the laughing-stock of Newton County."

Dan patted her hand comfortingly. "Crystal, honey, if I didn't believe that promotion was a sure thing, I'd never have announced it. Clyde Chapman agreed with me that you're the very best person for the job. I've never known of an instance when Washington overrode a district supervisor's recommendation."

"Yeah, relax, Crystal," Rich Patterson said with a teasing grin. Rich was the Oak Ridge district's timber supervisor, but more than that, he was a good friend to both Crystal and Dan. "I'll be calling you boss before the week is out."

"Boss, huh?" Crystal considered the notion with a grin. "Tell me, Ranger Dan, should I be a beneficent despot, or a harsh, unyielding tyrant?"

"Do I get to vote on that?" Rich asked forlornly.

"No," Crystal told him flatly, and everybody laughed.

Chuckling, Dan said, "Just remember that you can catch more flies with honey than you can with vinegar, and you'll make a fine boss."

"*If* I get the job," she added, but the others, in unison, shouted, "The job is yours!"

"All right! All right!" she said, laughing as she held up her hands to ward off their vehemence. "The job is mine. I worked for it, I earned it. I deserve it. The job is mine."

"That's my girl."

"And if something goes wrong—" She started to add a cushioning disclaimer, but everyone at the table shouted her down.

"What could possibly go wrong?" Rich asked.

"That's right," Dan said. "What could possibly go wrong?"

Laughing at their optimism, Crystal ran one hand through her short black bangs, and finally allowed herself to start believing. Being a ranger in charge of her own forest was what she wanted more than anything else in the world. Maybe Naomi, Dan and Rich were right. She'd been promised the job; maybe it was time to put the past behind her and stop expecting the worst.

Raising a glass of club soda, she proposed a toast. "All right, everybody! You win. Here's to Crystal Elliot, the new district ranger of the Osage National Forest!"

"Here, here!" Rich said as four beer mugs clanked against her glass.

FROM THE WINDOW of his boss's office, Nick Hanford surveyed the Washington skyline for what he hoped would be the last time. The city was pretty, sometimes even inspiring, but on restless days like this one, Nick felt as though he would kill for the sight of a tree that didn't have a monument casting a shadow on it. Three years was just too long for a country boy to stay in the city.

It was also too long for a father to be away from his only child, as his recent trip to Kentucky had graphically illustrated. Two months ago he'd gone down to pick up his fourteen-year-old daughter to take her on a Christmas vacation, and the resulting chain of events had turned Nick Hanford inside out. It was for Trisha's sake more than his own that he wanted to get out of Washington as quickly as possible. He only hoped that his old friend, Rex Teirnan, head of the U.S. Forest Service, would agree to help him.

"Nick! Welcome home!" Rex said enthusiastically as he entered his office and closed the door behind him.

"I didn't think you'd be able to wrap things up and get back so quickly," the older man commented as they shook hands and took seats on opposite sides of his desk. "How did the hearing go?" he asked anxiously.

Nick's smile faded. "I'm sorry to say that it didn't go at all, Rex. My ex-wife's lawyer finagled another three-week extension out of the judge, so I still don't have a decision yet." *Or my daughter,* he thought glumly.

"That's too bad," Rex said sympathetically. He knew very well what his friend had been going through these last few months, and another delay wasn't going to help his state of mind. "You know you don't have to worry about the time off. Take whatever you need until this is settled."

"Thanks, Rex," Nick said with a weary smile. "But I'm afraid time off is the least of my worries. I'm going to have to ask a big favor of you."

"Ask away."

Nick took a deep breath, steeling himself because Rex wasn't going to like this one bit. "I need to transfer out of Washington and get back into the field as soon as possible."

"What!" Rex exclaimed. "This is a little sudden, isn't it?"

"No, Rex," he answered patiently. "I've been thinking about a transfer for some time, now, and this business with Trisha has just forced me to make a decision a little sooner than I might have otherwise. My lawyer and I agree that I'll have a better chance of getting custody if

I leave Washington. Not only that, it will be much better for Trisha."

Rex frowned and leaned back in his chair. "Why?"

Nick sighed and stood, moving restlessly toward the windows. "Trisha has lived in small towns all her life, and the few times she's visited me here she absolutely hated the city."

"You mean she's threatening that she won't come live with you if it means living in Washington?"

"No, nothing like that," he said, shaking his head. "Trisha's emotions are so bottled up that she refuses to express an opinion one way or the other."

"Then why do you want a transfer?"

"Leaving Marjorie is going to be very traumatic for Trisha. I think it might be easier for her to handle if I take her someplace a little closer to her mother," Nick explained, leaning against the windowsill, his long legs stretched out in front of him. He looked a great deal more casual than he felt. The thought of having his alcoholic ex-wife within a thousand miles of his daughter made him physically ill, but at the moment, Trisha's needs had to come first. "And it's not going to be easy for her to leave her school and her friends, either. Trisha is very shy, and bringing her to a big, unfamiliar city is only going to make it harder for her to adjust."

"She'll have just as many adjustment problems in a small town," Rex argued, but Nick shook his head and laughed shortly.

"Are you kidding? The problems aren't even comparable! I was thirty-five when I moved to the city, and I didn't think I'd ever adapt."

"But you did," Rex said with a broad gesture toward Nick that took in everything from his salon-styled hair to the tailored suit that fit his massive physique like a glove.

Three years ago Nick Hanford arrived in Washington wearing blue jeans and cowboy boots, looking very much like a combination cowboy-mountain man; rough, rugged, and all country at heart. At six foot seven, with a muscular build that was the envy of every man who saw him, Nick was still undeniably rugged looking, but he had adapted to city life so well that no one would ever accuse him of being "countrified" anymore. "Who says you can't make a silk purse out of a sow's ear?" he asked with a grin.

Nick chuckled. "Thanks for the assessment, Rex, but I didn't come here for a fashion commentary."

"I know," the older man said ruefully. "You're here to ask for a demotion from an important, high profile job in administration to a respectable, but definitely low-profile district ranger position. That's a major career setback, Nick."

"Not for me it isn't," he replied firmly, rising from the windowsill to return to the chair by Rex's desk. "This job was supposed to be temporary, remember? I'm a ranger at heart, and that's all I've ever wanted to be."

"But I need you here. You're performing an invaluable service for the Department of Agriculture," Rex argued.

"Wrong," Nick shot back. "Three years ago when you pulled me out of the field to head the new Wilderness Experience program I was invaluable. Now I'm redundant. The program is running smoothly, and with the administration's budget cuts there's very little room for growth. You don't need me anymore."

"That's not true," the department head told him.

"Yes, it is." Nick leaned forward in his chair. "Rex, I'm grateful to you for bringing me to Washington. It's given me insight into the workings of the department that

I would never have had, otherwise. But I'm a ranger, not a bureaucrat. I wasn't cut out for big-scale diplomacy, and I wasn't cut out for the city, either.''

"But you've adapted nicely to your captivity," Rex pointed out with a sly smile.

"Because I knew it was only temporary. That was our agreement. I was supposed to come to Washington, set up the program, then hightail it back to the woods where I belong. You do recall agreeing to those terms, don't you?''

"I remember, Nick," Rex said wearily, as though he'd regretted that promise a hundred times since then. "But once you were here and I saw how much good you could do, I hoped you'd stay."

Nick shook his head. "I'm sorry, Rex, but for my sake and Trisha's, I think it's time to move on." He paused for a moment, then asked, "Do you know why I took this job in the first place?''

Rex looked a little surprised. "Because it was a wonderful opportunity."

"No." Nick shook his head and stood, pacing uneasily toward the windows like a caged animal. Talking about problems and exposing his emotions wasn't something that came easily to him, but in this one instance he felt it was important to make Rex understand exactly what was going on inside his head. He could demand a transfer and his boss would have to comply, but Rex had done a lot for Nick over the years, and he deserved more than a simple ultimatum.

Staring sightlessly at the Washington skyline, he explained, "Rex, when you asked me to take this job, Marjorie and I had been divorced for less than a year, and I was still in a state of emotional shock because I hadn't been able to get custody of my daughter. Marjorie had taken Trisha back to Kentucky, and quite frankly, I was a mess. I'd failed as a husband and a father. I was rattling around all alone in a big old Colorado farmhouse, trying to figure out what deficiency in my character had driven my wife to the bottle. And the worst part was that I was worrying incessantly about what effect Marjorie's drinking was having on our daughter.''

He turned and looked at his boss. ''And then you came along with a glamorous job offer, and I snapped it up because I saw it as a way to escape my personal woes. I had never wanted to go into the administration end of the Service, but this was new and exciting. I thought that if I could bury myself in something challenging and succeed, I'd escape all those feelings of failure.''

Rex sighed deeply, touched by his friend's confession. ''I hope your three years here have proven to you that you're anything but a failure, Nick.''

He grinned. ''Don't worry, Rex. My ego is in good shape. Professionally, I'm proud of the work I've done with the Wilderness Experience, and personally, I realized a long time ago that Marjorie's drinking wasn't my fault. God knows I wasn't a perfect husband, but I didn't create her problems.'' His expression became serious. ''What I have done, though, is ignore Trisha for too long. I *thought* I was keeping in touch with her, but I wasn't. Not really. Trisha has become so good at hiding her emotions that I had no idea how bad things had gotten for her. But when I went to pick her up for our vacation and saw what . . . what Marjorie—''

Nick stopped abruptly, unable to say any more, overwhelmed by the rage that always swept through him every time he thought of what Marjorie had done to their sweet, shy daughter. He stared out at the Washington skyline, but what he was really seeing was his daughter's bruised, battered face. The image was burned into his memory.

Trisha had tried to claim that she'd hurt herself when she'd slipped on a patch of ice and fallen down the back porch stairs, but Nick had known better. With coaxing, she had finally admitted that Marjorie had been unhappy about Nick taking her away for Christmas. She had wanted Trisha to cancel the trip and stay home, and when Trisha had refused Marjorie had flown into a drunken rage and hit her daughter—not once, but several times, and not with her hand, but with a rolled up magazine.

Trisha had also tearfully admitted that where once her mother had gotten drunk only occasionally, now, she was rarely sober. What Nick hadn't been able to get Trisha to admit was that this wasn't the first time Marjorie had hurt her.

What should have been a wonderful father-daughter vacation had turned into a two-week nightmare in Kentucky as Nick began a battle for custody of his daughter. His first impulse had been to bring Trisha to Washington while he sued for custody, but the lawyer he had consulted strongly advised against that. He could take his daughter anywhere he wanted while he had her for vacation, but once his two weeks were up, Trisha would have to be returned to her mother. At best, Nick would have been accused of violating the divorce custody agreement; at worst, he could have been charged with kidnapping.

The lawyer had reported Marjorie for child abuse and petitioned the court for temporary custody until an investigation and hearing could be held, but that maneuver had only been partially successful. Marjorie's family had a lot of clout in western Kentucky, and the best Nick had been able to obtain was a temporary order placing Trisha in the custody of her maternal grandparents until the case could be resolved.

And then the delaying tactics had started. Unlike big city court systems, under which it could take years to get a case on the docket, getting a case before the judge in little Gilford County, Kentucky, was a fairly quick procedure. Unfortunately, Marjorie's high-powered lawyer had managed to obtain not one, but two postponements. Clearly they were hoping that if they could stall the process long enough, Nick would get fed up with flying back and forth between Kentucky and Washington.

Nick's lawyer wanted to use this delay to his client's advantage, though. A reassignment to one of the National Forest districts in the Midwest would provide two strong factors that might help them win the case. Not only would Nick be showing a concern for his daughter's state of mind by moving her to a small community rather than an unfamiliar, intimidating city, but he would also be displaying a commitment to allowing Trisha to maintain contact with her mother—something that was very important to his daughter, though Nick was having difficulty understanding why.

And unfortunately, Rex Teirnan was having difficulty understanding a few things, too. Or at least that was how it appeared to Nick until his friend joined him at the window. "I assume you want this transfer immediately," he said, resigned to the fact that he was about to lose a valuable administrator and a good friend.

Nick managed a smile and turned to him. "The sooner the better. I know it's asking a lot, but I'd like to be relocated by the time I go back to court next month."

"That's a tall order, Nick," Rex said with a shake of his head. "There's not a lot of turnover in the Service on the district level. It's going to take a while to get you back into one of the big forests."

Nick shook his head. This was one contingency he was fully prepared for. He had come straight from the airport to the office, but before he'd arranged for this appointment, he'd spent a few minutes at the computer. "I'm not looking for a glamour job, Rex. Every ranger district in the country has its own charm, and its own set of problems to be identified, addressed, and solved. As far as a job is concerned, that's all I'm looking for. I just want a home for Trisha—and for me." He grinned. "And I think I know just the place."

Rex rolled his eyes and returned to his chair. "I should have guessed that you already had something in mind. In all the time I've known you, never once have you come to a meeting without being fully prepared. Where is this new home you think you've found?" he asked, turning to his computer.

"The Oak Ridge district of the Osage," Nick replied. "Daniel Gatlin has already turned in his resignation, and will be leaving his post at the end of next week. According to the computer, no one has been assigned to replace him yet. It's the only immediate vacancy in the area I'm looking for, and I want it."

Rex punched the appropriate buttons to verify Nick's information. "You're right." He swiveled his chair and looked up at the man towering over him. "Are you sure this is what you want, Nick?"

"I'm positive. Oak Ridge is only a five or six hour drive from Gilford."

"But it's in Arkansas," Rex warned, as though that alone might be enough to dissuade him, but Nick only laughed.

"Rex, you've been in the city too long. Arkansas was admitted to the union quite some time ago, and it contains some of the most beautiful forest land in the country. Oak Ridge is right in the middle of the Ozarks—and I can't think of a better place for a country boy like me."

This time it was Rex's turn to laugh. "Well, if you're going to convince the folks in Oak Ridge that you're one of them, you'd better lose the suit and the Italian loafers, my friend."

Nick clapped him on the shoulder and chuckled. "Believe it or not, Rex, people in Arkansas wear suits and shoes, too. But if it'll make you feel any better, I'll tell you a little secret." He sat on the edge of the desk and leaned over confidentially. "You may have taken this boy out of the country, but you never succeeded in taking the country out of the boy."

Smiling, Rex stood and offered his hand. "And I'll tell you a little secret," he said as they clasped hands warmly. "I never for a minute thought that I had. Come on. Let's get out of here and go down to Mario's. I want to drink a toast to the new district ranger of the Osage National Forest. What do you say, Ranger Hanford?"

"I say, let's go," he replied heartily. They trooped out as Nick ran the title over in his mind. *Ranger* Hanford. It had such a wonderful ring to it that he regretted not having made the decision to transfer out sooner. He belonged in the forest, not in an office in a big city of concrete. Washington had been good for him and good to him, but now he was going home. It would be a new home, granted, but that didn't matter. At long last, he'd have fresh air, trees, wildlife…and most important of all, his daughter.

To Nick, it felt like the beginning of a whole new life.

CHAPTER TWO

CRYSTAL PULLED her pickup off the highway and drove up the hill to the headquarters of the Oak Ridge district of the Osage National Forest. The small, attractive building made of stone and wood sat just on the outskirts of Oak Ridge, Arkansas, a community of about nine thousand, and the forest district snaked around the town in scattered tracts that consumed a big chunk of Newton County and its neighboring counties.

Though it wasn't quite eight o'clock, the small parking lot was already full—a fact that was unusual, but not surprising. Normally, Crystal was the first to arrive. She liked opening up the office and spending a few quiet moments reviewing her work schedule before things got hectic.

But this particular morning wasn't usual, and everyone knew it. It was the first of April. As of today, Dan Gatlin was no longer the district ranger. And neither was Crystal Elliot, despite the promises that had been made to her. Some pencil pusher with a lot of clout in the Washington office had decided he wanted to come down from D.C. and play in the woods for a while.

He probably heard that the bass fishing at Silver Springs is expected to be good this year, Crystal thought, trying to swallow the knot of bitterness that had been stuck in her throat since she'd heard the announcement last week. No matter how hard she tried, though, the lump wouldn't go away. Her reasonable, logical self told her that the disappointment would pass, but emotionally, she was devastated; she had allowed herself to believe that her fondest dream was about to come true, only to have that dream shattered.

Until her reasonable self won out, the best she could do was smile and be a good sport about it. Plastering that smile firmly in place, she took a deep breath of the unseasonably cold morning air and breezed into the office.

"'Morning, Crystal," Mary Alice Caufield said as she came down the hall toward the small visitors' lobby. Mary Alice had been Dan's secretary for the last ten years, and everyone had expected her to be Crystal's as well.

"Good morning," Crystal replied with a chipper lilt in her voice. "Any word on the new boss, yet?"

"Only that he'll be in sometime this morning," the secretary replied as she rummaged through the drawers of her desk behind the waist-high reception counter. She found her purse, then straightened and favored Crystal with a pitying look—the kind she'd been receiving for a week now.

It's coming, Crystal thought. The obligatory, "Gee, honey, you must really feel bad" speech. Unable to bear another one, Crystal cut her off. "Is there any coffee?"

Mary Alice nodded. "If you hurry. I only made a half a pot—I'm on my way to the store now to get another can, or this crowd won't survive the morning."

"Then you're the one who'd better hurry. I think I hear a surly lynch mob forming already," she warned Mary Alice as she bustled out the front door, chuckling.

Slipping out of her sheepskin jacket, Crystal moved quickly through the reception area, pointedly ignoring the small office where, until yesterday, Dan Gatlin had sat behind a battered oak desk. She tried not to think about how empty the whole office would be without his smiling presence, and she absolutely refused to entertain thoughts about how she'd expected to be sitting at that desk today.

She entered the rabbit warren of offices and cubbyholes in the center of the building and hung her jacket on the coatrack with a dozen others, then moved into the small kitchen next to her office to pour a fortifying cup of coffee. She spoke to everyone she passed, but noted that while most of the staff were at their desks, few of them really seemed to be working. All minds were focused on the imminent arrival of the new district ranger.

"'Morning, Rich," she called out as she passed her friend's desk, then took a right turn into her own office just across the hall. Automatically she brought her computer on-line and checked to see if there were any messages waiting for her. Sipping her coffee as she sat at the terminal, Crystal read through a directive from headquarters that had come in yesterday afternoon while she'd been in the field.

"Seems too quiet this morning, doesn't it?" Rich said just as she finished the letter. He was lounging at the door of her office, coffee cup in hand.

Crystal grinned at him. "You're never here in the morning, Rich. How would you know that?" Normally Rich spent the first part of his day doing on-site inspections of the logging operations, and rarely came into the office until noon.

He cocked his head in the direction of Dan's vacant office around the corner. "You know what I mean."

Her smile faded. "Yeah. It's going to seem strange without him," she said, turning her attention to some mail that had been left on her desk yesterday afternoon, organizing the correspondence into neat piles.

Rich frowned. He'd expected a little more from Crystal this morning—a surly frown, a sulky posture, a few irritable words...something...anything but her usual pleasant demeanor. After the dirty trick the main office had pulled on her, she deserved to indulge in one temper tantrum at the very least. As far as he knew, though, Crystal had taken the bad news like a brave little trooper, and that just wasn't human. She had to feel *some* resentment, and Rich considered it his duty as Crystal's friend to find it and force her to air her disappointment.

Moving into the office, he planted one hip on the edge of her desk and waited for her to acknowledge him.

Crystal saw the lean masculine thigh invade her territory, and she looked up questioningly. "Something on your mind, Rich?"

He shook his head, amazed. "How can you be so calm? Any minute now, a glamour boy desk jockey from D.C. is going to walk through the front door and take the job that should have been yours. You haven't said a single solitary word about it since the news came down from the district supervisor."

She gave him a tolerant smile. "What do you expect me to do, Rich? Go out to the highway and set up a detour so District Ranger Nicholas E. Hanford won't be able to find the place? Or better yet, how about putting land mines in the parking lot? That would take care of him once and for all."

Rich chuckled. "How can you joke at a time like this?"

"Look, Chicken Little, the sky isn't falling—yet."

"But—"

"No buts, Rich," she said patiently. "This is the Forest Service, and though it's not as regimented as the Army, it's still a branch of the federal government. One of the first things you learn is that you have absolutely no say over your fate within the Service. If the powers that be say 'Jump,' you say, 'How high?' If they say 'You've been reassigned to Timbuktu,' you say, 'When do I leave?'"

Rich sighed with disgust. "And if they say, 'You've been put in charge of your own district,' then snatch that promotion away, you just roll over and play dead, right?"

"Exactly."

"It's not fair," he grumbled. "It's like an April Fool's joke that isn't at all funny."

Was I ever that young and naive? Crystal wondered wistfully. "Who said life is supposed to be fair, Rich? The good guys don't always win, no one lives happily ever after, and on occasion, lightning *does* strike the same spot twice."

Rich started to ask her how someone so vivacious and lovely could also be so cynical, but he stopped just in time. Crystal didn't talk much about herself or her past, but other people did. In the three years he'd been assigned to the Osage, he'd heard all the rumors about her that refused to languish and die. Rich's own upbringing hadn't exactly been straight out of *Leave it to Beaver*, but if even half of what people said about Crystal's early life was true, she had every reason in the world to be a little cynical.

Despite all that, though, and despite the pleasure he received from knowing she considered him a good friend, Rich didn't really understand what made Crystal Elliot tick. She seemed completely open and friendly, yet she rarely let anyone inside her head. It was a little frustrating at times.

Sighing heavily, he thrust those thoughts aside. "It's still not right, Crystal. Dan's job should have gone to you."

"But it didn't," she replied, perusing a letter from a local high school inviting her to speak at Career Day.

"And you're not bitter about it?" he asked, incredulous.

Crystal tried once again to swallow the conspicuous lump in her throat. To camouflage the effort, she scrawled a brief message on the letter from the high school. "Not at all. That's the way the cookie crumbles."

"Boy, you're just full of platitudes today, aren't you?"

She grinned at him. "I'm just full of it, period."

Seeing that he was getting nowhere, Rich tried another tack. "Why do you think Hanford's coming here?"

"I don't have a clue."

"But he's a real hotshot in D.C.—head of his own program, and everything."

Looking for an excuse to escape Rich's relentless questioning, Crystal picked up the Career Day letter and stood. "Maybe he's coming here for his health."

"Get real. It's not for his health or his career," Rich said, following Crystal as she waltzed out of her office and down the corridor toward the front of the building. "Dan Gatlin was a district ranger for forty years and he never made the national news even once, but this Hanford guy is a real big shot with the press. For a while there after he launched the Wilderness Experience campaign, I saw more of him on the nightly news than I did Dan Rather. Why would he give all that up?"

Crystal had wondered about that, too. Rich was exaggerating the extent of Hanford's publicity exposure, but he did have a point. It didn't make sense that a high-profile project director with a wonderful glamour job in D.C. would willingly accept a position in one of the smallest ranger districts in the country. Unless, of course, the glamour-boy had screwed up somehow and had been sent back into the ranks as punishment.

Crystal had no intention of voicing that theory aloud, though. "I don't know why he's joining us lowly peons at the bottom of the heap, Rich, but I'd advise you to get back to your desk and try to look busy so that when the new boss arrives he won't think he's inherited a couple of gold bricks."

"You're right," he said, but followed Crystal into the reception area anyway because he really didn't have anywhere to go, or any particular time to be there. "But listen, if you change your mind about putting land mines in the parking lot, let me know."

"Why? Are you going to help me?" Crystal asked as she tossed the letter into Mary Alice's In basket.

"No, I just want to move my pickup first."

Crystal laughed, and that was all the encouragement Rich needed to launch into an amusing tirade of all the other devious things she could do to the new ranger. Leaning against the reception desk, Crystal laughed out loud—a deep, musical, throaty laugh that filled the room, lit up her face, and made twenty-seven-year-old Rich Patterson wish he were a few years older and a couple of inches taller.

That laugh—and the heart-stopping things it did to Crystal's face—had only begun to subside when Nick Hanford opened the door and stopped, taking in the room and the man and woman who had frozen at the sound of the door. He froze for a moment, too, and returned their curious stares. A Mexican standoff.

Having seen Hanford a few times on TV, Crystal recognized her new boss immediately. If she wouldn't have, the green cotton-duck pants and the khaki shirt peeking out from beneath his open corduroy coat would have been a dead giveaway. She'd known he was good-looking. What television hadn't given her any clue about was his more-than-impressive size.

Crystal's smile faded as she watched him automatically duck his head to keep from hitting it against the door frame. It was a movement almost, but not quite, unnecessary. The door was a standard six feet, eight inches high, and Nick Hanford took up all but a fraction of it. She wasn't sure about the dimensions of the door's width, but the new district ranger's massive shoulders took up most of that, too. If the sun had been behind him, his entrance would have darkened the room.

He was, quite simply, the biggest man Crystal had ever seen. He was also, undeniably, one of the handsomest. Television hadn't come close to capturing the magnetic aura that surrounded him.

Automatically Rich drew his shoulders a little straighter—a gesture that could have indicated respect for a superior officer, or a masculine ego trying to compete with another male of the species who outclassed him by a mile. Rich was five foot ten, young, and athletically built. He had absolutely nothing to be self-conscious about physically, but Crystal suspected that if Arnold Schwarzenegger had been confronted with this newcomer, he probably would have straightened his shoulders, too.

"Good morning. I'm Nick Hanford."

That seemed to shake them from their momentary stupor. As Crystal straightened, Rich stepped across the room with his hand outstretched. "Rich Patterson."

"Pleasure to meet you, Rich." He quickly took measure of the younger man, apparently liking what he saw, then turned his brown-eyed gaze toward the other occupant of the room.

Crystal hesitated only a fraction of a second beneath his mildly speculative look, then stepped forward with her hand extended. "Crystal Elliot," she said as he met her halfway and swallowed her slender hand in his longer, larger one. "Welcome to the Osage, Ranger Hanford."

He cracked a delighted smile that highlighted a network of lines in his face—lines that told Crystal this was a man who liked to smile. "Ranger Hanford," he repeated as though he was trying the title on for size—something he'd been doing for about a week. "You have no idea how good that sounds to me. It's nice to be here, Ms. Elliot."

Their clasped hands dropped away, but they stood there a moment, caught in a little web of silence as they assessed each other.

His skin was as pale as Crystal would have expected from anyone who'd spent too much time behind a desk, but it also had a rough, leathery quality to it that indicated he'd once spent a lot of time in the sun. His eyes were a fascinating shade of brown, the color of milk chocolate, but they were set a tiny bit too close together. That was a fortunate twist of genetic fate, Crystal decided, because that flaw saved his face from being altogether too perfect. He had a chiseled jaw, high cheekbones, full lips, a broad forehead, and perfectly styled soft brown hair. The most disconcerting thing about him, though, was his height.

Being six feet tall, Crystal rarely had to look up to anyone. As a child, she'd suffered through countless Amazon and Jolly Green Giant jokes. She'd marched third from the last in the processional at her high-school graduation, followed only by two stars of the basketball team. She was accustomed to looking down at most people—even men—or meeting them eye to eye, or on occasion focusing up an inch or so to return a man's gaze.

This was unheard of, though! Crystal actually had to tilt her head to look into Hanford's handsome face. Just standing close to him made her feel small and delicate—a feeling that was totally alien . . . and incredibly erotic. Both sensations were as disconcerting as they were thrilling.

Or maybe they were disconcerting *because* they were thrilling. Crystal didn't want to consider that possibility. *Men like this don't grow on trees,* she thought, then added a hasty, *Thank God.* If they did, her nervous system probably wouldn't be able to stand the strain.

Her thorough inspection of him took no more than an instant, but Crystal got the impression that Nick Hanford had spent that time evaluating her in much the same manner. Though she hated herself for it, Crystal wondered if he liked what he saw.

To avoid that thought, she stepped back toward the reception desk. "Did you have any trouble finding the station, Ranger Hanford?"

"None at all," he replied pleasantly, knowing he was going to have to ignore the instantaneous tug of attraction he'd felt the moment he'd seen Crystal Elliot. She was a beautiful woman in a very unconventional way. Her pretty face was framed by shoulder-length black hair and feathery bangs, and her wide, almond-shaped eyes were an arresting shade of blue-violet. She was unusu-

Journey with Harlequin into the past and discover stories of cowboys and captains, pirates and princes in the romantic tradition of Harlequin.

ally tall, but her long legs and subtle curves appealed to
Nick, mostly because she didn't show the slightest sign of
being embarrassed by her height. He knew from experience that such self-confidence wasn't always easy to come
by.

She was gorgeous, but she was also looking at him in
a very businesslike manner, and Nick thoroughly ap-
proved.

"Did you drive straight through from Washington,
sir?" Rich asked.

Nick dragged his gaze away from Crystal and turned
toward the young forester. "No. I stopped in Kentucky
and drove the rest of the way this morning." He didn't
feel the need to explain that he'd spent a couple of days
with his daughter.

"So you haven't had a chance to locate a place to live
yet," Crystal concluded.

"No." He slipped out of his coat and draped it over
one arm. "But that is my first priority. I understand
there's a small room here at the station I can use for a day
or two until I find something."

"That's right," Crystal confirmed. "The room is in
the back, if you'd like to see it. And naturally, you'll
want to meet the rest of the staff."

"Yes, I would—if you don't mind showing me
around."

"Not at all," she said politely.

"If you'll excuse me, I think I'll get back to work,"
Rich said. "It was nice meeting you, Ranger Hanford. If
I can do anything to help you get settled in, don't hesi-
tate to ask."

"Thanks, Rich. And please, call me Nick."

"All right, Nick. See you later." With a jaunty wave,
Rich disappeared down the hall.

Nick looked at Crystal. "Nice guy. Is everyone else on the staff going to be as friendly?"

"Why wouldn't they be?" Crystal looked up, and was suddenly hit by the most incredible, uncomfortable sensation. Her heart was doing a silly staccato drumroll, and she felt like a star-struck adolescent. Ridiculous! She had expected to have to fight a resentment of this man, not an attraction that was completely inappropriate and way out of the bounds of anything she'd ever experienced.

Fortunately the new district ranger didn't seem to notice that she was practically drooling over him. He shrugged. "Getting used to a new boss is never easy—particularly if the old boss was very popular. Was Ranger Gatlin well thought of?"

"*Very* well thought of, but I don't imagine that will prejudice anyone against you," Crystal replied, swallowing a surge of guilt. As far as she knew, she was the only person in Oak Ridge who had a reason to resent his assignment to the Osage.

"I hope you're right, but there's really only one way to find out." He grinned. "Shall we go meet the troops?"

His smile was so potent that Crystal had to look away from it. "Sure. This is your secretary's desk—she's out running an errand at the moment, but she should be right back. And the ranger's office . . . *your* office is right over there." She pointed to the door behind him, but began moving along the hall before he had the chance to look inside. "Everyone else is down here. We don't have a lot of space, so we all sort of work on top of each other. Normally a lot of the staff would be in the field this morning, but everyone was anxious to get a look at the new D.R."

She turned the corner and found the staff gathered in clusters throughout the room, all of them conversing quietly as they watched the door. Obviously Rich had already spread the word that the new district ranger had arrived. Crystal began her round of introductions, leading Hanford from one group to the next.

Nick filed the names and faces of his new staff, hoping that later he would be able to remember them all and the jobs they performed. At the same time, he tried to memorize the layout of the building. Most of the desks were clumped in the center of the large room, but two meeting rooms and several small offices lined the perimeter.

The office Crystal pointed out as her own was one of those. In fact, it was just around the corner from his. If the location of her office was of any significance, Crystal Elliot was fairly high up in the chain of command.

"And what do you do around here?" Nick asked when she had completed the last of her introductions.

"I'm primarily responsible for wildlife management, public relations, and recreation, but I also have a hand in several other areas."

"Who's in charge of the Wilderness Experience project?"

"Ranger Gatlin and I shared the responsibility for that one," Crystal told him as she stepped into the small kitchen adjacent to her office. Just inside the door, she stopped and looked up at Nick. "Of course, all that is subject to change now that you're here. Since you were director of the Wilderness Experience in Washington, I imagine you'll want to assume full control of the project."

Nick gave her a smile he hoped was reassuring. "As the new kid on the block, I don't think I'm in any position to make drastic changes yet. And as to the future—" he shrugged boyishly ''—I'm a great believer in the old saying, 'If it ain't broke, don't fix it.' ''

''That's good to hear,'' she said with a smile as she moved toward a door next to the refrigerator. ''The spare room is right here. We use it as an infirmary and for any specialist who comes into the area for only a day or two.'' She opened the door, flipped the light switch, then stepped aside to allow him to precede her. ''As you can see, it's not much.''

She was right. It wasn't much. One swift glance was all it took to survey the entire space. The block walls were institutional green, the ceiling was composed of acoustical tiles, and the only furnishings were a small table, a medicine cabinet, and a cot that made Nick cringe. It was a far cry from his own custom-made bed that accommodated his height, but until he found an apartment so that he could have his furniture shipped, he was going to be sleeping with his feet cold and dangling. It was not an appetizing prospect, but when he reminded himself of the reason he had made this move, cold feet didn't seem like much of a sacrifice.

Standing in the doorway, Crystal glanced from the bed to Nick and realized how uncomfortable it was going to be. Though she had no intention of being mean spirited toward the man who'd usurped her job, she couldn't help feeling a little satisfaction. Maybe a small dose of discomfort would send this pencil pusher back to the luxury and security of Washington.

Of course, Nick Hanford didn't exactly look like a pencil pusher; a log roller, maybe, but not a pencil pusher. He was a huge man, but there didn't seem to be an ounce of fat on him—everything was well-defined muscle. But then, Crystal reasoned, body building was all the rage now. Just because a man had muscles, it didn't mean that he had come by them doing a hard day's physical labor.

"Not exactly the Hilton," Nick observed as he turned his back on the room. "But it will do for a day or two."

"Will your wife be joining you as soon as you find a place to live?" Crystal asked, telling herself that she was only asking because everyone in town would want to know, and would expect her to have the answer.

"No," he told her, a small, dark shadow passing across his handsome face. "I'm divorced. But my daughter will be arriving in a few weeks." He stated it as fact, knowing it was a little premature to be so optimistic, but he refused to consider the possibility that he might lose his custody battle with Marjorie.

"How old is your daughter?" Crystal asked, feeling the need to make polite conversation.

"Fourteen. Her name is Trisha."

"That can be a tough age. I hope she doesn't have trouble adapting to life in a small town."

"Oh, that won't be a problem. She's never lived in anything but small towns," Nick answered, and saw the look of confusion that crossed Crystal's face. If he'd been living in Washington, where had his daughter been? To deflect the possibility that she might actually ask the question, Nick quickly changed the subject. "So, what about you?" he asked.

"What about me?"

"Are you married?"

"Oh. No. I'm a victim of the divorce courts, as well."

"Any kids?" he asked politely.

Crystal shook her head and smiled. "None. Are you going to tell me what I'm missing?" Another shadow crossed his face, and Crystal wondered what she'd said wrong.

"Let's just say that parenthood has its ups and downs."

"I've heard a rumor to that effect," she said, eliciting a smile from the new boss, and then a brief, uncomfortable pause stretched between them as they ran out of things to say. Suddenly it seemed to Crystal that the room was too small—or maybe it was just that Nick Hanford was too big and she was much too aware of him. She cleared her throat and stepped into the kitchen as she said brightly, "Well, that's enough small talk for one day. And that's also the end of the tour. Do you need help bringing your things in?"

"No, thanks. That can wait," Nick said, following her. "I'd rather get settled and take stock of the Osage."

"Then why don't I escort you back to your office?" She started for the lobby with Nick at her side, dwarfing her, making her feel small and feminine. It was such an unreasonably sexy feeling that Crystal tried valiantly to squelch it.

Halfway to the office, they ran into Mary Alice, who was hurrying toward the kitchen carrying a grocery sack, and Crystal made the appropriate introductions.

"It's a pleasure to meet you, Mrs. Caufield," Nick said, giving the plump, middle-aged lady a double dose of his most charming smile. "Until I figure out what's going on around here, I'm going to be depending on you a great deal."

"I'll do my best," Mary Alice said, her face taking on a flushed, girlish grin that made her look ten years younger.

This guy's charm must be universal, Crystal thought, relieved that she wasn't the only one whose heart seemed to beat a little faster in Ranger Hanford's presence. With a flustered giggle, the secretary mumbled something about putting away the coffee, and rushed off to the kitchen.

"She's a very good secretary," Crystal told Nick. "Dan... Ranger Gatlin, always said he'd be lost without her."

"I'm sure she'll be a big help to me."

With Crystal leading the way, they moved on. "I'm afraid you'll be disappointed in your office, Ranger Hanford. We don't get much money allocated to upgrading the station facilities." She stopped at the door and allowed Nick to pass in front of her. "As I said," she continued, "It's not much."

Nick took in the space that was only slightly larger than the sleeping room, but contrary to Crystal's assessment, he found the room very attractive. It's furnishings were comprised of an old oak desk, a metal file cabinet, a bookcase, and two old, but comfortable-looking armchairs. Potted plants and a tall ficus tree brightened the room considerably, as did the large window overlooking a grove of trees that hid the front of the building from the highway. Pleased by the pastoral scene, Nick walked slowly toward the window. "This is great. Just great."

His reaction surprised Crystal. She had wanted this office because of what it symbolized, not what it looked like. "I'm sure it's not what you're accustomed to in Washington."

Nick turned and favored her with a smile that creased his face in an absurdly handsome manner. "You're right. My office at headquarters couldn't compare with this. The view is great, and it's within a stone's throw of a forest in the Ozarks, a hundred miles from any major population center. After three years in the city, this office is heaven."

"You didn't like the city?" Crystal asked, wondering if his answer might provide some clue as to why he'd given up—or been forced to give up—his cushy job in Washington.

"The city was fine," Nick answered. "I just wasn't cut out to live in one for the rest of my life."

"I see," she said. "Well, unless you need me for something else, I'll get back to work."

"Go right ahead. And thanks for the tour."

"My pleasure, Ranger Hanford."

"I wish you'd call me Nick," he said pleasantly as she moved toward the door. "This place is so small that it seems silly to be so formal with each other."

"All right, Nick. I'm Crystal. Would you like me to send Mary Alice in?"

"Yes, thank you. I'm going to need a lot of filling in to bring me up to speed. My transfer came through so quickly that I didn't have a chance to study the Plan," he told her, referring to the individualized ten-year prospectus that outlined the needs and goals for each national forest district.

"Then you have your work cut out for you. Our Plan expires next year, and we're in the process of drafting a new one."

Nick whistled softly. "Oh, brother." Designing a Decade Plan was one of the hardest jobs a district ranger ever had to contend with. It required administrative skill and a vast knowledge of the forest. For Nick, the administrative skill was no problem, but he knew virtually nothing about the specific needs of this district. "You're right. I've stepped into the middle of a whopping big job."

Crystal grinned. "Are you sure you don't want to hightail it back to Washington?" she asked, and was suddenly appalled to realize that the question hadn't come out as the joke she'd intended it to be. Fortunately Nick didn't appear to notice.

"Not on your life," he said with a deep, resonant chuckle. "There's nothing I like better than a challenge."

"Good." *So much for scaring off the competition,* she thought glumly. But then, Hanford wasn't competing for the job Crystal wanted. He already had it.

"It's kind of strange, though," Nick said thoughtfully.

"What?"

He shrugged, remembering the file he'd read in Washington. Gatlin had put in forty years of service, but he hadn't reached mandatory retirement age yet. "It strikes me odd that a ranger would retire at such a critical time. Why did Ranger Gatlin decide to leave now, rather than wait until next year after the Plan was completed? You would think he'd want his influence to be felt long after he was gone."

The implied criticism—mild though it was—washed over Crystal like a bucket of ice water, and the surge of resentment she had anticipated feeling toward Nick Hanford finally arrived in full force. "I'm sure Ranger Gatlin felt that his replacement could handle the job," she said coldly. Nick Hanford had no right to criticize Dan Gatlin, just as he had no right to the job that should have been hers—the job Dan had felt comfortable leaving because he'd been convinced that Crystal would be his replacement. The strength of her sudden anger startled Crystal, and she quickly put a lid on it.

Nick realized immediately that he had put his foot into his mouth. Obviously he was replacing a man who had commanded a great deal of loyalty among his staff. "I'm sorry if that sounded critical," he said sincerely. "I'm sure Ranger Gatlin had good reasons for retiring when he did."

"Yes, he did," Crystal said tightly.

"I hope I'll get to meet him eventually."

"I'm sure you will. He said something about dropping by as soon as you were settled in."

"Good."

Crystal turned toward the door. "If you'll excuse me, Ranger Hanford, I really need to get back to work."

"Of course," he said, amazed at the change in her. She was trying hard to be polite, but obviously he had made her very angry and he really hated to get off on the wrong foot like this. "Ms. Elliot . . ."

Crystal stopped and turned to him. "Yes?"

"I really didn't mean to offend you with my comments about Ranger Gatlin."

Crystal took a deep breath. She was getting off to a bad start with the new boss, and that wasn't good. "And I didn't mean to be defensive," she said. "Sorry if I snapped at you."

"No harm done." Nick sat on the edge of his new desk and looked at her speculatively. "Ms. Elliot—"

"Crystal," she reminded him, making a peace offering.

He smiled. "Crystal, you're second in command around here, aren't you?"

"More or less," she admitted.

"Were you—" He paused, wondering how to phrase his question politely. "You mentioned something about Ranger Gatlin's replacement. Was someone in this office expecting to be promoted to district ranger?"

Crystal took a deep breath again, angry at herself this time for having allowed her temper to get out of hand.

Obviously she'd given away too much. But Hanford was going to hear the truth sooner or later, she reasoned, so it might as well come from her. "Yes," she admitted reluctantly. "I had been told by the district supervisor that the job was mine."

Nick frowned. The file on the Oak Ridge job opening had made no mention that a replacement had already been selected, otherwise he would never have taken the position. Mentally Nick cursed the supervisor who hadn't put Crystal's paperwork through soon enough. "I'm very sorry about that, Crystal. I had no idea someone else had been promised the job. If it's any consolation, I'm sure you'll receive that promotion to some other rangership very soon."

Crystal tried to smile at him. What he was offering was cold comfort, because she had no desire to leave Oak Ridge. This was her home. She had spent time in other districts, but this was the place she'd planned on spending the remainder of her career. Of course, Nick Hanford didn't know that, and it wasn't his fault that she had a special attachment to this particular forest. But with Dan and Naomi leaving, did she *really* have an attachment to the Osage? It was something worth thinking about. "Thanks," she said, knowing better than to burn her bridges behind her.

Nick realized that she was trying to be a good sport, and his respect rose a notch. "Listen, if there's anything I can do to facilitate your promotion, just let me know. There are quite a few people scattered through the Service who owe me favors."

"I appreciate the offer, but I haven't applied anywhere else yet. For the time being I'd rather leave things as they are," she said, filing his offer for future reference. She wasn't ready to give up the hope that he might not remain in Oak Ridge long. However, if it eventually became obvious that he wasn't just a short-timer, she might start seriously considering a transfer.

"All right, but if you change your mind—"

"Crystal, get out here!" Mary Alice called, her voice filled with urgency. "We got trouble!"

Startled, Crystal and Nick both scrambled toward the door.

CHAPTER THREE

CRYSTAL WAS OUT of Nick's office like a shot. Emergencies were rare except during fire season, but Dan Gatlin had taught Crystal by word and deed how to deal with just about every type of problem that could arise. "What's wrong?"

Mary Alice was just hanging up the phone as she turned toward Crystal. "Raymond Fisk just called. He went out to check his herd this morning and saw the Whipley boys headed into the wilderness preserve carrying shotguns."

"Damn!" Crystal swore, automatically dashing down the corridor for her coat and asking, "How long ago?"

"About an hour."

"All right. Call Tony at the Juvenile Office, then get hold of Lonnie at the stable and tell him to saddle Cinnamon for me." Slipping into her coat, Crystal started out, but a loud cough stopped her. It wasn't until she turned and saw Nick standing casually at his office door that she remembered it wasn't her place to issue orders.

Nick's smile was a pleasant mixture of tolerance and confusion. "Might I be let in on the nature of this emergency?"

Crystal's shoulders drooped a little. "Of course. Sorry." She stepped away from the door, chafing with embarrassment and the sudden strain of inactivity. She wanted to deal with this problem, not stand around discussing it.

"Earlier this week we got a call from Tony Manguson, the county juvenile officer, warning us that he'd heard a rumor that the Whipley brothers—two incorrigible delinquents—had been bragging about going up to the lake at Silver Springs to kill themselves a bald eagle or two," she told him, then added as an afterthought, "Silver Springs is part of our forest land. It's—"

"I know. It's part of the Wilderness Experience project," he said. As head of the program, Nick had been responsible for approving the Oak Ridge district's plans to upgrade the primitive campsites and hiking and riding trails in that particular area. Consequently Silver Springs was the only part of the district that Nick knew anything at all about.

"Then you also know that we've got a nesting pair of bald eagles on the lake," she said, urgency coloring her voice. "I notified everyone in the area to be on the lookout for the Whipley boys, and the Juvenile Officer promised he'd have a talk with them, but apparently he couldn't locate them or his talk didn't do much good. Either way, we've got a problem, and it has to be dealt with quickly."

Nick nodded and moved away from his office door. "I take it from your instructions to Mary Alice that the only way to reach the lake is on horseback."

"That's right," Crystal answered, stepping to the huge map that covered one wall of the reception room. "Dan Gatlin has a farm right here—" she pointed to a small section of land about twenty miles north of Oak Ridge "—in a meadow adjacent to the forest. The fastest way to get to Silver Springs—" she traced a line farther north "—is to cut across Dan's place."

"How long will it take?"

"About thirty minutes to the stables, and another two hours to the lake," Crystal answered, anxious to be off.

Nick moved down the hall to the rack where he'd hung his coat earlier. "Then we'd better get going. By the time we get to the horses the boys will have almost a two-hour head start."

Stunned, Crystal sputtered for a moment before she could get out, "But the only way to catch up with them is on horseback."

"So you said." Nick shrugged on his coat. "Does Ranger Gatlin have a horse he might trust me with?"

"Probably," she answered dubiously. The ride to Silver Springs was long and difficult. She needed to cover the rough terrain fast, and this Washington appointee was only going to slow her down.

"Good," Nick said, turning to Mary Alice, who had been watching and evaluating the new ranger's approach to the situation. "When you call the stable, ask if they can have a horse ready for me, too, please."

"Should I go ahead and call the Juvenile Officer, as well?" she asked.

"If that's your usual course of action in these situations," Nick answered. "I'm the new kid on the block, remember. I trust Crystal's judgment on this." His tone suggested that he was only willing to trust her until her judgment proved fallible.

If Crystal had been unsure about the course of action she'd dictated, she might have been intimidated by his statement, but she wasn't. She was going to do whatever it took to save those eagles. Still doubtful about Ranger Hanford's ability to keep up with her, she said, "It's quite a long trip up to the lake, sir. I'll be gone the better part of the day."

Nick noted that she said "I'll," not "we'll," and "sir," not "Nick." But there wasn't time to wonder why she didn't want him to accompany her. "What better way is there for me to get to know the forest than to make the trip with a native guide? The paperwork can wait, the eagles can't."

Realizing she couldn't deter him, Crystal finally gave up. She almost, but not quite, succeeded in masking her irritated sigh. "Then let's get going. Mary Alice, tell Lonnie to saddle Goliath for Ranger Hanford."

Fishing the keys to one of the Forest Service Jeeps out of the pocket of her khaki trousers, she headed for the door.

Once outside, Crystal quickened her pace, taking long steps around the side of the building and heading up the hill toward the vehicle in back. Given her long-legged gait, most people had to run to keep up with her when she was in high gear, but not Nick Hanford. He kept pace with her so easily that it was a little irritating. His stride seemed almost casual, and it was clear that, had he chosen to do so, he could have left her behind with only the smallest effort.

Studiously avoiding looking at the man at her side, Crystal led him past the large building that housed the district's fire trucks and other emergency equipment. Her Jeep was parked with the rest of the fleet of bright green vehicles just behind the fire shed, and she headed toward it without a word.

"Goliath, eh?" Nick commented, just trying to fill the uncomfortable silence. "That sounds like a horse that should just about fit me."

"He's a big gelding. He knows the terrain, and he's a very gentle, steady mount," Crystal said as she climbed into the driver's seat.

"Good." Personally Nick would have preferred a horse with a little spirit, but since he hadn't been in the saddle for a long time and didn't know the area they'd be riding in, Crystal's choice was probably correct. He circled the Jeep to the passenger side and climbed in. "Tell me about Ranger Gatlin's farm," he suggested, once again filling an uncomfortable silence.

Crystal sighed as she put the Jeep in gear and roared out of the parking lot, down the hill, and onto the highway. She didn't mean to be unfriendly, but she was worried about the eagles, and about her inability to let go of her resentment toward Nick. "It's not really a working farm—just a lot of meadowland and a few stands of timber. He has a terrific stable, though, with a lot of good breeding stock."

"What breed?"

"Quarter horses," she said, studiously keeping her eye on the traffic to avoid looking at Nick. His broad shoulders seemed to fill up the front seat; once again she felt small and uncomfortable.

As she always did when she was at a disadvantage, Crystal took the initiative and began talking, pointing out places of interest along the way. Nick asked questions, but confined them to general things about Oak Ridge and the Osage National Forest. Some of Crystal's discomfort began to evaporate when it became clear that Ranger Hanford was no stranger to the everyday workings of a forest station.

By the time Crystal pulled off a winding, hilly two-lane blacktop onto the gravel road that led to Dan's farm, they were actually chatting pleasantly. They topped a rise, getting an excellent view of the picturesque valley below, and Nick smiled.

"Now, that's what I call beautiful," he said with so much sincerity that Crystal's opinion of him rose considerably. She loved this valley and everything in it; particularly the quaint, two-story farmhouse, painted white, with clapboard shutters and trim in country blue that dominated the postcard-perfect setting. An old-fashioned veranda circled the front and sides of the house, and enormous oaks and pecan trees—just beginning to don their spring finery—sheltered and shaded it.

Near the house sat several outbuildings, one of them a two-car garage, newer than the farmhouse, but built in the same simple style. To the left, well away from the other structures, was the stable—a long building with a steeply sloping roof and a hayloft at one end.

"It is pretty, isn't it?" Crystal said lovingly.

"It's incredible. Is this Ranger Gatlin's place?" he asked, instantly in love with the beautiful valley and the tall, wooded hills that rose around it.

Crystal nodded, and Nick glanced at her, wanting to see if the surprisingly warm timbre of her voice matched the look on her face. It did. *The valley isn't the only beautiful thing in sight,* he realized. The smile that lit up Crystal's face was dazzling, and what made it all the more attractive was that she was completely unconscious of it.

"I can certainly understand why you chose to board your horse here. I'd use any excuse I could think of to come here, too."

Pleased that he could appreciate the charm of the valley, Crystal glanced at him with her smile still in place. "I spent the happiest years of my life on this farm," she told him. "It's very special to me."

Nick's dark eyebrows went up in surprise. "Really? You grew up in Oak Ridge?"

"Yes."

Nick suddenly felt like a fool for having suggested to Crystal that she could look forward to a promotion to another district. If Oak Ridge was her home, it was no wonder she'd reacted so strangely when he'd offered to help her find another job. But that subject seemed best left alone for the time being, so instead he asked, "Are you related to Ranger Gatlin?"

"Sort of," she said, focusing her attention back on the road as she took the Jeep down the steep hill with all the speed and certainty of someone who had traveled the road often. She glanced at Nick again just long enough to see his look of curiosity, and decided she might as well tell him what he'd learn sooner or later. "Dan and his wife, Naomi, are my foster parents. They only have one child of their own, but they had a big hand in raising several others—including me and Lonnie Macklin, who runs the stable."

There were questions Nick wanted to ask about how Crystal had come into the care of foster parents, but that didn't seem appropriate. Instead he commented, "Well, they certainly chose the perfect spot to raise a bunch of kids. I can think of all kinds of mischief I could have gotten into in a place like this."

"Oh?" Crystal couldn't resist an impudent grin. "Were you a troublemaker?"

Nick grinned, too. "I got into my fair share. My parents were in their late forties when I was born, so I didn't have a lot of supervision during my turbulent teen years. How about you? If I had to guess, I'd say that you never got into trouble a day in your life."

"You'd be right. I was the perfect child," she told him as she took a road that forked away from the house and placed them right in front of the stable. "I had to be," she said quietly, her voice cryptically sad.

Nick wanted to ask what she meant, but Crystal had already shut off the engine and was climbing out of the Jeep. Two men came out the stable—one barely out of his teens, the other much older, with the weather-beaten face of an outdoorsman. *Dan Gatlin,* Nick decided. He had a look of authority that was unmistakable.

"Dan! What are you doing down here?" Crystal asked as she hurried toward him. "I thought Mom had you cleaning out the attic this morning?"

"I escaped," he said with a broad grin. "Lonnie called and told me there was trouble brewing at the lake, so I thought I'd better come down and see if you needed any advice."

Crystal laughed. "You just wanted to get out of cleaning the attic."

"No, I just like giving you advice," Dan returned teasingly. "And I also thought it might be a good opportunity to meet Ranger Hanford." He turned his full attention to the mountainous man ambling up behind Crystal.

"Then let me do the honors," she said, quickly introducing Nick to Dan and the young man with him. Lonnie mumbled a grudging hello, but Dan's reception was much warmer.

"Welcome to the Osage, Ranger Hanford."

"Thank you. It's a pleasure to meet you," Nick said, shaking hands with both men before he said to Dan, "I was hoping we'd have a chance to get together sometime soon."

"I'd like that. I'm sure you must have a million questions."

"That I do," Nick said ruefully. "I had hoped to arrive in Oak Ridge before you officially retired, but I couldn't manage to get here any earlier."

Lonnie Macklin cleared his throat uncomfortably, drawing a curious look from Nick as the boy said, "Listen, Crystal, I got the horses saddled and ready to go."

"Good." She looked at her foster father. "We're really pressed for time, Dan. The Whipley boys have a big jump on us."

"Right, right. Ranger Hanford and I can get to know each other later. You two better hit the trail—what there is of it."

His enthusiastic tone sounded curiously forced, and Crystal felt a sudden surge of sympathy for him. It couldn't be easy to stand by and watch someone else go off to do the job that had once been his. For his sake, as well as her own, Crystal turned to Nick. "You know, Ranger Hanford, it's really not necessary for you to accompany me. If you'd rather stay here and talk to Dan—"

"No offense to Ranger Gatlin," Nick said with a grin at both of them, "but I'd rather get a look at this wilderness area—if you've got a horse for me, that is."

Dan clapped Nick on the back and led him around the side of the stable. "Sure do. Goliath is saddled and waiting. You just point him toward Silver Springs, and he'll do the rest."

The horses—a huge black gelding with a white blaze and fetlocks, and a beautiful bay mare—were tethered to a rail below the hayloft. Goliath and Cinnamon. Nick didn't have to be told which was which, or that they were both fine animals.

Crystal watched Ranger Hanford approach the horses confidently, singling out Goliath to speak to in hushed, reassuring tones. He looked the horse over, stroking his neck, patting his rump, checking the cinch; then he put on the gloves that had been stuffed into his pocket, and mounted with the ease of a man who had spent a lot of time in a saddle.

Maybe he'll do all right, after all, Crystal thought, unsure whether she was pleased that he wouldn't slow her down or disappointed that he wasn't the greenhorn she'd expected him to be.

"There's fresh water in the canteens," Lonnie told her as she checked Cinnamon's cinch. "I put a first-aid kit in your saddlebags." He had also secured a rolled up army blanket behind each saddle in case of an emergency.

"Naomi sent some sandwiches down, too," Dan added. "You can't possibly make it back before midafternoon."

"Trust Mom to think of the practical side of any emergency," Crystal said with an affectionate smile as she pulled on her gloves. "Tell her I said thanks. See you later!"

She swung easily into the saddle and urged Cinnamon into a trot. Nick fell in beside her as she led them away from the stable into an open meadow behind the farmhouse. There, she picked up speed, and before long, the bay and the gelding were galloping neck in neck. Crystal glanced at her companion long enough to decide that he was an exceptional horseman.

She had a sudden urge to coax Cinnamon into high gear and turn their ride into a race just to see how good Hanford really was, but she resisted that urge. She couldn't risk tiring the horses just to satisfy a whim. This was business, not pleasure, though Crystal couldn't deny that she was enjoying herself tremendously.

But then, she always enjoyed taking Cinnamon out for a good gallop, she reasoned. What she was experiencing didn't have anything to do with the handsome man keeping pace with her, glancing at her from time to time with a smile that showed his own unbridled pleasure.

The horses were barely winded when they reached the edge of the meadow and Crystal slowed to a trot. Nick followed suit, patting Goliath's neck in praise, but looking with envy at Crystal's bay. "That's a lot of horse you got there. I had the feeling you could have left old Goliath and me eating your dust if you'd wanted to."

"That's true. Goliath wasn't built for speed, but before the day is over, I think you'll appreciate many of his other fine qualities."

And she was right. In the first two hours they spent traveling circuitously through the Silver Springs Wildlife Preserve, Nick saw just about every kind of terrain he could have expected to see, but Goliath took it all in stride. The trail they followed was an old logging road that could barely be called a trail at all. The heavily wooded landscape was peppered with outcroppings of boulders worthy of the Rockies, and years of disuse had washed away sections of the old road entirely. At times they followed trickling streams that mysteriously dried up after a few hundred yards. Gentle slopes gave way to steep ones. Rocky trails became soft beds of moss and carpets of early spring wildflowers.

The trees rose around them like tall gray ghosts. They were just beginning to bud, giving the forest a fuzzy green hue, but here and there the shocking pink of redbud trees and the creamy white of dogwoods in full bloom bathed the hills in vibrant color.

Though the climb was uneven, it was clear that they were traveling steadily upward. A hiking trail began periodically intersecting the riding trail, and Crystal informed Nick that this was the route the Whipley boys would have taken.

"How many trails are there to the lake?" he asked.

"Four. The two on this side that intersect, a hiking trail on the east side, and another old logging road that comes in from the north," she answered without turning to look at him. They were riding single file up a rocky ledge and she knew better than to take her eye off the narrow path. The drop off to her left wasn't terribly deep, but it was steep enough to make a careless rider wish he'd stayed home.

When they finally reached the top of the ridge, Crystal stopped and waited for Nick to catch up. "How are you doing?"

He grinned at her. "Fine. Though I will admit I'm a little out of practice. There aren't many districts left in the country where access is so restricted." By mutual consent, they dismounted to give the horses a breather, and Nick used the time to study the rugged terrain. "This is beautiful country. It always amazes me to find virtually untouched land like this. Silver Springs must be pretty small to have escaped development into a resort area."

"Actually it's bigger than you might think, but until about thirty years ago, all this land was owned by a very eccentric old man who lived up at the lake and guarded his privacy like a miser hoards gold. He willed it to the government with the proviso that it be allowed to remain a wilderness area."

"Lucky us." Nick smiled, and Crystal couldn't help smiling, too. He really had incredible eyes. Their color was nothing special, but the natural warmth and humor in them was hard to resist.

"This place has always been very special to me."

"I guess you spent a lot of time here when you were a kid. I know I would have."

"Dan brought me here a lot," she admitted, her expression turning wistful. "He taught me about trees and animals, but his real goal was to teach me about myself."

"How old were you when you came to live with the Gatlins?" Nick asked, curious to know more about her.

Crystal didn't want to go into the sordid story of her childhood, so she answered his question as pleasantly but succinctly as possible. "Twelve. The Gatlins are the most wonderful people in the world." In order to deflect more questions, she gestured to a barely discernible trail. "We'd better keep moving. Let's walk the horses for a while."

"Sure." Obviously she didn't want to talk about her past, and Nick had no problem with respecting her privacy. "Tell me about these two delinquents we're chasing," he suggested, switching the conversation to something neutral.

Crystal groaned. "Bobby and Lewis Whipley. They're troublemakers of the first order. They probably would have been sent off to reform school years ago if their father hadn't bought their way out every scrape they've ever gotten into."

"Which leads them to believe that they're completely above the law." Nick guessed.

"That's right."

"How old are they?"

"Fifteen and sixteen, I think, but I'm not sure which one is older. They're both as mean as junkyard dogs," she told him, her voice growing hard as she thought about what the boys were planning to do. "God, this makes me mad."

"I know what you mean," Nick said, but Crystal gave him a piercing look.

"Do you really? Do you have any idea what those birds they want to kill represent? They're the only resident pair of eagles in this part of the state! If they've already started nesting, one gunshot is all it will take to drive them out of the area for good—and that's assuming that the boys don't actually kill one of them outright!"

Her vehemence surprised Nick. "Hey, I'm on your side, remember? I get sick every time I think about how stupid people like the Whipleys have systematically pushed the bald eagle to the edge of extinction."

"Sorry," Crystal muttered when she realized she'd practically yelled at Nick. "This is just something I take very personally. I'm the one who found the birds last year, and I spent a big part of the summer studying them. They're not just an endangered species to me, these are *my* eagles."

Nick could appreciate her feelings, but felt obliged to warn her, "That's a dangerous sentiment, Crystal. Commitment to wildlife is one thing, but personal attachment is something quite different. Those birds belong to Nature, not you."

"I know that, and I'm perfectly willing to let them meet their fate in the wild—whatever it may be. I don't want to tame them and make them pets. I just want them to live without the interference of man. They deserve that much, at least."

"Well, I certainly can't argue with you about that."

"You'd better not," Crystal advised him with a laugh. "I once took a hickory switch to a hunter who was taking potshots at hawks up here. That little lapse in judgment has earned me quite a reputation in these parts."

"I can imagine it would." Nick laughed, appreciating the fact that Crystal stood up for what she believed in but at the same time didn't take herself too seriously.

"What about you?" Crystal asked. "Have you ever had a lapse in judgment for a good cause?"

"One or two," he admitted. "When I was working in the Arapaho, I once threw a guy out of a bar for bragging about the number of golden eagles he'd killed that winter."

"You worked in the Arapaho National Forest?" she asked with obvious surprise.

Nick nodded. "I was a ranger there for six years before I went to Washington."

Crystal was dumbfounded. At one time or another, every forester in the service had wanted to work in the Rocky Mountains. It was roughly equivalent to a small-town politician dreaming of becoming governor. "What in the world are you doing down here in Arkansas?" she asked incredulously before she even realized the words were out. "You've been a project director in Washington and you've had one of the most glamorous ranger assignments in the country. How did you end up here?"

"You sound like Rex Teirnan," Nick said with a lop-sided grin. "Arkansas isn't exactly the end of the world, you know."

"It is to some people."

"Well, not to me. Would you believe I actually requested this district?"

Crystal came to a dead stop and looked at him. "No."

If nothing else, Nick had to admire her honesty. "You think I was sent here as punishment," he said, stating it as fact, not as a question.

Crystal hesitated only a moment before answering. "I had considered the possibility."

"I'm happy to say that's not the case," he replied without seeming to have taken offense. "I really did request this district, Crystal, and I'm truly sorry that I knocked you out of a promotion."

"I'll get over the disappointment," she said offhandedly, stroking Cinnamon's neck. "Now, we'd better mount up again and get going."

"All right." Nick remounted Goliath and watched with admiration as Crystal swung easily into the saddle. She was an excellent horsewoman. She also seemed to be an honest, forthright person, and he admired that, too. "Listen, Crystal, since you're second in command around here you're going to have to know about this anyway because I'll be taking some personal time off in a couple of weeks—"

She turned in the saddle and looked at him. "What?"

"I'm involved in a legal fight with my ex-wife over custody of our daughter. They're living in Kentucky, and I requested a transfer to this area because—" He paused, not wanting to get into the reasons because they were so complicated—and messy. "Well, let's just say it has to do with the custody battle, and leave it at that. My reasons for wanting this assignment are personal, but that doesn't mean I won't give this job everything I've got."

"That's good to know," she said, wondering why he was fighting for custody of his daughter. Was the girl being used as a pawn in a game between bitter parents, or was Nick Hanford a devoted father who had his child's best interests at heart? Something about the look of pain that flashed through his eyes and the hard set of his jaw made Crystal suspect it was the latter. On the surface, Nick was warm and friendly, but underneath he had problems that were weighing heavily on him. "And you don't have to worry, Nick. No one will hear about your personal business from me.''

"Thanks. I'd appreciate that." He gestured toward the trail. "Shall we press on?"

With Crystal leading the way, they finally made it to the crest of Saddleback Ridge, where Nick got his first look at Silver Springs. Sparkling in the sunlight, the lake stretched out beneath them, beautiful and untouched by the hand of man. A network of cliffs and heavily wooded shores formed an irregular boundary, and from his vantage point on the ridge, Nick couldn't see any way to reach the water.

"This is incredible," he murmured as Crystal dismounted and withdrew a pair of high-powered binoculars from her saddlebags. Nick held out his hand, and she handed him Cinnamon's reins.

"As far as I'm concerned, it's the most beautiful, peaceful spot on earth." Stepping closer to the sheer drop-off, she raised the binoculars.

"You looking for the boys or the eagles?"

"Eagles first, boys second," she muttered.

"Can you see their nest from here?"

"Yes." Crystal held her breath as she scanned the western shore of the lake until she found what she was looking for. "It's empty."

"I don't know about you, but I'll take that as a good sign," Nick said as he dismounted and tethered both horses. "The boys couldn't be too far ahead of us, and if they'd done any shooting, we'd have heard them. Hopefully your eagles are out hunting." He joined her at the edge of the cliff and she handed him the binoculars. They stood side by side as Crystal pointed out landmarks that helped him narrow down the location of the nest. From this angle and distance it was impossible to tell if there were any eggs in the nest, but the eagles would have been impossible to miss.

"I hope you're right," she said, scanning the woods again for any sight of the delinquents. Unfortunately there was very little unobstructed shoreline visible to her. They returned to the horses and followed Saddleback Ridge until it finally led them down a gentle slope where they caught only occasional glimpses of the lake through the trees. And then the forest finally gave way, and Nick found himself staring at an oasis of serenity as the lake stretched out in front of him.

"Beautiful, isn't it?" Crystal asked reverently, and Nick was just about to reply when the first shot echoed across the lake and reverberated through the woods like a crack of heat lightning.

CHAPTER FOUR

"Damn!" Crystal muttered as Cinnamon and Goliath shied at the sound. A second shot closely followed the first, and Crystal struggled to maintain control of her horse as she searched the sky, praying she wouldn't see one of her eagles plummeting toward the earth.

"The shots came from down here...somewhere in those rocks, I think," Nick said, but Crystal was looking skyward.

"There! They're shooting at hawks," she said, pointing almost directly overhead to the two beautiful red-tailed hawks that had been soaring on the air currents until the shots had startled them into serious flight. She held her breath, praying they would make it out of range, but just when she thought they had escaped unharmed, a third shot rang out. Crystal emitted a strangled cry of pain as the larger hawk flapped her wings erratically and fell out of the sky into the woods.

Before Nick could completely comprehend what was happening, Crystal was thundering down the irregular shoreline, blithely dodging trees that jutted onto the lake. He followed her as quickly as he dared, but she knew this area like the back of her hand, and Nick did not. He kept her in sight, but she gained on him steadily until finally she swerved into the woods just short of a cliff that soared twenty-five or thirty feet into the air.

"Crystal!" He called out to her, but she was gone and he was left to follow her trail.

Crystal charged uphill, headed for the spot where the steep incline intersected with the Staircase, a series of flat-topped cliffs that overlooked the lake. By the time she arrived, she could hear voices above her, and she quickly dismounted, secured Cinnamon's reins to a birch sapling, and scrambled up the nearly vertical bank to the smooth, sloping surface that jutted out over the lake.

Near the edge, Bobby and Lewis Whipley were so absorbed in celebrating their kill that they hadn't even heard Crystal coming until the scrape of her boots on the rock captured their attention. They whirled around, and their laughter died abruptly as they saw her bearing down on them with fury written all over her face.

"Oh, damn it! It's the bird lady," Lewis muttered, and both boys began frantically searching for an avenue of escape. Unfortunately for them, there was no easy exit. Behind them was a straight drop into the water, and to their left was a sheer rock face. To their right, the rocks rose about seven feet to another plateau, and beyond that, another, and another, like a giant stairway to the sky.

It was a fairly simple climb from one step up to the next, and the boys realized the only way out was up.

"Don't even think about it, boys!" she said harshly as they dodged to the right. Her tone of absolute authority stopped them in their tracks, and they stood still, watching her uncertainly as she approached. Bobby held his shotgun loosely as though he'd nearly forgotten about it, but it was pointed in Crystal's general direction, so she stopped a dozen feet away, eyeing the gun.

"We were only havin' some fun, Crystal," Bobby said defensively. "We didn't hit nothin'."

"I know better than that, Bobby," she said with disgust, holding out one hand. "Unload the shotgun and give it to me."

The boys looked at each other, silently debating whether or not to obey, and Lewis said defiantly, "You can't do that, lady. You can't take our—"

"I said jack the shells out of the chamber and hand it over!" she roared. Her voice echoed across the silent lake, and Bobby quickly broke the gun open, removed the shells, and held the shotgun out to her. "You boys are in big trouble," she said as she took the gun.

"We didn't do nothin'," Lewis argued, squaring his shoulders defiantly.

"Save it for the judge," Crystal snapped. "Now come on."

She pointed downhill, waiting for them to precede her, but the boys suddenly decided to do things the hard way. They bolted for the ledge, intending to climb the steps, and Crystal cursed under her breath as she respectfully laid the shotgun at her feet and charged after them. They didn't have enough of a head start to get any farther than halfway up to the second level before Crystal was right behind them. Placing one foot on the rock wall for leverage, she reached up and snagged both boys by their identical camouflage hunting vests. Fortunately they were fairly small for their age, and one good yank was all it took to pull them off balance and send them tumbling to the ground.

Crystal pivoted, ready to pounce on them again if they tried to run, and despite her anger it was everything she could do to keep from laughing at the scene in front of her. The boys had automatically rolled to their knees and found themselves looking down at the large pair of work boots that had taken root in front of them. They froze, then slowly craned their necks up to the face of the man towering over them. It was such a long journey that it seemed to take forever, and their shock was so obvious that Crystal actually did have to smother a laugh.

"Hello, boys," Nick said pleasantly, though there was nothing friendly about the uncompromising way he was looking at them. "I wouldn't try going anywhere if I were you. You're in enough trouble as it is." His glance moved up to Crystal, pinning her with a dark look that seemed to say "Don't laugh, you're in trouble, too." Her amusement faded, and she wondered what on earth she'd done to anger him. She returned his hard look with a puzzled frown, but he didn't seem inclined to enlighten her.

He reached down and grabbed a handful of the boys' vests and helped them none-too-gently to their feet while Crystal retrieved their shotgun.

"Who are you?" Lewis asked, trying unsuccessfully to work up a little belligerence toward the stranger who towered over him by a good twelve inches.

"I'm Nick Hanford, the new district ranger."

"Huh?" Bobby frowned and looked at Crystal. "I heard *you* were the new ranger."

Nick shot her a puzzled glance, but she pointedly avoided looking at him. "Well, you heard wrong," she said, swallowing a small surge of embarrassment as she silently cursed Dan Gatlin for the premature public announcement he'd made at the Lakeside Bar and Grill. "Now, come on, boys, let's go."

Resigned to their fate the boys retrieved their backpacks from the edge of the cliff, then trudged down the rock ledge with Crystal and Nick right behind. "Are you going to turn us over to Tony?" Lewis asked, referring to the Juvenile Officer.

"You bet we are," Crystal answered. "But first you've got some work to do."

"Work?" Bobby's head swiveled around. "What work?"

"You're going to find that bird you shot and make sure she's not suffering," she told them, wondering what Nick thought of the decision she'd made without consulting him. The answer to her question came quickly.

"That's right," he said, supporting her totally. "We're going to comb these woods until we find her."

"But that could take days!" Lewis exclaimed.

"Then we'll come back tomorrow," Nick said casually, though he really didn't think it would be necessary to return. He had a pretty clear image of where the hawk had gone down, and he was certain that Crystal did, too.

Nick's unexpected presence had shifted the balance of power significantly, and Bobby and Lewis were harboring no more thoughts of escape as their captors herded them down the embankment. Unfortunately Nick's presence did nothing to improve their attitudes. Arms akimbo, Bobby stared mutinously at Crystal. "Okay, Bird Lady, how are we supposed to find that eagle?"

"Eagle?" Crystal said incredulously. Watching a beautiful hawk blown out of the sky had made her heartsick and angry, but somehow Bobby's ignorance brought on a whole new set of conflicting emotions—the strongest of them, sadness. These boys had thoughtlessly set out to destroy something rare and beautiful without any concept of the damage they were doing—and showed not the slightest sign of remorse.

It was all Crystal could do to remain calm as she told him, "That was a hawk, Bobby. You didn't kill an eagle."

"And it's lucky that you didn't," Nick added, exchanging a glance with Crystal that told her his thoughts were almost identical. The boy's ignorance was pathetic. "Killing an eagle is a felony that carries a mandatory ten-thousand-dollar fine, plus a jail term."

"We ain't seventeen, so you can't send us to jail," Bobby said belligerently, but Lewis swallowed hard and looked at his brother.

"Ten thousand dollars?" he said weakly.

"That's right," Crystal replied. "Now let's get moving. The hawk went down behind that ridge." She pointed south. "We'll have to leave the horses here and go on foot."

Reluctantly they began trudging up the hill with Nick and Crystal close behind.

"I'm hungry," Bobby whined.

"Too bad," Crystal said. "We'll eat something after we've found the hawk."

Bobby snickered and poked his brother in the ribs. "I wonder what hawk meat tastes like?"

Crystal smothered an outraged gasp and fought the urge to inflict bodily injury on the insensitive little smart aleck. Her hands were knotted into angry fists, and she was surprised when Nick placed his hand on her coat sleeve and gave her arm a reassuring squeeze. His hand was large, but surprisingly gentle, and he was giving her an endearingly crooked little smile. Crystal felt her anger drain away, to be replaced by an emotion that was much softer—and a lot more pleasant.

"It's not worth the trouble," he whispered.

"I know," she said, managing a strained smile. She wasn't accustomed to feeling such tender emotions for anyone—and particularly not a man she'd known so briefly. Instead of thinking about that, though, she concentrated on her irritation with the Whipleys. "But it would feel so good to give them just one good whack."

"You can say that again."

Realizing they had sunk into hotter water, the boys quickened their pace slightly to put a little distance between themselves and their captors. Crystal's first instinct was to keep up with them, but since she couldn't shake her anger she decided that a little space might help. Nick apparently had the same thought, because he lagged behind, too, until about a dozen yards separated them from the boys, and then they picked up their pace, keeping a steady distance between them.

Nick's motive was a little different from Crystal's, though. He wanted a moment to talk to her out of the boys' earshot.

"That was a pretty reckless stunt you pulled back there," he commented seriously, keeping his voice low.

Crystal glanced at him and found that his face was set into very stern lines. "What stunt?"

"Those boys had a loaded shotgun, but you stormed after them like Teddy Roosevelt leading the charge up San Juan Hill. Unfortunately you left your troops behind," he said, tapping his chest to indicate her cavalry contingent of one lone soldier.

"I'm sorry," she said sincerely, realizing how completely she had usurped Nick's authority in this situation. He had every right to reprimand her, and she appreciated the fact that he was doing it in a manner that didn't put her completely on the defensive. "I'm used to taking the initiative in things like this, and I was just so damned angry that I didn't think."

Nick nodded. "I know you were angry. So was I. But you could have gotten yourself killed."

"Bobby never would have shot me," she argued.

"You don't know that for sure. You could have startled them into doing something stupid."

"I really don't agree with you," Crystal stated reasonably, "but I do realize that it was wrong to leave you behind."

Nick gave her a grin that signaled the end of his reprimand. "I've been left behind before. And you did do a good job rounding up the boys. I thought I was going to crack up when you plucked them off the cliff like a couple of dog ticks."

Crystal shrugged, suddenly embarrassed. Her actions hadn't been what anyone would call feminine, and for some strange reason it bothered her that Nick had witnessed her unladylike behavior. "I just did what was necessary."

Nick sensed her embarrassment and wondered at its source. Rather than comment on it, though, he changed the subject. "Why did the boys call you Bird Lady?"

"Oh, that," she fanned the air with one hand. "I'm a licensed raptor rehabilitator, and since I'm the only one in the area, any time anyone finds a wounded hawk or owl, it's brought to me." She grinned at him. "I also get my fair share of barn swallows, blue jays, and robins—hence the nickname Bird Lady. Not very flattering, is it?"

"I don't know. I think it's kinda cute."

Crystal groaned. "Oh, please. Nothing about me has been cute since I was five years old."

Nick chuckled and found that he couldn't argue with her. Nothing about Crystal Elliot was even remotely cute. She was strikingly beautiful, strong, capable, and almost aristocratically graceful, but she wasn't cute. "I stand corrected," he replied. "So tell me about your rehabilitation project."

Keeping one eye on the boys ahead of them, Crystal obliged Nick. "I don't know if you could call it a 'project' or not. I don't get more than a dozen raptors a year."

"How many do you have now?"

"Two. A barn owl and an adorable little American kestrel."

"What's wrong with them?" he asked, genuinely curious.

"The kestrel had some stress points on his primary wing tips, and somehow he broke them off."

"So he'll be fine as soon as he goes through a molt," Nick assumed.

"That's right," she said, impressed by the depth of his knowledge about birds of prey. "The barn owl has been a much more difficult case, though. He flew into the windshield of a pickup truck and dislocated his shoulder. I think he's healing nicely, but he's a real handful."

Nick chuckled. "I can imagine. Barn owls aren't known for their good-natured dispositions."

Crystal laughed, too. "I'll say. He spreads his wings, goes into an attack display, and rushes at me every time I enter his pen."

"You're a brave lady," he said with an admiring grin. "A full-grown barn owl has a wing span of nearly four feet. I don't think I'd want to be locked in a room alone with one."

"I've gotten used to fending for myself in small quarters," she replied.

Crystal's love of her avocation was obvious. The warmth of her voice and the lively sparkle in her eyes were so compelling, Nick felt a surge of attraction to her that was so strong he had a hard time suppressing it.

The Whipley boys, who had never been out of Crystal's thoughts or sight, reached the top of the hill and were just starting to disappear down the other side. She called for them to wait, and when the boys stopped as directed, she and Nick quickened their pace.

"I think the hawk went down in this little valley. Do you want to direct the search, or shall I?" she asked quietly, and received a look from Nick that she found impossible to read.

"Thanks."

Crystal frowned. "For what?"

"For recognizing that I might have a need to establish a little authority over the boys."

"You did that with just one look," she told him ruefully.

"Well, I'm glad you think so, and I really don't feel the need to control this operation just for the sake of my image, but under the circumstances, it was very considerate of you to offer."

They were getting closer to the boys, and Crystal stopped so that she wouldn't be overheard. Keeping her voice low, she looked at him seriously. "Listen, Nick, I don't have any hard feelings toward you because you took this job. I'm disappointed, yes. And I had expected to be resentful because I thought you were just a paper pusher from Washington, but that's obviously not the case. You know your way around the forest, and you're also very good at handling people. I respect that."

"Coming from you, that means a lot, Crystal," he said sincerely, and his obvious approval of her made Crystal feel warm all over.

"Thank you," she replied, growing a little uncomfortable with the way he made her feel. "I just wanted you to know that I have no intention of trying to undermine your authority or enter into a tug of war with you."

"That's very reassuring. Not everyone who had a big promotion taken away as you did would be so generous."

Crystal tried to shrug off his compliment. "I'll get over it."

"I hope so. I'm really going to need your help and support in getting settled into this job."

"You've got it," she promised, and was a little surprised to realize that she meant it completely.

Nick smiled and his dark brown eyes twinkled with warm lights that made Crystal's heart do a small staccato drumroll.

Under Nick's guidance the foursome spread out and began covering the rough terrain. Nearly an hour later as they crossed a shallow brook the cry of a distressed hawk brought them all to a dead stop.

"Over here!" Lewis yelled. "It's alive. Right here. Jeez, I almost stepped on it!"

Hurrying along the stream bank, Crystal wondered how Lewis Whipley had ever survived to reach his mid-teens. A hawk eighteen inches long would be a little hard to miss. "Stay back," she instructed calmly. "You're frightening her." And indeed, the hawk was wild-eyed with fear. She was alert, but in shock, with her head swiveling this way and that in confusion. One wing was draped uselessly at its side.

Approaching the hawk slowly, Crystal removed her gloves from her pocket and slipped them on as she continued speaking to the bird in low, soothing tones. "Easy girl. I'm not going to hurt you. Don't be afraid. I just want to help."

Standing a respectful distance away to keep from alarming the hawk further, Nick watched Crystal in amazement. She knelt, and the hawk did not protest. In fact, it seemed greatly soothed by Crystal's presence. For a moment, Nick almost came to believe that she had some rapport with it, for the bird seemed to grow calm at the sound of her voice, and stayed very still as Crystal slowly reached out her right hand.

That hand was only inches from the hawk's head when the magical rapport proved to be nothing more than illusion. The hawk struck abruptly, its powerful beak— especially designed to tear animal flesh—clamping onto Crystal's hand. Both boys jumped back, startled by the sudden attack, but Crystal didn't even flinch. She had been expecting no less, and was ready for it. Protected by the gloves, she allowed the hawk to grip her right hand while the left one quickly encircled the bird's back and shoulders. Startled, the hawk let go of the glove and Crystal quickly immobilized it.

"Could you give me a hand, Nick?" she asked.

"Gladly." He knelt opposite her, drawing on his gloves. "What do you want me to do?"

"Hold her here," she instructed, transferring control of the bird's legs to Nick. "But be careful. I think a piece of shot must have broken her left tarsus. Can you help me get this glove off?"

Nick hesitated a moment. "Are you sure that's a good idea?" he asked, thinking about the damage the hawk's beak and razor-sharp talons could inflict.

"I can't examine her with the glove on," she replied, and Nick acquiesced, using his free hand to remove her glove.

With Nick helping her control the hawk, Crystal quickly conducted her examination.

"How bad is it?" Nick prompted when she seemed to have completed her inspection.

"I can't say for sure. She may have just the broken wing and leg."

"Do you have a vet who can set them?"

A smile spread slowly across Crystal's face. Nick understood without being told that she was not going to destroy the hawk; she was going to take it home and try to save its life. "Actually I do that myself. We just have to transport her down the mountain as gently as possible."

"What would you suggest?"

"We need something to wrap her in," she answered, concerned about the hawk's shallow breathing and the rapid heartbeat she could feel thumping beneath her hand. "She's really stressed, but she'll calm down if we immobilize her and cover her head."

"Our coats would smother her, wouldn't they?"

Crystal nodded. "I'm afraid so."

"I've got an idea. Here. Put this back on," Nick said, clumsily helping her into her glove. When her hand was once again protected, Crystal took hold of the hawk's legs and watched as Nick stood. Quickly he slipped out of his coat, tossed it to Lewis, and began unbuttoning his long-sleeved khaki shirt.

Stunned, Crystal watched as he undressed. Her hold on the hawk never faltered, but rescuing birds of prey was the last thing on her mind as Nick stripped down to his white undershirt, then blithely pulled it over his head. His physique was nothing short of magnificent, from the sinewy cords of muscles that rippled from his forearms and broad shoulders, across the perfectly defined contours of his chest, down to his flat stomach and lean waist. A soft brown matt of hair dusted his chest and tapered down to a narrow vertical band until it disappeared beneath his dark green trousers.

Working out of doors as much as she did, Crystal had seen a lot of men bare chested, but never one who looked as perfect as Nick Hanford—or one who stole her breath away quite so completely. At that moment he epitomized the very essence of masculine strength; it was impossible not to wonder what it would be like to touch him . . . and to be touched by him.

The thought was so erotic and so startling that Crystal looked away from him, pretending to be absorbed in controlling the red-tailed hawk, who was actually quite still.

"Brrr..." Nick shivered as he quickly put his shirt and coat back on. "Is it always this cold in April?"

"Not usually," Crystal replied, not daring to look at him.

"Just my luck, I guess." With the help of the utility knife he always carried, he split the front of the T-shirt open and spread it out on the ground next to Crystal.

"Thanks," she murmured, placing the hawk on the shirt. With his arms and hands tangling with Crystal's, Nick helped her immobilize the bird, and suddenly, Crystal was all thumbs. Her awareness of the man who was pressed shoulder to shoulder with her was completely unnerving. She tried not to flinch whenever Nick's hands brushed against hers, but by the time they had finished, Nick was looking at her a little strangely.

"You think that will do it?" he asked as Crystal folded the material over the bird's head.

She nodded and cradled the hawk in her arms like a newborn infant. "I think she's calming down already. We'd better return to the horses and get her down the mountain, though."

"All right. Let's go." Nick stood and placed one hand on Crystal's elbow to steady her as she rose.

It took only a few minutes to return to the spot where they'd left the horses. The boys were complaining incessantly about being hungry, so Nick led Goliath and Cinnamon down to the lake and spread one of the blankets in a sunny spot that provided a breathtaking view of the lake. Crystal laid the hawk on a soft bed of leaves while Nick took Naomi's sandwiches from the saddlebags.

"All rl-lght! A picnic!" Bobby said, and earned a sharp look from both Crystal and Nick.

"This isn't a fun day at the beach, boys," Nick told them. "Just sit down and eat. You've got a long walk ahead of you."

Digging into their backpacks, the boys came up with several smashed bags of potato chips and their canteens. Crystal and Nick washed their hands in the crystal-clear lake, then settled onto the blanket, and the boys chose a spot a short distance away.

"Mrs. Gatlin packed enough sandwiches for a small army," Nick said quietly, leaning toward Crystal. "Should we be kind and share, or let the boys make do with potato chip crumbs?"

Crystal glanced at Bobby and Lewis. "I guess we'll share," she said with a resigned sigh. "I was never very successful at being an ogre."

Nick chuckled and picked up two of the plastic-wrapped sandwiches. "Heads up, boys." He tossed them one at a time.

They grunted what could have been thank-yous, and fell on the sandwiches ravenously.

Enjoying the serene setting and a chance to relax, Nick and Crystal ate Naomi's delicious chicken salad sandwiches in silence. Unfortunately it didn't take long enough to finish their lunch. "I wish we could stay here the rest of the day, but we really should be getting back," Nick said, stifling a yawn as he leaned back on both elbows.

"You say that, but you're not moving," Crystal returned in a teasing tone, gathering up the plastic wrap and napkins.

"Just two more minutes," he pleaded. "The thought of another three hours in the saddle is definitely slowing me down."

Crystal eyed him mischievously. "You could always walk back and let Bobby ride Goliath."

"Over my dead b—" He stopped abruptly, staring skyward. "Crystal, look!"

She glanced up, and a broad, happy smile lit her face. High above them, two eagles were soaring on the shifting air currents, playfully dodging this way and that, slowly descending toward the lake.

"Wow!"

"Would you look at that!" the boys exclaimed simultaneously.

"Be quiet and don't move," Crystal told them. "Just watch." And they did watch quietly as the eagles separated, one heading across the lake to the nest while the other swooped lower, growing larger and larger as it descended toward them. Two and a half feet long, with a wing span of nearly seven feet, the eagle cast a huge shadow as it soared over them, its white head standing out in bold contrast to its dark body and wings.

Taking no notice of the humans nearby, the magnificent bird skimmed the water, its wings lapping the surface occasionally, sending rippling circles outward, until finally its great wings arched as its talons shot forward, plunging into the water. With stunning accuracy, the eagle struck its prey, then flapped furiously to resume its flight. It soared up and away toward the nest, leaving four breathless humans behind, enthralled and sadly earthbound.

"Incredible," Nick said quietly, more to himself than anyone else. "That's the reason I joined the Forest Service."

Crystal looked at him and smiled, for once not embarrassed by the knot of emotion that clogged her throat. "Me, too." They stared at each other for a long moment, each savoring the pleasure of having found a kindred spirit. It was an experience Crystal had shared with very few people in her life—and none of them made her feel quite the way Nick Hanford did. With difficulty, she looked away from him and focused on the boys, who were still staring across the lake, hoping for another glimpse of the raptor.

"That's what you came up here to kill," she said without censure, just as a statement of fact. "If you had succeeded, her mate would have flown away, and no other visitor to this lake would ever have had the chance to see what you just saw."

To his credit, Lewis ducked his head in shame, but any remorse Bobby Whipley felt was deeply buried beneath a stronger need to prove to the world how tough he was. "It was just a big bird with a white head." He sneered. "I don't know what all the fuss is about."

Crystal looked at him with pity as she stood. "And you probably never will," she said sadly. "Come on. It's time to head for home."

CHAPTER FIVE

IT WAS AFTER FOUR by the time Nick and Crystal herded their charges across the meadow toward the Gatlins' farm. The boys were so tired they were practically stumbling, even though their captors had generously allowed them to travel horseback part of the way. Even the horses seemed grateful for the slow pace Nick and Crystal were setting. Using the army blanket, Crystal had made a little bed for the hawk, and everyone had taken turns carrying her, as well.

"Looks like they've been expecting us," Nick commented as Dan and Naomi slipped off the back porch and Lonnie Macklin at the stable all began hurrying toward them.

"Mom's probably been pacing the floor. If we hadn't taken time to look for the hawk, we'd have been back two hours ago," Crystal replied, trying to flex her numb hand without disturbing the hawk in her arms. She'd been carrying the bird for nearly half an hour, and her arm was beginning to lose feeling.

Nick noticed the movement and cocked his head toward the hawk. "You need me to take her?"

"No thanks, we're almost there," she answered, then called out a greeting to her foster parents, who had stopped to wait for them at the edge of the yard.

"Hi, honey!" Dan called back, but Naomi caught a glimpse of the bundle Crystal was carrying, and clutched her husband's arm.

"Oh, no," she moaned. The blanket being used as a cushion made the bird look much larger than it actually was. "They wounded one of the eagles, Dan. Crystal must be heartbroken." Dressed in sneakers, a red flannel shirt and the worn-out pair of blue jeans she'd been cleaning the attic in, Naomi hurried toward her foster daughter with Dan at her side.

As they neared, Crystal and Nick brought the horses to a standstill. "Did they get the eagles, honey?" Dan asked as Naomi approached Crystal from the left side and held up her arms to receive the wounded bird.

Keeping a tight rein on Cinnamon, Crystal leaned down and passed the bird to her mother. "No, we were lucky this time," she answered. "The boys thought they had bagged an eagle, but they only managed to wound a red-tailed hawk."

Gently cradling the bundled-up bird, Naomi turned to the two culprits who were skulking behind the horses, hoping to go unnoticed. "Oh, boys, how could you?" It wasn't a condemnation, just a simple question that seemed to suggest that somehow she had expected better from them.

Naomi was a small, attractive woman with a generous amount of silver in her hair and huge sky-blue eyes. There was nothing the least bit intimidating about her, but Nick was astonished to see that one look from her and a few softly spoken words were enough to make both boys hang their heads in shame. Clearly this was a woman who was well suited to raising a big brood of kids. Nick doubted that she had ever had to raise her voice to get a child to do exactly what she wanted him to do.

"Sorry if we worried you folks, but it took us quite a while to find the hawk," Nick said as he dismounted.

"Oh, no problem," Dan replied. "I'm just glad you did. If there's any chance at all of saving the poor thing, Crystal will do it. She's something of a miracle worker."

Dan's pride in his daughter's accomplishments was obvious, and Nick couldn't help smiling. "I don't doubt that for a minute. So far, I haven't found anything that Crystal *can't* do," he said, looking up at her.

"Thanks," she mumbled. Embarrassed by the praise, she turned her attention to the boys. "Come on, guys, let's get up to the house so I can call Tony and let him know we're bringing you in."

"You won't have to do that, Crystal," Dan told her as she dismounted. "Tony called about half an hour ago, wondering whether or not you'd found the boys, and he said he'd just drive on out. He should be here anytime now."

"Great, that'll save us a trip to the detention center." They started toward the house just as Lonnie finally caught up with them. Only a little out of breath from his long jog from the stable, he took charge of the horses and mumbled something about giving them a good rub down.

"I'd be glad to give you a hand, Lonnie. It's the least I can do," Nick said as he removed the boys' shotgun from its makeshift holster on Crystal's saddle.

Lonnie waited impatiently, refusing to look at Nick. "No need," he muttered shortly. "I can do it. That's my job."

He led the horses away, and Nick looked after him, puzzled. He hadn't thought much about the boy's cool attitude this morning, but now he wondered what was wrong. Unable to imagine what he'd done to offend Lonnie, Nick glanced at Crystal to see her reaction, but she was already several yards ahead of him, deep in conversation with Naomi, discussing treatment of the hawk.

Dan had lagged behind, though. "Nick..." he said, drawing his attention away from Crystal. "Listen, I'm sorry Lonnie has been so rude. Don't give it a second thought—he'll come around eventually. Crystal's like a sister to him, and he's very protective of her."

Nick frowned. "Crystal? Why would he think she needs to be protected from me?"

"Well, not protected, exactly, but..." Dan sighed heavily, not really sure how much he should say. When they had learned that Crystal's job had been usurped by an outsider, Lonnie hadn't taken the news nearly as well as Crystal had. Lonnie was very much a loner, but he was so fiercely defensive of his family that he had decided to hate the new ranger sight unseen.

But Dan didn't want to say that to Nick. His premature announcement of the promotion had already caused Crystal enough embarrassment, and Dan didn't feel that it was his place to tell his daughter's new boss that he had taken her job. If Crystal wanted him to know, she'd tell him herself.

Nick heard Dan's hesitation and finally realized the source of the problem. "Oh, I get it. Lonnie is bent out of shape because I kept Crystal from getting promoted."

Dan looked at him in surprise. "She told you about that?"

Nick nodded. "Yeah. I can't tell you how bad I feel about it. When I requested this assignment, I had no idea the post had already been promised to someone else. The paperwork hadn't gone into the computer, so I had no way of knowing."

Dan didn't doubt that Nick's regret was genuine. "It was just bad timing all around, I guess. But you really don't have to worry about Crystal, Nick. She's the ultimate team player—I've never known her to hold a grudge in her entire life."

"Unlike Lonnie?" Nick asked with a grin.

Dan laughed. "Believe it or not, he's really a good kid."

"Oh, I believe it," Nick replied. "I admire loyalty."

"That's good to hear."

"Crystal told me that you and Mrs. Gatlin have raised a lot of foster kids," Nick commented as they moved on toward the house. "Does Lonnie still live here with you?"

Dan nodded. "He built a little apartment in the stable."

"What about Crystal?" he asked, remembering how beautiful she'd looked as she talked about how much she loved the farm.

"She lives here, too, in the main house. She had an apartment in town for a while, but when she decided to start her raptor rehabilitation program Naomi and I convinced her it made a lot more sense for her to move back home." The crunch of gravel drew Dan's attention to the driveway. "Oh, good. There's Tony Manguson. Come on, I'll introduce you."

Naomi had already headed into the house to settle their new patient into a recovery box, but Crystal and the boys had seen the juvenile officer's car coming and were waiting in the yard.

"Hello, Crystal," Tony said warmly as he got out of his car and came around to the other side. Thirty-five, twice divorced, and currently single, Tony Manguson was an all-around nice guy—friendly, outgoing, and more than passably handsome. Over the years, Crystal had dated him casually a number of times—when he was between divorces—but she had never allowed their relationship to go beyond friendship. "I got your message this morning, and I was beginning to get worried about you."

"We made it just fine, but thanks for being concerned," she replied amiably. Quickly she filled Tony in on what had happened at Silver Springs, and the juvenile officer herded the boys into his car. "I don't want them to get off easy, Tony," she said firmly as soon as the boys were out of earshot.

"Neither do I, but Bob Whipley has the best lawyer in the county and enough money to buy the boys out of just about any trouble they could ever get in."

"That's not fair," she said, then realized how ridiculous the statement was. No one knew better than she did that when it came to juvenile justice in Newton County, life was seldom fair. She and her brother, Tommy J., were proof of that.

"I agree with you, Crystal," Tony said as Nick and Dan joined them. He gave Dan a friendly smile and shot a curious look at Nick, but didn't stop what he was saying to Crystal. "I'll process them into detention and hold them until juvenile court meets on Thursday. I'm going to need your testimony at the hearing."

"All right. Nick was a witness, too. Will you need him?"

"Nick?" he questioned.

"That's me," Nick said, extending his hand. "I'm Nick Hanford, the new district ranger. It's nice to meet you, Tony."

"The new ranger...?" Tony shook hands perfunctorily as he frowned and glanced at Crystal. "But I thought you . . .'' His voice trailed off when he realized he'd put his foot in his mouth.

"That's my fault, Tony," Dan spoke up, feeling sick at heart. "The announcement of Crystal's promotion was a little premature."

"Announcement?" Nick asked.

Dan nodded. "The district supervisor assured me the job was Crystal's, and I very stupidly announced it at my retirement party a couple of weeks ago."

"Dan, it's not your fault," Crystal insisted, then looked pointedly at Nick, who was clearly upset. "It's not *anybody's* fault."

"That's very gracious of you, Crystal," Nick said, but her absolution didn't assuage his guilt, which was growing steadily. He'd never dreamed that her promotion expectations had been made common knowledge. Not only was she having to deal with her natural disappointment about not getting the job, but she also had embarrassing moments like this to contend with. Knowing that everyone in her hometown was feeling sorry for her couldn't be easy for her. No wonder she had been cool toward him when they'd met. It was a miracle she was even willing to speak to him.

"Well, I still feel bad about it," Dan said. "If I hadn't opened my big mouth—"

"Dan, please, just let it go," Crystal begged him, laying a reassuring hand on his arm. "It's not important."

"But it is important, honey. It's made things worse for you, and it may even cause some resentment against Nick."

"I've handled bigger problems than this, Dan, believe me," Nick said wryly. "Crystal is right. It's not something you should worry about. We'll do our jobs and eventually it will all blow over. The only thing that's really important is that Crystal isn't holding a grudge against me. All things considered, I'd say that's pretty remarkable."

"Crystal is a pretty remarkable lady," Tony said sharply, not at all pleased with the way the new ranger was looking at Crystal.

Nick heard the note of warning in Tony's voice that clearly said "hands off, she's spoken for," and was more than a little disappointed to learn that Crystal had a man in her life. Of course, she was so beautiful and so much fun to be with that it was only to be expected, but it was still disappointing. Tony Manguson was a lucky man.

Crystal heard the strange note in Tony's voice, too, but she wasn't really sure what it meant. "Listen, if you guys want to stand here and sing my praises all evening, you go right ahead," she said with a grin. "But I've got to go inside and get some nourishment into that hawk."

"And I've got to get the boys to the center," Tony said, remembering his charges in the car. "Nice meeting you, Hanford. I'll see you in court Thursday."

"Oh, I'll be there. It's important that I take a firm stand on illegal hunting in the wilderness preserve."

Dan gave him an approving smile, and Tony bade everyone a pleasant farewell as he jumped into his car and sped off.

"Come on in the house, Nick," Crystal invited. "I'll get you something to drink while I take care of the hawk—if you don't mind waiting, that is," she said, realizing that he'd spent his entire first day at work away from the station.

"I don't mind," he replied, matching his gait to hers as they moved toward the house. "We couldn't make it back to town before quitting time, anyway, and actually, I'm anxious to see what you do with the hawk."

"At this point, there's not much I can do," she said, leading him through the squeaky door to the screened-in back porch. Dan brought up the rear as they entered Naomi's homey kitchen. "I'll force-feed her a good dose of raw eggs and liquid vitamin supplements in a solution of Gatorade, and let her rest a few hours."

"Here, let me have your coats. I'll hang them in the front closet while you two look after the hawk. I'll be upstairs, moving some boxes out of the attic if you need me, honey," Dan said. Taking their coats, he disappeared through a swinging door.

"This a great kitchen," Nick said, leaning against the counter by the door as Crystal washed her hands at the sink. "I haven't seen one like it in years." Except for the modern appliances, the room looked exactly as it must have when the old house was built. The countertops were all constructed of tiny porcelain tiles, the huge cabinets were painted white and the floor was an old-fashioned linoleum that had seen a lot of wear but was still in excellent condition. Frilly yellow curtains were tied back from the window over the sink, and there was a matching curtain on the window of the back door.

"I love this old house," Crystal told him as she poured two glasses of iced tea and handed one to Nick, then started gathering ingredients for the hawk's dinner. "It's big and drafty, but I wouldn't trade it for any mansion in the world. There's nothing on earth as enjoyable as opening the windows on a cool spring day and letting the breeze sweep through, or sitting in the porch swing at sunset, watching the squirrels playing and listening to birds singing." Crystal realized she was getting a little carried away and laughed at herself. "That must sound very boring to you after so many years in the city."

"Actually that sounds like my definition of heaven," Nick said, utterly captivated by the look of joy on her face. "Living in the city had its advantages, I guess, but I'm just a country boy at heart."

She gave him a smile that said she understood exactly what he meant. He returned that smile, his dark eyes crinkling at the corners in a way that fascinated Crystal. Before she realized what was happening, they were simply staring at each other, caught in a little web of sweet, entirely sexual tension that seemed to have sprung up from nowhere. It was delightful and exhilarating, but it was also quite disturbing. She'd known Nick for less than a day! How could she possibly be experiencing an attraction this overwhelming?

Completely against her will, she remembered the sight of Nick when he removed his shirt up at Silver Springs. Every muscular contour had been burned into her memory in delicious detail. Embarrassment flooded through her, and she quickly returned to her task. Unfortunately her sensual awareness of him just wouldn't go away.

Crystal wasn't the only one who found the tension discomfiting. Nick cleared his throat and reminded himself sternly that his life was too unstable right now to even consider embarking on a romantic relationship. Yet he couldn't keep from admiring everything about Crystal as she worked around the kitchen. The effect she was having on his senses was nothing short of alarming. "What can I do to help?" he asked when she finished mixing the hawk's lunch.

"Just be ready to give me a hand if I get into any trouble," she replied, moving through a large dining room into a beautiful glassed-in sun porch. Nick followed her, but when she knelt in front of a well-ventilated cardboard box in the middle of the room it quickly became obvious that she was more than capable of handling the job alone. Nick watched in awe as she immobilized the hawk and force-fed it with a large syringe, then returned it to the recovery box to rest.

Because he seemed interested in her hobby, Crystal pointed out her raptor cages in the backyard and told him a little more about her setup.

"This is very impressive, Crystal," he told her as they returned to the kitchen. "It must take up a lot of your spare time."

"It does, but it's well worth it. And, of course, I have a lot of help." A troubled shadow passed over her face. "I'm not sure how I'm going to manage when Mom and Dan leave next month."

"Where are they headed?"

"Arizona."

"Vacation?" he questioned, though something about the sad look on Crystal's face told him otherwise.

"No, they're moving out there permanently. Mom's father passed away a few years ago and left her the family ranch outside Mesa, so Dan, Mom, and their son, Casey, are going to take a stab at breeding quarter horses. Casey's already there." She managed a grin. "This is how Dan always planned to spend his retirement, so it's kind of a dream come true for them."

Nick returned her smile, but he couldn't help feeling a stab of sympathy for her. She was obviously trying to be cheerful about the imminent departure of her parents, but clearly it wasn't going to be easy for her to watch them go.

"There you are, honey," Naomi said brightly as she bounced into the kitchen. "Sorry I disappeared on you. I had just got the hawk settled in when Doris Simpkins called."

"And you're already off the phone?" Crystal said facetiously.

Naomi chuckled. "Miracles do still happen. So, did you get the hawk fed? And did you get Ranger Hanford something to drink?"

"Yes—to both questions," Crystal answered. "And I don't think you two were ever really introduced. Nick Hanford, this is my mother, Naomi Gatlin."

Naomi offered her hand, only to have it swallowed by Nick's. "Welcome to Oak Ridge, Nick."

"It's a pleasure to be here. If my first day on the job is any indication, this is going to be a pretty terrific assignment."

"I certainly wouldn't contradict you," Naomi replied. "This community has been very good to Dan and me."

"That's because you've been so good to the community," Crystal told her with a fond smile.

Naomi waved off the compliment and looked at Nick. "Has Crystal invited you to stay for supper yet?"

The question caught Nick off guard, and before he could answer, Crystal said, "No, Mom, I hadn't gotten around to that yet." She looked at Nick. "You will join us, won't you?"

"That's very nice of you, but actually I'd really like to get back to the office, shower, and get into some clothes that haven't spent the day on a horse."

Crystal pursed her lips thoughtfully. "That's a nice plan, but I'm afraid there's one little flaw in it."

Nick lowered his head and sighed as he realized what she was about to say. "There's no shower at the station, right?"

"Sorry."

He shook his head. "I should have realized that this morning. I guess I'll be checking into a motel tonight, after all."

"Don't be silly," Naomi scolded mildly. "Bring a change of clothes out here and use our shower."

Nick smiled. Apparently there was no end to the Gatlins' generosity. "That's very kind of you, but I couldn't impose. I had planned to stay in the infirmary at the office for a day or two until I found a place to live, but since there's no shower there, I'm going to have to get a motel room anyway. I might as well do it this evening."

"All right, then, but that still doesn't mean you can't come to dinner," Naomi said. "There's no reason for you to eat alone in a restaurant your first night in Oak Ridge, and I know you and Dan have a lot to talk about, so it's settled. Right, Crystal?" She looked at her daughter for support.

Crystal folded her arms across her chest and leaned against the counter. "Absolutely."

Nick laughed with delight. "I can see that I'm outnumbered, but I really do need to start looking for an apartment tonight. May I please take a rain check?"

"Sure," Crystal said, remembering that Nick had told her he was trying to get custody of his daughter. If that was true, finding a place to live had to be his first priority, and she respected that. Still, she couldn't help being a little disappointed that he wasn't staying. And then she couldn't help being irritated with herself for being disappointed. Nick Hanford was her boss, not her boyfriend, and she was going to have to keep that fact firmly in mind.

Naomi knew when to give up, too. "All right, I'll let you off the hook tonight, but I insist you come back one night this week."

"I wouldn't miss it for the world," Nick told her, totally captivated by the older woman's dancing eyes and spritely personality. "Are you ready to head back to town, Crystal?"

"Let's go." She collected their coats and they walked down the lane to the stable where they'd left the Jeep.

"I think I've fallen in love with your mother," Nick said, only half joking.

"Don't feel bad. Everyone does. When I was in high school I always had the nagging suspicion that boys only wanted to date me so that they could be around Mom."

Nick gave her a skeptical look. "I seriously doubt that, Crystal. With your looks and personality, you probably had to beat the boys off with a stick—and you probably still do."

She laughed airily. "Yep, that's me. The femme fatale of Oak Ridge, Arkansas." She lowered her voice confidentially, as though she was imparting a deep, dark secret. "It's the uniform that drives 'em wild."

Nick laughed, too, but his eyes were dead serious when he told her, "No, it isn't, Crystal. With or without the uniform, you are one incredible lady."

"Thank you." Crystal swallowed hard and wondered if she'd only imagined the flirtatious innuendo in his comment. The memory of Nick without his shirt flashed in her mind again, and suddenly she was wondering what it was going to take to squash her outrageous attraction to him. Nick was her boss; she'd be seeing him every day for the next few months, probably even the next few years. How long could anyone be expected to fight his kind of sex appeal?

Feeling like a silly schoolgirl with a ridiculous crush, Crystal climbed into the Jeep and drove Nick back to town.

The thirty-minute ride had never seemed longer.

WITH ONE TOWEL wrapped around his waist and another draped over his shoulders, Nick stepped out of the bathroom and headed straight for the telephone beside the bed. After Crystal had dropped him off at the office, she had given him directions to the Oak Ridge Inn, a modern, two-story motel where he'd had no trouble obtaining a simple but comfortably furnished room. Hoping a little hot water would work some magic on the muscles that were protesting after nearly six hours on horseback, he'd jumped into the shower immediately.

Now, he was refreshed and ready to face an evening of apartment hunting. The prospect wasn't as appealing as dining with Crystal Elliot and her delightful foster parents, but finding a place for Trisha to live was his first priority. A copy of the *Oak Ridge Daily News* was lying on the bed, but before he started pouring over the classified ads, he had a phone call to make to his daughter. He'd spent two days with her in Kentucky before driving on to Oak Ridge, and when he'd returned Trisha to her temporary home at her grandparents' yesterday she had made him swear that he'd call to let her know he arrived safely.

In one way, Nick had been amused and touched by her almost maternal concern, but mostly he'd been disturbed by it. Fourteen-year-old girls were supposed to be obsessed with their appearance and their latest crush on a rock star or the captain of the high-school basketball team. But instead, Nick's daughter had been so traumatized by his ex-wife that she had become more parent than child. That was only one of the reasons Nick considered it so vital that he get custody of Trisha. He had to give her the sense of security Marjorie had denied her; he had to find some way to let his little girl be a teenager again.

Though he knew it was too much to hope for, Nick sat on the side of the bed and dialed his former in-laws number, praying that Trisha would answer the phone. None of his confrontations with Marjorie's parents had been pleasant, and he'd just as soon not have to endure another of Charles or Lois Keating's tirades about how cruel Nick was being to Marjorie and Trisha.

The phone rang twice before a gravelly male voice came on the line. "Keating residence."

Nick sighed wearily. So much for doing this the easy way. "Hello, Charles, this is Nick. May I speak with Trisha, please?"

The voice turned decidedly frosty. "Hello, Nick. Apparently you made the trip all right."

"Yes, and I promised Trisha I'd call and let her know that."

"I'll be happy to pass your message along to her," Charles told him. "Trisha is still eating supper."

Nick gritted his teeth. "Well, I'm sorry I interrupted your meal, Charles, but I'd rather talk to Trisha myself. Now, if you'll just call her to the—"

"I don't suppose you realize or care that your daughter is very upset about this whole ordeal you've forced on all of us," Charles said irritably.

"Of course I realize it!" Nick snapped. He'd heard the same argument so many times that he'd lost all patience with Charles, who insisted on turning a blind eye and a deaf ear to his daughter's problems. "But Trisha was upset long before I started the custody suit. Good Lord, she's been physically and emotionally abused by an alcoholic mother. She's got a right to be upset, and so have I!"

"Damn it, that's an unfounded accusation—"

"Take your head out of the sand, Charles, and face the facts," Nick shouted, coming to his feet in frustration and anger. "Your daughter is an alcoholic!"

Nick could almost visualize the portly man draw his shoulders back. "If Marjorie drinks a little too much sometimes, it's because she had such a lousy husband."

If the statement hadn't been so pathetic, Nick might have laughed. He and Marjorie had been divorced for four years, yet he was still getting all the blame. "Charles, we've had this conversation before—too many times, in fact. I'm not going to get into it again. Now put my daughter on the phone immediately. You managed to get temporary custody of her, but that legal agreement says that I can see her or talk to her anytime I want, so you call her to the phone or my lawyer will be in touch with the judge first thing tomorrow morning to let him know that you have violated the terms of his temporary custody order."

"All right," Charles said between gritted teeth. "But you're not going to win this fight, Nick. I will not allow you to humiliate my daughter and the entire Keating family."

Nick sighed again. "If you don't want the humiliation of having Marjorie's alcoholism and child abuse made public, all you have to do is get her to quietly and legally transfer custody to me. Now, get Trisha to the phone, or the next number I dial will be my lawyer's."

Nick jerked the phone away from his ear as the receiver was slammed onto the hard oak surface of the telephone table. The open line cackled with static, and it was several minutes before Trisha finally came to the phone. Nick heard a click as she picked up an extension.

"Okay, Grandpa, I got it," she called out. "You can hang up now." Neither she nor Nick spoke until they heard the telltale click of the other phone. "Hi, Daddy."

Just the sound of his daughter's voice calmed Nick, and he sat once again on the side of the bed. "Hi, sweetheart. Were you getting worried about me?"

"No, I just figured you had a really long day," she answered reasonably. "How did it go? Do you think you're going to like being a ranger again?"

Nick chuckled. "I think I'm going to love it. You won't believe what I did today." He told her about Crystal, and about the emergency trip they'd made to Silver Springs on horseback.

Trisha, whose first love was horses, wanted to know everything there was to know about the horse he'd ridden. It wasn't until after she was satisfied that she had a good mental image of Goliath and how the big black gelding had handled that she allowed Nick to continue with his confrontation of the Whipley boys.

"They really killed a hawk?" she asked with genuine concern. Trisha had the softest heart Nick had ever encountered, and he was proud of her compassion.

"No, they only wounded it," he reassured her, and went on to explain Crystal's rehabilitation program.

"Gee, that's neat. When I move to Oak Ridge, do you think Ms. Elliot might let me see some of her birds?"

Her assumption that she would soon be living with him gave Nick a warm constriction in the area of his heart. Despite Trisha's reluctance to abandon her "sick" mother, she was obviously already anticipating the day she would come to live with him. "I think that can probably be arranged, sweetheart."

"And do you think that maybe—" She stopped abruptly and became very quiet.

"What, honey?"

"Nothing," she answered brightly, but Nick knew better than to accept her cheerful tone at face value. Over the past two months he'd come to realize that when Trisha was at her bubbliest it usually meant that she was only trying to cover up something that hurt too badly to confront.

"Come on, sweetheart, tell me what you were going to say."

There was another pause, hesitant this time. "It really wasn't anything important, Daddy. I was just thinking that . . . well, when I come to live with you I'm going to have to leave Morning Glory here with Grandma and Grandpa, so I kinda wondered if maybe Ms. Elliot would let me ride one of her horses sometime. But it really doesn't matter, Daddy," she said in a rush. "Really it doesn't."

"Of course it matters, Trisha," he said, touched and angered by her conciliatory tone. She tried so hard not to impose on anyone, not to cause anyone worry, or make demands of any kind, when, in fact, she had every right to be upset about leaving behind the beautiful thorough-bred Charles had given her two years ago. "I promise you that just as soon as we get settled in, I'll find a good stable so that we can bring Morning Glory here. I would never deprive you of your horse, sweetheart. I know how much she means to you."

"Thank you, Daddy," she said with obvious relief.

"And in the meantime, I'll see if I can't work out something with Crystal to rent a couple of horses so that we can take a trip up to Silver Springs—just the two of us. Would you like that?"

"Oh, yeah. That would be great."

Nick could see Trisha's smile as clearly as if she had been in the room with him. They talked a few minutes longer and he gave her his phone number at the Oak Ridge Inn to go with the number he had already given her for the ranger station. As they said goodbye, Nick promised her that it wouldn't be long before they were together for good.

He said it with absolute confidence, but as he hung up he realized that he'd just made a promise he wasn't completely certain he could keep.

CHAPTER SIX

"HOW COULD HE DO THAT? How could he just let them go?" Nick asked with obvious annoyance as he and Crystal left the courtroom of Juvenile Judge Wilson Adams. Their footsteps echoed in the cavernous halls of the century-old courthouse.

"The Whipleys have the best lawyer in the county," Crystal replied. "Tony was afraid this would happen."

"But they broke the law, and obviously it's not the first time."

"And it probably won't be the last."

They reached the head of the stairs and Nick stopped, not sure what to make of Crystal's attitude. "Are you as nonchalant about this as you sound?"

Crystal leaned against the sturdy oak banister and sighed. "Of course I'm not nonchalant, but I know better than to let my expectations get too high."

Nick frowned, thinking back to Tuesday morning when she'd come into his office to inform him that the hawk had died sometime during the night. That hawk's survival had been important to her, yet she had delivered the news as dispassionately as she would have given a weather report. He'd suspected then that Crystal was adept at hiding her emotions, and he wondered if this was just another example of that ability. "So, you're not surprised that Bobby and Lewis got off scot-free?"

"Technically they didn't," she replied evenly. "They got a one hundred and fifty dollar fine."

"Which their daddy will pay without blinking an eye."

"That's right."

"And the boys will have learned nothing," Nick said with disgust.

"Right again."

"And you don't have a problem with that?"

Crystal sighed again and glanced around to make certain no one was within earshot. "Yes, I have a big problem with that, Nick. But I also have a little experience with juvenile justice in this county, so I know better than to expect too much."

She started down the stairs and Nick followed her, reflecting on what had happened in court. The hearing had been short and informal. Tony Manguson had presented the charges against the boys, and then he'd asked Crystal to recount what had happened at the lake. The pinch-faced, gray-haired Judge Adams had listened attentively to her, but the moment Nick had been asked to verify her story, Adams's attention had shifted elsewhere, as though Nick's testimony was of absolutely no interest to him.

All week long, Nick had been encountering similar attitudes. No one was overtly unfriendly toward him, but after four days in Oak Ridge, he knew that carving out his own niche here wasn't going to be easy. Dan Gatlin had left some mighty big footprints, and everyone had been eager for Crystal Elliot to fill them. Crystal's unflagging support had gone a long way toward quelling the resentment, and Nick had been taking it in stride—until a very disturbing thought suddenly occurred to him.

"Crystal—" He touched her arm just as she reached the first landing, and they stopped again. "Do you think the judge's decision had anything to do with me?"

Crystal had noticed Adams's cool attitude toward Nick, as well, but she told him honestly, "I don't think so. This is a small community, and people tend to be a little suspicious of outsiders. I don't think the judge would let that affect his decision, though. Apparently Adams doesn't think that killing a hawk is a serious crime. That's a common sentiment, by the way. You'd better get used to it."

Nick smiled wryly. "I've been around the block once or twice, Crystal. Believe me, this isn't the first time I've encountered that attitude. I guess I was just hoping that things had changed a little in the last three years."

"Elsewhere, maybe, but not around here. Don't take it personally, Nick."

"Yeah, but it feels personal," he admitted with a frown. "What happens in this forest district is my responsibility, and that judge just passed along a message that it's okay to kill wildlife illegally on *my* land."

Crystal grinned, remembering a similar conversation they'd had on Monday; only then, they'd been talking about eagles, and the shoe had been on the other foot. "*Your* land? Isn't that a—" what had he called it? "—a dangerous sentiment?"

Nick laughed. "You know what I mean."

Their eyes met and held as a little thread of understanding passed between them. Whether they were working in Nick's office or making on-site inspections of the forest, their awareness of each other never seemed to evaporate. "Yeah, I do know. Come on, let's get back to the station."

They started downstairs again, but before they reached the first floor, Tony called to them from the top of the stairs, and they stopped to wait for him. He was grinning from ear to ear as he bounced down the stairs. "I've got some good news for you, Crystal. After you left, I had a little talk with the judge and got him to issue a warning to the Whipleys. If they're caught again with a gun on Forest Service land, they'll automatically get ninety days detention.''

"Well, that's something," Crystal said. "Did you also remind Bob Whipley, Senior, that he'll be out ten thousand dollars if his boys kill an eagle?"

"I did. And I think he took that seriously."

"Let's hope it does some good," Nick commented. It hadn't escaped his notice that Tony had addressed his "good news" to Crystal only.

"Amen. I guess you two are headed back to the station now."

"Yes." Crystal nodded as she checked her watch. It was nearly five, but she had some work to finish up before she could quit for the day.

"Well, I really appreciate you coming down. I'm just sorry it didn't go better for us." He looked at Crystal, turning his back to Nick completely. "I'll give you a call later, okay, hon?"

"Okay," she said guardedly, a little surprised by his casual use of an affectionate endearment because it suggested an intimacy that did not exist between them. To the best of her recollection, Tony had never before called her "hon, honey, sweetie," or anything even remotely similar since she'd broken him of the habit of calling her "Legs" by threatening to break one of his.

He waved goodbye, then hurried off to the court clerk's office to file some documents, and Nick escorted Crystal out to the parking lot across the street from the old courthouse.

"How long have you and Tony been dating?" he asked casually, telling himself he was just making polite conversation. In truth, it was a question he'd been itching to ask all week.

Crystal frowned. "What makes you think we're dating?"

"You mean you're not?"

"No."

"Hmm." Nick couldn't hide a pleased smile. "I would have sworn that you were."

"Why?"

"Tony's behavior has been a little . . . territorial, that's all."

Of course, Crystal thought. Now, it made sense—not just that he'd called her "hon," but that business on Monday, too, when he'd told Nick how remarkable she was. Nick had gotten the impression that they were dating because that was the impression Tony had wanted him to have. "Boy, do I feel naive," she muttered as she moved to the passenger side of the Jeep. She'd been leaving the driving to Nick so that he could learn his way around Oak Ridge.

Leaning his forearms against the roof, Nick studied Crystal intently. Despite the time they'd spent together and the easy camaraderie they'd developed, he still didn't have the slightest clue as to what made her tick or why she carefully hid her emotions. He thoroughly enjoyed her complete lack of feminine artifice, though. Until he'd met the lovely, statuesque Crystal Elliot, he'd never known that a sunny, unaffected personality could be such an aphrodisiac. "There's no reason you should feel naive. The signals Tony has been sending were all for my benefit, not yours. He was trying to warn off the competition."

Crystal mirrored Nick's position and they faced each other squarely over the top of the Jeep. "I'm not the grand prize in a contest—at least not that I know of."

"Maybe you should tell Tony that when he calls you for a date this weekend."

A disbelieving smile spread slowly across Crystal's face. "You're awfully sure of yourself."

"No," he corrected her. "I'm just sure of Tony. If you're not already dating him, you will be invited to do so soon, because he is definitely interested in you, Crystal."

Her smile turned to puzzlement. "Tony and I haven't dated in years. I can't imagine why he'd be acting territorial now."

"Ah, but you have dated in the past."

"Casually," she admitted.

"Well, believe me, Crystal, a sense of competition will do wonders for resurrecting a man's interest in a woman."

"And he sees you as competition?"

"That's right."

"Why?"

There was a tiny pause. "Probably because he senses that I find you very attractive," he replied. Crystal looked distinctly uncomfortable, but Nick couldn't tell if she was bothered by the fact that he was attracted to her or just that he had admitted it so honestly. Before she could formulate a reply, he continued. "However, just because I find you attractive doesn't mean that I have to do anything about it."

"I wish you wouldn't," she said, applying a little honesty of her own.

"Don't worry. I have more than I can handle right now with this new job and the custody hearing I'm involved in. Dating is the last thing on my mind."

"Good," she said firmly, and Nick assumed a wounded air.

"You don't have to say it as though it would be a fate worse than death."

Crystal couldn't keep from laughing. Nick Hanford was the most appealing man she'd ever met, and she'd been fighting a growing attraction to him all week. It felt good to have the situation out into the open. "Oh, I can think of a lot of things that would be much worse than dating you, Nick, but it's just not a wise idea. My life is pretty complicated right now, too."

"Your life isn't complicated, Crystal, it's just plain hectic," he told her. To the best of his knowledge, she hadn't been free one single evening all week. In addition to her full-time job and her avocation as a raptor rehabilitator, she also taught an adult education course in bird watching at the local junior college on alternating Monday nights and Saturday mornings. On Tuesdays, she took an aerobics course, and on Wednesday he'd heard Mary Alice Caufield mention some kind of meeting they were both attending that night. Crystal had a very full life. Maybe even too full, but that wasn't his judgment to make.

"I like to keep busy," she explained lightly.

"There's a big difference between keeping busy and being a workaholic, Crystal."

Nick couldn't have explained what happened at that instant because Crystal's expression didn't change, but he suddenly felt as though an asbestos curtain had fallen between them, completely severing the feelings of friendship and attraction that had been there a moment before. "Well, whatever my life is or isn't, it'll be a lot simpler if we keep our relationship professional, with maybe a little touch of friendship thrown in for good measure."

"My sentiments, exactly. But does that mean I'm still invited out to your place for dinner tonight?"

"Well, of course," she said with a smile. "Mom's been pestering me all week about getting you back out to the farm. If you don't show up, I'll be in big trouble."

Nick opened the car door and slipped in as Crystal did the same. "Then I guess we'll be seeing each other tonight." He started the engine and looked at her. "But it's not a date."

"It's not *that* kind of a date," she corrected him, a smile tugging at the corners of her mouth.

Nick nodded. "All right. Just so we've got the record straight."

Crystal fastened her seat belt. "I think it is, now."

Nick reached for the gearshift, then stopped and twisted on the seat. His grin was all male and heart-stoppingly roguish. "Do you want to place any bets on how long we can keep it straight?"

She looked at him for a moment, wishing she could take the bet. But considering the way Nick made her feel, she knew better than to place money on how long they'd be able to ignore their attraction. "No. No bets," she said, cursing her honesty and her quickening pulse. With one firm response she could have completely laid to rest the subject of dating now, and possibly forever. Her brain told her to do just that, but every feminine instinct she possessed had screamed at her to leave the door open just a crack.

"Me, neither." Smiling with satisfaction, Nick put the car in gear and sped out of the parking lot.

KNOWING HE WAS fifteen minutes late, Nick crossed the horseshoe veranda of the Gatlin farmhouse and knocked on the front door. Crystal answered almost immediately, and Nick took a step back, a little shocked. It was the first time he'd seen Crystal out of uniform, and she looked impossibly pretty in a deep red blouse and casual skirt. With a bright smile and a cheery welcome, she ushered him through a long hall into a huge living room that was furnished in a homey Early American style with lots of photographs on the walls and a beautiful fireplace with a solid oak mantel. It was a comfortable room, and the fire in the hearth made it even more cheery and welcoming.

"Did you have any trouble finding us?" she asked as she took his coat and hung it in the hall closet. "I know the road looks a lot different after dark."

He gave her an unashamedly sheepish grin. "I'll say. I took two wrong turns and had to stop once for directions. I've been getting around in town pretty good, but until I learn all these back roads I may have to pin a note to my lapel saying 'Lost: One Forest Ranger—if found, please return to the Oak Ridge Ranger Station.'"

Crystal laughed. "I'm sorry, but we don't have enough money in our budget to pay a reward for your return. You're on your own."

"Gee, thanks," he said, chuckling as he looked around. "So, where is everyone? Have I missed supper?"

"Not a chance. I just finished setting the table and Dan's helping Mom in the kitchen."

"Can I do something to help?"

"Not that I know of. Just make yourself comfortable until it's time to eat."

"Thanks." Nick stepped over to the fireplace, not because he was particularly cold, but because it was so inviting. He started to say just that, but when he looked up into the pair of deer antlers that were mounted over the mantel, the compliment died on his lips. There, staring back at him were a pair of round, yellow eyes set in a fluffy ball of feathers.

Crystal had an adorable little saw-whet owl in her living room. Even though the bird was sitting perfectly still, it never crossed Nick's mind that it might be stuffed.

"Uh, Crystal—" The wide yellow eyes blinked once, then twice, and before Nick could fully comprehend what was happening, the owl lurched off its antler perch and landed on his shoulder. Nick turned his head slowly to look at the owl just as the owl looked at him, and they found each other nose-to-beak.

Crystal couldn't keep from laughing. "I see you've met Pippin," she said between giggles.

Nick wasn't afraid of the little owl that was only an inch away from his face, placidly trying to stare him down, but he didn't want to do anything to startle it. Without moving anything but his lips, he replied, "I wasn't really given a choice in the matter."

"I'm sorry, I should have warned you. She's such a little flirt. Here, let me take her," Crystal said, moving toward him.

"Oh, you don't have to do that," he said with a grin. "Pippin and I seem to be getting along just fine." Moving carefully, he stepped to the sofa and sat. When Pippin found herself facing the wall, she turned around and settled into a comfortable roosting position.

"I think you've made a friend," Crystal said, admiring Nick's immediate acceptance of the owl. Most visitors to the Gatlin household preferred to enjoy the adorable little creature from a distance.

"Where did you get her?"

Crystal joined him on the sofa. "Her nest tree was felled by a timber cutting operation last year, and Pippin's wing was permanently damaged before she ever fledged. She's never going to be capable of anything more than short flights," she said sadly. "I don't keep birds that can't be rehabilitated because I just don't have the facilities for them, but I had to make an exception with Pippin. I just couldn't bring myself to destroy her. She's the only really affectionate raptor I've ever had."

As though to illustrate Crystal's point, Pippin lowered her head and pressed it against Nick's cheek. "You're right, she's a real charmer." He scratched the back of the owl's neck and received a series of quiet, satisfied whistles for his effort.

"Hello, Nick. I see you're getting acquainted with our favorite house pest," Dan said jovially as he entered the living room and spotted Pippin making herself at home on Nick's shoulder.

"Don't pay any attention to Dan," Crystal said with an airy wave. "He loves that bird more than I do. In fact, he's the one who convinced me we should keep her."

"A decision I have never stopped regretting," he teased, dropping one hand on Crystal's shoulder. "Naomi sent me in to round you two up for supper."

"Well, I know better than to keep a cook waiting," Nick said, cocking his head toward the owl. "Does Pippin eat with the rest of the family?"

"Not if Mom has anything to say about it," Crystal replied, leaning toward Nick to relieve him of the bird. The movement brought them so close that Nick could smell the subtle scent of peaches that clung to Crystal's hair. A shaft of pure, unadulterated desire pierced him when their eyes met, and he knew from the darkening of her eyes that Crystal was experiencing the same thing.

Her gaze darted away as though what she had seen in his eyes and felt in her own heart were too potent to linger over. Her hand trembling, she pressed one finger against the bird's tarsus, and the little owl came to her obediently.

"Dan, why don't you show Nick where he can wash up," she suggested as she stood quickly and returned Pippin to her antler perch. Dan complied, and Crystal stood for a moment at the fireplace as she watched the two men leave the living room.

When they were gone, she pressed one hand against her heart, which was beating much too rapidly. She and Nick had agreed that they wouldn't pursue their attraction, so obviously, this kind of reaction had to stop.

"But I think that's going to be easier said than done, Pippin," she murmured, then hurried to join the others.

When he'd learned that Nick was dining with them, Lonnie had decided to eat dinner in town, so only Dan, Naomi, Nick and Crystal gathered around the big table in the dining room. Naomi asked that they join hands for grace, and Crystal reluctantly complied. Placing her hand in Dan's on her left was no problem, but touching Nick, sitting to her right, was something quite different. Crystal had always been embarrassed that her hands were so much larger than most women's, but when her fingers slipped into Nick's palm, she once again experienced the totally alien feeling of being small and delicate. His hand swallowed her smaller one, and his touch tingled all the way up her arm. She was immensely grateful that Naomi kept the blessing short.

Oven-barbecued chicken was passed around the table along with bowls of vegetables that had been canned from Naomi's garden last year. This was the first real chance Dan and Nick had had to talk, and the conversation immediately turned to "shop talk." They discussed everything from timber cuts and logging contracts to the problems of wildlife management and recreational facilities.

They were nearly finished with the main course when Nick looked at his hostess. "We must be boring you to tears."

Naomi gave him an indulgent smile. "Oh, I'm used to it. Dan and Crystal do this all the time, but I think we are due for a change of subject. How do you like Oak Ridge so far?"

"I like the town a lot—it's a comfortable size. Small enough to give everyone a feeling of community, but big enough to have a few of the amenities—like a shopping mall and movie theaters. About the only thing I haven't found to my liking is the drastic housing shortage."

"You haven't had any luck finding a place to live yet?" Naomi asked with a touch of surprise.

Nick shook his head. "I've looked at several apartments and even a few houses, and haven't found a thing that I'd want to move my daughter into."

"What, exactly, are you looking for?" Dan asked, helping himself to one final serving of green beans that had been cooked with bacon drippings and new potatoes.

"For right now, a roomy, two-bedroom apartment in a nice neighborhood will do. Of course, eventually, I'd like to have a place out in the country like this so that Trisha can keep the horse her grandparents gave her.

She's a little upset about having to leave Morning Glory behind.''

"How old is she?'' Naomi asked.

"Fourteen.''

She gave him a knowledgeable smile. "Then you do have a problem. Girls and their horses are inseparable at that age. When Crystal was fourteen, she had a pretty little filly named Sugar, and it was everything Dan and I could do to keep her from sleeping in the stable with it.''

Nick smiled. "That sounds just like Trisha. Sometimes I think that she and Morning Glory are joined at the hip.''

"When will your family be joining you?'' Dan asked, a little concerned by the knowledge that Nick had a child, because that probably meant that he had a wife, too. Dan had noticed the looks that had passed between Nick and Crystal, and he would have sworn that the new ranger was unattached. They hadn't been flirting, exactly, but it was clear that they were attracted to each other. The last thing Dan wanted was for Crystal to get hurt.

Nick's answer dispelled Dan's worries, though. "Trisha will be here in about two weeks, hopefully,'' he explained. "She's been living with my ex-wife since our divorce four years ago.''

Crystal noticed the little cloud of worry that passed over Nick's face. He hadn't mentioned the custody fight to Dan and Naomi, but obviously it was a source of great concern. Touched by his anxiety, she said, "You're more than welcome to board Trisha's horse here, Nick. Dan's going to be taking all of his stock to Arizona in a few weeks, so there'll be more than enough room in the stable.''

"That's right,'' Dan said enthusiastically. "We're already boarding several horses, and Lonnie is staying on to help Crystal for a while. Boarding Trisha's horse here wouldn't be a permanent solution, of course, but it would do for a while.'' A thought occurred to him and he looked at Nick speculatively. ''You know, if you're really serious about wanting a home in the country and you were willing to consider buying property, you might think about this place.''

Crystal froze for an instant as her spirits took a nose dive into her own private pit of despair. Dan and Naomi were selling the house with her blessing and at her insistence, but that didn't lessen the agony of losing her home. True to form, though, she fought the fist of pain that wrapped around her heart and pretended that nothing was wrong.

Nick frowned. ''You're selling the farm?''

''I'm afraid so,'' Dan replied. ''Are you at all interested?''

''Well, of course I'm interested, but...'' His voice trailed off and he glanced at Crystal, who had started stacking empty plates and bowls, seemingly oblivious to the conversation. ''I hadn't really given it any thought, but when I heard that you two were going to Arizona, I just assumed Crystal would be staying on here.''

''Me? No.'' She gave Nick a bright smile. ''They've been trying for months to talk me into buying the house, but I wouldn't have this old white elephant on a bet. It's far too big for just one person. You really should consider it, though. It's a great place to raise a child who loves horses.''

Her manner was charming and her eyes were twinkling, but Nick wasn't fooled for a minute. The look on Crystal's face was almost identical to the one Trisha wore when she was trying too hard to be cheerful because something was too painful to face. Nick knew without being told that the thought of losing her home was driving a stake through Crystal's heart.

"Well! I'm ready for dessert," she announced brightly, pushing her chair back from the table. "Mom, why don't you and Dan see if you can convince Nick to stable Morning Glory with us while I bring in the pie. Hope you like strawberry-rhubarb, Nick," she said as she sailed out of the room with both hands full of empty dishes.

They watched her go, then Naomi pushed away from the table. "I'd better give her a hand. Excuse me, Nick."

"Certainly."

The swinging door was still dancing back and forth as Naomi slipped into the kitchen and saw Crystal at the sink with her shoulders slumped and her hands braced on the edge of the counter.

"Oh, honey, are you all right?"

Startled, Crystal straightened and whirled around. "Mom! I didn't hear you come in. Why don't you go back out and keep Nick company? I can handle the dessert."

"You didn't answer my question," Naomi said, moving to her.

Crystal tried to smile reassuringly, but she'd never been successful in hiding her feelings from this perceptive, loving woman. "I'm fine, Mom."

"No, you're trying to pretend that you're fine, but you're not." She opened a cabinet and removed four dessert plates. "I could kick Dan for mentioning that the house is for sale."

"Why? He's got a hot prospect out there. The farm is going to sell sooner or later, and sooner will be a lot better for you and Dan."

Naomi set the plates on the counter and looked at her. "Crystal you know that Dan and I are more than willing to work out some kind of arrangement with you—"

"Mom, stop it," Crystal demanded gently. "We've been over this a dozen times, and it's a closed subject as far as I'm concerned. As much as I love this house, and as much as it hurts me to think that I won't be living here much longer, I just can't afford to pay you what it's worth. And not only that, it really is too big for just one person. I can't bear the thought of rattling around here all by myself after you're gone. So please—" she gave Naomi a big hug "—let's just drop it, okay?"

"But I can't stand knowing how much all of this is hurting you, Crystal."

Crystal didn't have to be told that "this" meant the upcoming move to Arizona. "You're doing what's right for you and Dan. He's always dreamed of running a ranch with Casey, and you've always dreamed of living out your retirement at home where you grew up. Your family is out there."

"But you're here," Naomi replied, tears welling in her eyes. "And I'm having a real hard time imagining what my life is going to be like without you in it every day. I'm going to miss you so much, honey. I suppose it's selfish, but it would be a lot easier on me if I knew that you were living in this house where you belong."

"Oh, Mom . . ." Crystal took her hand, fighting back her own tears. "At this moment, I'm not really sure where I belong. To tell you the truth, I've been thinking about leaving, too."

Naomi was surprised, but she quickly realized that she shouldn't be. "Because Nick got the job instead of you?"

Crystal nodded. "At first I thought maybe he'd stay here a few months and then move on, but that's not going to happen. He requested this district specifically, so if I'm ever going to get a district of my own, I don't have any choice but to transfer." She smiled. "Clyde Chapman called me yesterday and told me he'd let me know as soon as another ranger position opened up. So you see, there's a good chance that I may be gone soon, too. You really don't have to worry about leaving me."

Naomi placed one hand on Crystal's arm while the other swiped at the tears that were stinging her eyes. "I can't help but worry about you, honey. You're my daughter."

Crystal hugged her again as she blinked back more tears. She was so very lucky that Dan and Naomi had taken her into their home and their hearts. And she was more grateful to them than she could ever express. Without the love and security they had given her so freely, her life would have turned out so differently.

Unbidden, she thought of her brother; sweet, confused, misguided Tommy J., who was lying in a cold, dark grave because he hadn't been able to escape the influence of their no-account father, Tom Bass. Dan and Naomi had tried to make a home for Tommy J., too, but he hadn't been able to adjust. Time after time he had run back to his father, until finally the social workers had given up and allowed him to remain in the custody of a man who wasn't fit to raise a dog, let alone a child. Tom Bass had died years ago, but his legacy had lived on in Tom, Junior. Alcoholism was like that. It destroyed lives, it tore families to shreds, it left painful scars that could never be completely healed, and sometimes it even killed. Tommy J. was proof of that.

And it could have been me, Crystal thought as Naomi shooed her onto the back porch to fetch a gallon of ice cream from the freezer. *I could have been the one Tom Bass single-handedly destroyed.*

Brushing aside the painful, depressing thoughts of her brother, Crystal focused on how lucky she was and helped Naomi serve dessert.

CHAPTER SEVEN

"THIS REALLY HAS BEEN a terrific evening, Crystal," Nick said as he followed her into the hall. He'd already said good-night to the Gatlins, but it was going to be a little more difficult to say it to Crystal. "It's been a long time since I've had this much fun. I guess I needed to relax more than I realized."

"We're all really glad you came. Especially Pippin," she replied, handing him his coat. Without stopping to examine her motives, she impetuously slipped into her own jacket. "Come on, I'll walk you to the car." She flipped on the outside lights and they moved onto the porch.

"You have an incredible family," he told her casually as they sauntered to the steps. "I can see now why Dan earned so much respect in his thirty years here. I've only known him a few days, and already I know that I'll miss him when he goes to Arizona." He stopped at the bottom of the stairs and looked at her. "I can only imagine what it's going to do to you."

Crystal shrugged. She wasn't ready yet to confront the incredible pain that was looming on the horizon. "It's not going to be easy, but eventually, every bird has to leave the nest." She grinned. "Only in this case, the nest is leaving me."

Nick didn't return her smile. "Listen, Crystal, about the house being for sale..."

"Did you and Dan talk about his terms?" When Crystal and Naomi had returned to the dining room with dessert, the men had been discussing the entirely non-threatening topic of bass fishing, and the subject of the house had never come up again.

"Briefly," he replied. "But I just want you to know, we didn't come to an agreement. It's just too soon for me to think about buying property." Nick looked off toward the vague silhouette of the stable in the distance. When he spoke again, his voice sounded incredibly weary. "Frankly I'm not sure I'm going to be able to get custody of my daughter, and even if I do, I can't make a decision like this without consulting her."

"That's understandable," Crystal said as they continued walking toward Nick's Bronco.

"What I'm trying to say is that your home is safe from me—for a while, at least."

Crystal was surprised to learn that her song and dance at the dining table hadn't fooled Nick for a minute. Usually she was much better at covering her emotions. Or maybe Nick Hanford was just more perceptive than most people. Whichever was the truth, Crystal didn't see any point in denying that she'd been upset. "Nick, if you do consider buying the farm, I hope you won't let my silly feelings affect your decision."

"Your feelings aren't silly, Crystal."

"Maybe not, but the fact remains that eventually this place is going to be sold. If you want it, there's no reason why you shouldn't have it."

Nick stopped by his car door and turned to her. "This is a terribly presumptuous question, but why aren't you buying it?"

"A lot of reasons," she replied, leaning against the hood of the car. "This farm is Dan and Naomi's nest egg.

What with all the foster kids they've taken in over the years, they weren't able to save much, but they'd always planned to sell the farm and let that money see them through their retirement. If I'd allow it, they'd *give* me this place, or at the very least, they'd carry the mortgage and let me pay it off a little at a time, but I can't do that. Dan wants to breed horses, and that takes capital.''

"Couldn't you get a bank loan?''

Crystal shook her head. "I've got some money saved, but it's not enough for a decent down payment. And besides, I wasn't kidding when I said this place was too much for one person. Believe me, I've given it a lot of thought. I know I'm doing the right thing.''

Nick looked at her closely. The porch light cast odd shadows that added a hint of mystery to her lovely face, but he could still see her sincerity. "Knowing it in your head and accepting it in your heart are two different things, though, aren't they?''

Again, Crystal was stunned by how well he understood her. "Yes, they are,'' she murmured.

"I'll be giving it some more thought—the house, I mean—but Dan and I did reach an agreement about boarding Trisha's horse. She's going to jump for joy when I tell her I've found a temporary home for Morning Glory. Having her horse here will really ease her transition into a new life.''

"Getting custody of your daughter is very important to you, isn't it?''

Nick nodded. "It's the most important thing in my life. My ex-wife has some . . . problems that are really hurting Trisha. I just can't allow that to happen.''

Since he didn't offer more, Crystal didn't press him. "Well, if there's anything I can do to help, I hope you'll let me know.''

"You can keep your ear to the ground and let me know if you hear of any apartments for rent."

"Listen, if I know Mom, she's probably on the phone trying to scrounge up a perfect place for a man and his teenage daughter."

Nick slapped his hands against his thighs. "Well then, my problems are obviously solved. I doubt that there's anything Naomi can't do if she sets her mind to it."

Crystal smiled. "You are an excellent judge of people, Ranger Hanford."

The expression on Nick's face softened into something Crystal wasn't sure she should examine too closely. "Sometimes better than others," he answered quietly. A long pause stretched between them as they studied each other, and just when Crystal was sure he was going to step toward her, he did exactly the opposite. "Well . . . good night, Crystal," he said, opening the car door.

"'Night, Nick." She returned to the porch and stopped. For a moment there, she'd been sure he was going to kiss her, but something had changed his mind. A strange sensation of loneliness and longing seeped into her consciousness as she turned and watched his car disappear into the night.

BLINKING AGAINST the bright sunlight, Crystal circled the Oak Ridge Inn, looking for Nick's blue Bronco. It wasn't there.

"Damn it, Nick, where are you?" She'd been searching for nearly an hour, and she'd run out of places to look. He wasn't at the station, and she hadn't seen his automobile at any of the restaurants or shops along the Strip—the mile-long stretch of highway that served as Oak Ridge's main shopping district. His Bronco wasn't downtown, and this was Crystal's second trip to his motel. If it hadn't been so important that she locate him, she would have given up half an hour ago; the weather had turned much warmer, and Crystal knew a lot of ways to spend a perfect spring day that were more fun than driving aimlessly around Oak Ridge.

But the message she wanted to deliver *was* important. Early this morning she'd learned about a vacant apartment that sounded absolutely perfect. She'd been tromping through the woods with her bird-watching class when she'd overheard one of her pupils, a friendly middle-aged man named Harry Carlisle, mention that he was in the process of renovating one of the apartments he owned because the former tenants had nearly destroyed the attractive little duplex.

Crystal hadn't even known that Harry owned rental property, but she had practically pounced on him to get the details. It would be several more days before the apartment was ready for occupancy, but it sounded ideal. Harry was going to be painting the apartment this afternoon, and he had suggested that Crystal bring Nick by to take a look.

Only she couldn't find Nick!

In desperation, she finally pulled a pad and pencil from her glove compartment and wrote him a note, then dashed in to the registration desk to get Nick's room number. She drove around to his room near the back, taped the message to his door, and returned to her truck—just as he pulled into the parking lot.

Laughing and waving, she flagged him down. "Boy, you are one hard fella to find," she said as he rolled down the window and grinned at her.

"Well, if I'd known you were looking, I'd have made myself more available. What's up?"

"Have you been apartment hunting all day?"

He nodded. "Sure have."

"Any luck?"

"Not even a nibble."

Crystal's smile widened. "That's good, because I think I may have found something."

"Hallelujah!" Nick whooped. "What is it, where is it, is the landlord going to have reservations about renting to a single man and a teenage girl who are new in town, and when can I see it?"

Crystal took his questions in order, ticking them off on her fingers one by one. "It's a spacious duplex that's in the last stages of renovation. It's less than a half a mile from the ranger station. Your prospective landlord is one of my students, so he knows that if he doesn't rent to you, I'll flunk him. And in answer to your last question, Mr. Carlisle is on the premises at this very moment awaiting your arrival."

"Crystal, you're a miracle worker! It sounds like the answer to my prayers. Come on, get in," he said, removing a city map and several newspapers from the passenger seat. "Let's go see this gem before someone else snaps it up."

"All right. Just give me a minute to get my purse and lock the truck." She hurried back to the little cherry-red pickup, then climbed into Nick's Bronco. "I really hope I'm not leading you on a wild-goose chase," she said as Nick drove out of the parking lot and turned in the direction of the ranger station.

"Don't worry about it. I've chased so many wild geese this week that I'm getting to be an old hand at it." Traffic was heavy, but he took his eyes off the road long enough to give her a warm smile. "I really appreciate you going to all this trouble for me, Crystal."

"It's no big deal," she said with a shrug. "I know how important it is that you find a place to live."

Nick shook his head. "I suppose I was being a little unrealistic, but I really didn't think it would take this long."

"Maybe this will be the end of your search. I'll keep my fingers crossed. Turn right up here just before you get to the ranger station." She told him what little she knew about the duplex as she directed him through a maze of streets in one of the older sections of town. One final right turn brought them to Riverdale Lane, and she pointed to a long stucco building at the end of the quiet, dead-end street. "There it is."

"This looks like a great neighborhood, Crystal," Nick said, looking appreciatively at the well-kept houses and neatly manicured lawns. Enormous oaks and maples lined the street, and the lane ended just short of a wild thicket of trees, bushes and brambles.

"There's a little runoff creek just on the other side of the thicket," she told him.

Nick pulled onto the driveway behind a battered pickup. The house was old, but seemed to be in excellent condition. It had been built in a decidedly Spanish style with a red tile roof and lots of decorative wrought iron on the arched windows and doors. An enormous archway leading to a two-car garage cut the duplex in half, and the two apartments sat on opposite ends of the arch. It was a well-thought-out arrangement that would provide both tenants with quite a bit of privacy.

"So far, so good." Nick climbed out of the Bronco and followed Crystal up the driveway. Harry Carlisle, dressed in paint-stained overalls, met them at the door, and after a hearty welcome, ushered them through the apartment. All the carpets had been removed and would be replaced as soon as the painting had been completed, but other than that, the house looked wonderful to Nick. It had high ceilings, big windows, arched entrances, and lots of recessed bookshelves in the living room. A kitchen and dining room were combined into one big, sunny space, and the two bedrooms sat on opposite ends of a long hall, with a spacious bathroom in between. Best of all, there was a charming flagstone patio in the side yard. The dense underbrush by the creek made the area seem completely isolated from the world.

Nick couldn't have asked for anything more perfect if he'd designed it himself. The rent was more than reasonable, and Harry Carlisle came across as a landlord who was committed to keeping his property in tip-top condition. Most importantly, thanks to Crystal's recommendation, Carlisle had no reservations about renting to someone new in town. Nick wrote out a check for the security deposit and first month's rent, and Harry told him he could plan to start moving in on Friday.

The entire transaction took less than thirty minutes. Nick could hardly believe that his week-long search was finally over.

"Crystal, you're wonderful!" Jubilantly he swept her into his arms and waltzed her down the flagstone walk.

"Nick, what are you doing!" she exclaimed. With his hand firmly at her back, he had her spinning in circles, and it was everything she could do to keep from tripping over her own feet.

"I'm dancing for joy."

"You're scaring the hell out of your new neighbors—that's what you're doing!" She swiveled her head, trying to see if anyone was watching them, but Nick was moving too fast.

"I don't care. I'm so happy, I feel like celebrating," he said, slipping both arms around Crystal's waist. Before she knew what was happening, he had lifted her off the ground, her body crushed against his in a giant bear hug.

Of their own volition, her arms slipped around his neck. "Nick! Put me down!" she ordered, but what she really wanted to say was *Don't put me down. Don't ever put me down, because this feels wonderful!* Crystal was absolutely giddy. She'd never been held by anyone who had this much strength. No one had ever swept her off her feet—literally or figuratively. Nick was holding her as though she weighed no more than a feather, and his face was only a whisper from hers.

"Thank you, Crystal. You just can't imagine what finding this apartment means to me. You're terrific." He gave her a simple kiss of thanks. But when he drew back and their eyes met again—hers wide with wonder and his twinkling with happiness—their embrace took on a whole new meaning. Suddenly Nick's elation drained away, only to be replaced by a feeling that was much more primal. Holding Crystal, having her body pressed against his, felt much too good.

He lowered her to the ground and stepped back. "Sorry. I don't usually get that carried away."

Crystal regained her equilibrium quickly and gave him a droll look. "Neither do I."

Nick's laughter broke the sensual tension between them, and they started toward the car. "Tell you what... Why don't I express my gratitude in a more practical manner? Let me take you out to dinner tonight."

Crystal's heart leaped at the prospect, but she wondered if it would be wise. "Nick..."

He stopped in front of the Bronco. "Dinner and a movie. What do you say?" He gave her an engaging grin that was impossible to resist.

"I thought we agreed that we weren't going to date?"

"So who's dating? This is just one friend saying thanks to another for solving a very important problem."

"Yeah, but that's still 'dating,' Nick."

Leaning one hip against the hood of the car, he regarded her mischievously. "It doesn't have to be *that* kind of a date," he said.

"Really? Then why are you looking at me like a cat who's about to swallow a canary?" she asked with a mock suspicion that told Nick she was eventually going to accept his invitation.

"Who, me?" His expression was the very essence of innocence.

"Yes, you."

"You have a very distrustful nature, Crystal. I'm just looking for a way to say thank-you."

"You've already done that." *In spades,* she thought. Her body was still tingling from his embrace.

"Oh, come on," he said, moving around the car. "Will you agree to go if I promise not to make a pass at you?"

With a world-weary sigh, Crystal moved to the car. "All right."

"Good." Nick raised his right hand, his expression serious. "Scout's honor, I do solemnly swear that I will not open one single door for you, I will not hold your hand during the movie, and when I take you home I will not make any attempt to kiss you good-night."

Crystal climbed into the car. "Gee, that sounds great," she said dryly. "Why don't I just stay home and watch TV?"

Laughing, Nick slid behind the steering wheel. "Shall I pick you up about six-thirty?"

"I'll be ready," she replied, watching Nick as he started the Bronco and backed out of the driveway. The sleeves of his sweater were pushed up to his elbows, displaying the fine network of dark hair that covered his powerful forearms and the back of his large hands. "Nick..."

He shifted into drive and looked at her. "What?"

"Were you really a Boy Scout?"

He grinned devilishly. "Never."

Crystal sighed, trying not to smile. "That's what I was afraid of."

THOUGH NICK HAD NEVER BEEN a Boy Scout, he took the pledge he'd made to Crystal quite seriously. They ate dinner at Oak Ridge's finest steak house and took in a movie at the four-theater cinema at the mall, and not once did he pull out a chair, open a door, or defer politely to her opinion on anything. They chose which movie to see by a democratic flip of a coin because Crystal wanted to see an English film that had just won ten Oscars and Nick had his heart set on a new Clint Eastwood adventure.

"You were right," she said with disgust as they left the theater. There was no crowd to fight, because nearly everyone else had given up on the movie after the first hour. "We should have gone to see Clint. How on earth did such a boring film win that many awards?"

Nick looked at her in surprise. "You didn't like it? I thought it was great."

Crystal was astonished. "You're kidding? Half of the movie was spent on those long, slow-motion shots of the scenery. It was beautiful country, but if I'd wanted to see a travelogue, I'd have stayed home and watched *National Geographic*."

"Well, yes, some of those scenes did go on a little too long, but I thought the movie had a lot to say about how people react to their environment and how they can be changed by it."

"If it had said it in half the time, I'd have liked it a lot better. I still think the Clint Eastwood picture would have been more fun."

It was well after eleven, the mall was closed, and the other movies had already ended. They had the parking lot all to themselves as they argued their way toward the car. Nick was unshakable in his appreciation of the movie, and Crystal was just as intractable in her dislike of it. Their opposing viewpoints made for lively conversation.

"And you didn't think William's suicide was disturbing?" Nick asked, digging the keys out of his pocket.

"Well, of course it was disturbing, but it was also stupid." She stopped by the car door and waited while Nick unlocked it. "No one kills himself because his dog gets run over by a truck."

"The dog's death was just a metaphor for the wife's betrayal," Nick argued as he opened the door and stepped back.

Crystal put her hands on her hips and faced Nick squarely. "Metaphor, schmetaphor. The cluck killed himself because of a dog." She stopped abruptly and gave him a big grin. "And you just opened a door for me."

"Omigod," Nick said, reaching out quickly to slam the door. "I'm sorry. I can't imagine what came over me. Sometimes I have these gentlemanly impulses that I just can't control! Please say you'll forgive me."

Crystal burst out laughing and opened the door herself. "All right, but just this once. Don't let it happen again."

"It won't. I swear," he promised contritely, but his eyes were dancing with merriment. "Is there anything I can do to make it up to you?"

"Just get in the car and drive."

With mock subservience that was so absurd it kept Crystal laughing, he scurried around the car and got in.

"You are so funny," she told him, still chuckling.

"So are you," he replied, turning on the seat. "I can't remember when I've ever enjoyed anyone's company more—even if you don't appreciate the subtleties of good filmmaking."

But I appreciate you, she thought, fascinated by the play of light and shadow across his flawlessly handsome face. Why had she ever thought that his eyes were too close together? They were perfect. They were warm and dark, and just one look from them made her want things she hadn't wanted in years.

Crystal's eyes were making Nick want things, too; most of all, at that a moment, a kiss. Convincing himself that just one would be enough, he leaned toward her and gently cupped her cheek in his hand.

"You promised," Crystal whispered when his lips were only a breath away from hers. The thought of pulling away never occurred to her.

"I promised I wouldn't kiss you when I took you home. But we're not home yet."

"No, we're not, are we?" She could hardly breathe.

His mouth touched hers sweetly, almost innocently, but there was nothing innocent about the rush of excitement that small contact brought them. Crystal's hand drifted up to Nick's arm as her eyes closed, and she gave herself over to the kiss. He plied at her lips gently, then withdrew, changed the angle of his head and kissed her again, more firmly this time, more insistently. Crystal opened to him, savoring the feel of the intimate invasion. She met his tongue with her own, testing the warmth of it, delighting in the taste. Her heart thundered in her ears, and a delirious ache tightened her breasts and settled, warm and moist, between her thighs.

When Nick finally pulled back, his eyes were dark and intense. "Crystal . . ."

"I think you should take me home now, Nick," she said breathlessly before she could change her mind and consent to something it was much too soon to even consider.

"I think so, too." He didn't move. "I don't *want* to, but I think I should."

Reluctantly he straightened and started the car. They spoke very little on the long ride back to the farm, but there was nothing strained or self-conscious about the silence. One thing was clear: the movie had been forgotten, but their sweet, potent kiss had not.

When they reached the farm, Nick walked Crystal to the door. The house was dark, but the porch light had been left on. "I'll see you Monday," Nick said, keeping a respectful distance.

"Right." She fished her keys out of her purse. "Good night. Thanks for a great evening."

"My pleasure."

"See you Monday." She opened the door and slipped inside.

"Right." The door closed and Nick returned to the car.

Leaning against the wall, Crystal closed her eyes and listened to the car as it drove away. She stayed there for several minutes until there was nothing to hear but the steady beating of her errant heart.

CHAPTER EIGHT

"HOW DID THE INSPECTION GO?" Mary Alice asked as Crystal returned to the station late Thursday morning.

"I am happy to report that the new picnic tables look great. We can start installing them next month," she replied, slipping out of the lightweight jacket that she really hadn't needed. The springlike weather they'd been having this week was almost too good to be true. "Did I get any calls while I was out?"

Mary Alice shook her head. "No, but Nick wants to see you."

"Okay." She quickly hung up her jacket, then rapped on the open door to Nick's office as she ducked her head inside. "You wanted to see me?"

Nick glanced up from the report he was studying and motioned her into the room. "Come on in and have a seat."

"What's up?" she asked, trying to be nonchalant as she settled into the chair in front of his desk. They'd done a pretty good job of avoiding each other since last Saturday night, and Crystal didn't think the discomfort she was feeling was all one-sided. Nick didn't look any more relaxed than she felt.

"Can you hold down the fort without me tomorrow afternoon?" he asked with obvious reluctance. "I hate to impose on you, but my furniture is arriving from

Washington tomorrow and I need to be at the new apartment so they can unload it.''

She gave him a reassuring smile, relieved that his reason for wanting to see her was something so simple. And so nonthreatening. "No problem.''

"Thanks. I really appreciate it, especially considering that I'm going to be out of the office most of next week, too.''

For the custody hearing in Kentucky, Crystal remembered. "Don't worry about anything. This place practically runs itself,'' she replied, studying him for some indication of how he felt about the upcoming hearing. They hadn't really talked about it—in fact, they hadn't spoken about anything other than business since their date. In Crystal's opinion, that was all for the best. She was still trying to convince herself that there was absolutely nothing special about the time they'd spent together or the kiss they'd shared that night.

She was hoping if she told herself that enough times, she'd finally begin to believe it. She'd be able to start sleeping again instead of tossing and turning. She'd stop getting all hot and bothered every time she thought about Nick Hanford, and her heart would stop palpitating every time she saw him. Eventually she'd stop tasting him and smelling him even in her fitful dreams. After all, it had just been an ordinary, run-of-the-mill, garden-variety kiss between two people who were becoming friends....

And pigs could fly.

Fortunately Nick seemed as intent as she on forgetting that it had happened. Or maybe he hadn't mentioned it because he didn't want to attach too much importance to it. Either way, Crystal knew that she was going to have to rid herself of the vexing romantic thoughts she was having about Nick because they were spoiling the easy camaraderie they'd developed. Nick had made it clear before their "date" that he wasn't interested in getting involved with anyone right now, and she had made it equally clear that she wasn't interested in entanglements, either.

So, why was she so disappointed that he hadn't asked her out again?

Knowing there was no answer for that question, Crystal started to rise. "Well, if that's all—"

"Actually there is something else. If you've got a minute."

"Sure." She sat back down, and was surprised when Nick rose and moved across the room to close the door.

"I need a woman's opinion on something," he admitted as he returned to the desk.

Crystal gave him a mischievous grin. "Are you trying to figure out whether or not I qualify?"

"Oh, you qualify, all right," he said with an ironic little laugh that made Crystal's heart skip a beat. At least he hadn't *completely* forgotten about their kiss. "It's just that I hate to impose on you."

"Well, why don't you tell me what it is, and I'll let you know if it's an imposition."

"All right. It's about Trisha and the wonderful apartment you found for us. You see, my apartment in Washington was only a one bedroom, and Trisha always slept on the sofa bed when she came to visit me there. But now, I've got to furnish a room for her, and I don't have the slightest idea where to start. A basic bedroom suite is no problem, but—" he gave Crystal the sheepish grin she found so engaging "—what do I do about curtains and a bedspread? Linens? Lamps? Wallhangings and all those other do-dads? What would a fourteen-year-old girl like?"

"Decorating the room herself," Crystal answered promptly, impressed by his concern. He seemed almost nervous about having everything perfect for Trisha, which was understandable. Nick wouldn't be normal if he wasn't a little frightened of the responsibility he was about to take on.

His caring attitude and the vulnerability she sensed in him touched Crystal on a very basic level. Her own father—her real one—had never felt the slightest sense of responsibility toward either of his children. Nick's daughter was very lucky. "I don't know Trisha, of course, but I can't imagine any fourteen-year-old girl who wouldn't go crazy over the idea of decorating her own room from scratch—furniture, curtains, do-dads, and all."

Nick thought about it for a moment. "Maybe you're right. It's just that I want everything to be perfect for her when she gets here. She'll be having to adjust to a new town, a new home.... The thought of her walking into an empty room seems a little bleak."

He had a point, and since Crystal didn't know anything about his daughter, she didn't feel comfortable pushing her own opinion any further. "Nick, if that's the way you feel about it, why don't you go ahead and buy a bedroom suite, some neutral curtains and a bedspread, then let Trisha pick out the rest herself. That way, her room won't be bleak, but there'll be lots of ways for her to add her own touches to it. I'll be glad to help you pick out some things if you want," she offered, then bit her tongue when a strange, uncomfortable expression came over Nick's face. Volunteering to help was a serious mistake. After all, he'd asked for her *opinion*, not her assistance. She had definitely overstepped her bounds.

Nick frowned, wondering what he should do—not only about the bedroom, but about Crystal's offer. Now he was sorry he'd brought the subject up. In fact, he was sorry about a number of things where Crystal Elliot was concerned—most of all, that he'd kissed her last Saturday. The memory of that one kiss was driving him crazy. He'd been on the verge of asking her out again a dozen times this week, and every time the thought popped into his head, he squelched it. Crystal was sweet, charming, fun to be with, and the most damnably desirable woman he'd ever met. But he had other things to worry about, like the custody suit, Marjorie and her parents, Trisha's emotional state, a new job, Trisha's new bedroom... Tossing a budding romance into the equation just wasn't smart.

And asking Crystal about the bedroom hadn't been smart, either. There was nothing intimate about furniture or curtains, but allowing Crystal to help him shop for those items *felt* intimate. That was the kind of thing a woman did for her lover, and Nick knew better than to give her the impression that their relationship was headed in that direction. When he'd asked her out last Saturday, he'd honestly believed they could keep things strictly platonic, but after he'd given in to the temptation to kiss her, he'd realized his folly—in spades. A platonic friendship was the last thing Nick wanted with Crystal, so he had to keep his distance.

"Thanks for offering," he said finally, trying to overcome an irrational feeling of resentment toward Crystal. It wasn't her fault that her very existence was driving him to distraction. "But I think I'll take your original advice and let Trisha go on a shopping spree when she gets here. Maybe this will feel more like home to her if she decorates the room herself. Thanks for the suggestion. I'll let you get back to work now."

Crystal knew a brush-off when she heard one, and her spirits plummeted. It was obvious that Nick thought she was trying to insinuate herself into his life, when nothing could have been further from the truth! She'd only offered to help him out of courtesy, but suddenly she felt as though she'd just made a pass at him and he'd turned her down flat. It was a humiliating feeling, and Crystal didn't like it one bit. Damn it, he was the one who'd brought the subject up in the first place!

Trying to control her irritation, she stood. "Glad I could be of help," she said more crisply than she'd intended. "See you later."

Nick watched her go, puzzled by her brisk departure. Was it his imagination, or was she mad about something? Had she expected him to jump at her offer of playing Daddy and Mommy Go Shopping? Was she upset because he hadn't followed up their last date with another invitation? Maybe she was just angry because he'd broken his promise and kissed her Saturday night.

Was it possible that she'd picked up on the irritation he felt over not being able to control his incredible attraction to her?

"You see, this is why I don't want to date," he muttered irritably, moving across the room to his file cabinet. "Women are too damned complicated." He retrieved the files he wanted and resisted the urge to slam the drawer shut. "You kiss one of them and they start hearing wedding bells."

You're being unfair, Nick, a reasonable little voice told him.

I don't care. I'm frustrated.

Well, don't take your raging hormones out on Crystal. She was only being nice.

I'll take my raging hormones out on anyone I damned well choose, thank you very much.

The little voice took on a smug tone. *But that's the problem, isn't it, Nicky? Crystal's the one who got you stirred up, and she's the only one who can put out the fire.*

I am not on fire.... I'm just a little scorched around the edges.

You want my advice?

No.

Well, I'll give it to you anyway. Define the problem.

That's the advice?

Yes. Figure out what's got you so upset, and maybe you'll realize that the solution is a lot simpler than you think.

Nick leaned back in his chair. Define the problem? All right. Crystal Elliot is the problem. There, that was simple enough.... Or was his attraction to her the problem?

Or was the real problem the fact that he was trying so hard to *fight* that attraction?

Ah, now you're getting somewhere, the smug little voice told him.

Oh, shut up. Ignoring his inner voice, he tried to get back to work.

CRYSTAL HELD HER TEMPER just long enough to reach her office. She shut the door calmly, quietly, and then looked around the room for something to throw. How dare that egotistical so-and-so treat her like some marriage-minded bimbo who was trying to corral him to the altar? She barely knew the man, for crying out loud! He was the one who had asked for her advice. He was also the one who had broken their no-dating pact by asking her to go out with him. And he was the one who had initiated that kiss on Saturday night!

Suddenly Crystal felt like a royal fool for having allowed Nick to set the course of their relationship.

But then again, why shouldn't she have allowed it? They had been attracted to each other—or so she'd thought. What was wrong with seeing him socially?

Nothing, unless it interfered with their ability to work together. And it appeared that just might be the case.

Or maybe Nick was simply under an incredible amount of pressure because of the custody hearing.

A wave of sympathy for him overcame her anger and Crystal settled in at her desk to get some work done. She was deeply attracted to Nick, and despite what had happened in his office, she was still pretty sure he was attracted to her, too. It would be wonderful if something special developed between them, but it certainly wouldn't destroy her if it didn't.

Resolving to maintain a wait-and-see attitude, she tried to get back to work.

NICK TOSSED another empty cardboard box into the garage and wandered back into the living room. His furniture had arrived yesterday, and was arranged to his satisfaction. Last night, he'd unpacked boxes and organized closets and drawers until long after midnight. All that remained were a few boxes of books and knick-knacks that had to be unpacked and distributed throughout the living room.

And then what? Hang a clock and a couple of pictures? And after that?

Nothing. One of the beauties of living life simply was that it made moving a relatively painless task. In another hour, Nick would be completely settled into his new apartment, with nothing to do but worry about the custody hearing. It seemed that the closer the moment came, the more agitated Nick became. Marjorie's lawyer's delay tactics had stretched the ordeal out inexorably, magnifying Nick's anxiety and dread. He wanted the endless wait over and done with. He wanted to put the ugliness behind him and get on with making a new life for Trisha and himself.

But before he could do that, he had to make it through an interminably long Saturday afternoon and night. Tomorrow would be better, because he'd be on the road to Kentucky, and Monday would be spent in conference with his lawyer. But how was he going to make it through today when he was as jittery as a drop of water on a pancake griddle?

Go for a jog through the neighborhood? That would kill an hour, and he could certainly use the exercise.

Shop for groceries? There was another hour and a half.

Nick glanced at his watch and discovered that it was just after twelve. A little quick math told him that the agenda he'd laid out thus far would carry him through to about four o'clock—if he took a long hot shower after his jog. If he dawdled at the grocery store he could probably keep himself occupied until four-thirty or five. And then what? Curl up on the sofa with a good book?

Not an appetizing idea. What he really wanted— needed—was distraction, people, music, gaiety, and most of all, someone to talk to to keep him from going crazy.

Face it, Hanford, you're scared as hell and you don't want to be alone.

Fear wasn't something Nick felt comfortable facing, but it was a sensation he'd experienced more and more frequently these last few months. He was afraid for

Trisha's safety. He was afraid she'd be emotionally scarred for life. He was afraid he wouldn't get custody of her...and though he hated to admit it, he was equally afraid that he *would* get custody.

Not a very noble sentiment.

He knew he had to get Trisha away from Marjorie and was willing to do anything in the world to see that his little girl was safe, but deep down he was terrified that he wasn't up to the job of being a good father. He was certainly out of practice, and he wasn't all that sure he'd been a good father to begin with.

When Marjorie had taken Trisha to Kentucky four years ago, Nick hadn't known if he'd survive. He'd known he was well rid of Marjorie, but his daughter was a different story. Trisha was the one and only reason he'd put up with the drunken binges and hysterical tirades that had frayed the fabric of their marriage for so long that finally there had been nothing left worth salvaging. He had demanded that Marjorie confront her drinking problem and get help, or get out.

Her choice had been to deny the existence of the problem and return to Kentucky, where she'd filed for divorce. She'd convinced her family that Nick's womanizing had been the real cause of the breakup, when nothing could have been further from the truth. Despite a wretched marriage, Nick had been completely faithful to Marjorie. He'd been tempted to cheat a number of times, and once he'd actually come close to sleeping with a vivacious newspaper reporter who'd been in town doing a story on the Arapaho National Forest. In the final analysis, he hadn't been able to go through with it, though. The concepts of honesty, loyalty, and fidelity had been firmly ingrained in him by his parents, and not even

Marjorie's total rejection of him sexually had allowed him to overcome his beliefs.

That brush with adultery had proved to Nick that he had to get out of his marriage, though. He knew he couldn't live with himself if he became an unfaithful husband, but he couldn't bear a loveless, sexless marriage in a home that was little more than a combat zone.

It hadn't started out that way, of course. He'd been working at his first assignment in a forest in western Kentucky when he'd met his future wife. Marjorie had been a beautiful, sweet, delicate young woman who had completely captured Nick's heart. She'd had an utterly feminine "poor little rich girl" quality about her, and a sadness that had made Nick want to protect her and make her happy. It had taken years for him to realize that her sadness was caused by a deep-seated insecurity, and that she had married him primarily because she'd wanted to escape the restrictive environment that had been created by her wealthy, overprotective parents.

They'd been married only a few months when Marjorie had started pushing Nick to ask for a transfer; she wanted out of Kentucky and away from her parents. For the sake of his career, Nick wanted to remain where he was until he was ready for promotion, but Marjorie hadn't wanted to wait that long, so he'd transferred to a forest in Minnesota. Unfortunately the delicate southern belle hadn't adapted well to her new environment, and she'd pressured Nick to move again.

Though transferring again would have been bad for his career, Nick might have complied just to keep peace had not Marjorie discovered she was pregnant. He convinced her to stay in Minnesota until after the baby was born, but by then he was almost eligible for promotion, so they stayed a while longer.

Marjorie had been a teetotaler when he'd met her, but that changed after Trisha's birth. She'd started to drink; just socially, at first, but it grew steadily worse, even after Nick was promoted to ranger and offered an excellent assignment in Louisiana. They moved south, but Marjorie wasn't happy there, either, and Nick began to suspect that his wife wasn't going to be happy anywhere—she simply wasn't capable of happiness.

By the time Trisha was six, it had become clear that Marjorie's drinking was completely out of hand. Nick confronted her with the fact that she had a problem, and Marjorie had agreed. She'd promised that if Nick would get them out of the small, cliquish town they were living in, she'd stop drinking. So Nick put in for another transfer and moved his family to Colorado, but the drinking didn't stop, and Nick finally refused to move again just to please Marjorie. He'd tried to convince her to seek help, but this time she denied the problem.

Everything became Nick's fault. She swore he'd never loved her. She accused him of having nonexistent affairs. His career meant more to him than she did. He loved Trisha more than he loved her. He'd married her for her money. He was a lousy lover who didn't know how to satisfy her needs....

The list went on and on, with the accusations becoming more and more outrageous, but Nick had stayed with Marjorie for Trisha's sake. His little girl meant the world to him, and for years he convinced himself that having two full-time parents—even ones who despised each other—was better than being a child from a broken home.

Finally, though, he hadn't been able to take any more. Trisha had been eleven when he'd delivered his ultimatum to Marjorie—get help so that they could try to salvage their marriage for Trisha's sake, or give him a divorce. Marjorie had returned home to be near the family she'd once wanted so desperately to escape, and Nick made the tragic error of allowing her to file for divorce. Her influential family had seen to it that Marjorie was portrayed as the neglected wife; Nick was the adulterous husband. He hadn't had a prayer of winning his custody suit in Marjorie's hometown.

But the powerful Keating family wouldn't succeed this time. Nick had proof that Marjorie had beaten her child. He'd managed to find witnesses who were willing to swear that she was frequently seen drunk in public. He had obtained copies of her bills at the country club that showed not only how much she drank, but proved that she left Trisha unsupervised for five or six nights out of every week.

He had a good case, but there was no guarantee that he'd win. Two months ago, Trisha had confessed that she wanted to come live with him, and had promised that she'd tell that to a judge. In the meantime, though, she'd been living with her grandparents, and they were undoubtedly putting fierce pressure on her. She was also seeing Marjorie regularly, and no one knew better than Nick how good she was at manipulating people, soliciting their sympathy, and inducing guilt. If Trisha was browbeaten into changing her mind, Nick would never win custody.

Was it any wonder that he felt as though he was sitting on pins and needles today? Was it any wonder he felt alone and disconnected? And more importantly, was there any way to escape his anxiety for even a little while?

He needed to get out of the apartment and find some way to distract himself. And he needed someone to talk to. It was as simple as that.

Nick had met a lot of people during his first two weeks in Oak Ridge, but there was only one person he knew well enough to call up and say, "Let's go out tonight and have a good time." There was only one person he was coming to think of as a friend, only one person he knew for a fact could make him laugh and take away the feeling that he was about to jump out of his skin.

Without stopping long enough to think about what he was doing and change his mind, Nick started looking for the directory that had been delivered along with his telephone yesterday.

FIGHTING THE SENSATION that she was about to tumble headlong down the stairs, Crystal shifted her hold on the huge cardboard box and prayed that no one had left anything on the steps below her.

"Oh, honey, that's heavy!" Naomi said, scurrying up the stairs toward her. "Let me help you."

"That's okay, Mom, I've got it," she said, but Naomi took hold of one side anyway and together they wrestled it down to the hall. "Okay, now what?" she asked, glancing at the two separate stacks of boxes that flanked the room. "Does it go with the stuff being donated to the Rescue Mission or the stuff being shipped to Arizona?"

"I have no idea. What's in it?"

"How should I know?" Crystal turned her head toward the stairs and yelled up. "Dan forgot to label it!"

Grinning, Dan appeared immediately at the top of the stairs, a roll of packing tape in one hand and a pair of scissors in the other. "Did somebody call me? What did I do wrong this time?"

"Honey, you sealed this box before you labeled the contents," Naomi replied.

"I think that's those sweaters you wanted to get rid of."

"Are you sure? It feels too heavy to be sweaters."

"Oh. Well, maybe it's the photograph albums and scrapbooks."

"No, I already put those in the dining room."

"Maybe it's—"

"Maybe we ought to put it down and open it, so we'll know for sure," Crystal said with a laugh. This chaos had been going on all morning and had reached ludicrous proportions.

"That's a good idea, honey," Naomi said.

They lowered the box just as the phone rang, and Crystal darted out of the hall, dodging boxes as she went. "I'll get that while you two play Sherlock Holmes. Whatever you do, don't donate the photograph albums to charity! I don't want those old pictures of me in a bathing suit to get into the wrong hands!" She snatched up the phone. "Gatlin's Sanitarium for the Temporarily Insane. May I help you, please?"

Nick's deep-throated laugh made Crystal's heart skip a beat. "You're in an awfully chipper mood today, Ms. Elliot."

"Nick! Hi." Crystal sank onto the arm of the sofa. "We're packing and loading...and moving stuff around today. It's sort of crazy here." Why was she suddenly feeling tongue-tied? Surely not because she'd been hoping he would call. Which she had been, of course. Her anger with him Thursday had evaporated almost as quickly as it had come when she realized that she had overreacted. Nick was under so much pressure that he was entitled to act a little strange now and then.

"You're helping Dan and Naomi get ready for their move?"

"That's right. They leave for Arizona two weeks from today—but that's a subject I don't even want to think about. How's *your* move coming along?"

"It's well in hand, thank you. In fact, I should finish up this afternoon."

"Great."

"Yeah." He paused a second. "But that means I have a whole evening ahead with nothing to do except sit around and think."

"And worry?" she asked sympathetically.

At the other end of the line, Nick was feeling better already. He'd known Crystal would understand. "Exactly. I thought maybe a little distraction would help— you know, get out and be around people. Have dinner...maybe listen to a little foot-stomping music."

Crystal knew exactly how he felt, but she wasn't sure just what he was getting at. After what had happened in his office Thursday, she didn't want to take anything for granted. "Nick, are you asking me to suggest someplace, or are you asking me to accompany you?" she asked cautiously.

He laughed again, this time at himself. "Boy, am I losing my touch. Believe it or not, Crystal, there was a time when I knew how to ask a lady out on a date."

"Oh, I believe you," she said a little too quickly, thinking of their last date. "I just didn't want to make any assumptions."

There was another pause, and when Nick spoke again his voice was soft and full of regret. "I'm sorry about what happened in the office the other day, Crystal. I know I offended you, but I really didn't mean to."

His genuine apology touched her. "It's all right, Nick. You're under a lot of strain. Let's just forget about it."

"All right. But where does that leave us on the subject of dinner tonight?"

"Well, if you're in a serious party mood, there's a little place called the Lakeside Bar and Grill out on Indian Lake. On Saturday nights, it features a live band that plays deafening country music, dancing, one or two fist-fights—guaranteed—and the best fried catfish and hush puppies in this part of the state. Does that sound like what you're looking for?"

"It sounds absolutely perfect—if you'll agree to join me."

Crystal smiled happily and was glad Nick couldn't see her at that moment. "Why don't you pick me up at seven?"

"I'll be there. See you later."

They hung up and Crystal returned to the hall just as Naomi came downstairs with another box. "Honey, will you help me get some of these into the dining room? We're running out of space here."

"Sure, Mom." She picked up a box from the "Arizona" pile and started down the hall with Naomi right behind her.

"Who was on the phone?"

"That was Nick."

"May I assume from the expression on your face that it wasn't a business call?" Naomi asked slyly.

Crystal chuckled and glanced over her shoulder. "Am I really that transparent?"

"Only to me, dear. Are you going out with him again tonight?"

She nodded. "I think he's a little…apprehensive about the trip he's making next week. I suggested we go to the Lakeside—that's enough to distract anybody from their troubles."

"I'll say." They stacked the boxes in the corner, and Naomi stopped to look closely at her daughter. "You really like Nick, don't you, honey?"

Crystal leaned against the dining-room table. "Yeah, I do. He seems like a very strong man—not just physically, but emotionally, too. He's great with people, and he's really funny...." She paused for a moment, and her expression became wistful. "I like him a lot."

"Is he the reason you turned down a date with Tony last weekend?"

Crystal shook her head in amazement. "Doesn't anything get past you? You know, years ago when we had a house full of kids, I could understand how it was possible for you to know everything that went on in our lives because there was always someone willing to snitch. But now, there's no one here to tell tales, and you still know everything!"

"Collecting information is what mothers do best," Naomi said smugly. "I would have made a great CIA agent. And you didn't answer my question."

Crystal sighed. "I turned Tony down because I don't see any point in dating him. I'm just someone he dates casually when he's between marriages and is looking for a new wife. We're never going to be anything more than friends."

Naomi's ears perked up at that. "Does that mean you're finally going to come out of hibernation and consider marriage again? You know, honey, just because things didn't work out with Roger doesn't mean that you have to give up on marriage completely."

"Mom, this has nothing to do with Roger, and I'm not considering marriage," she said in exasperation. Nothing could spoil her day quicker than the mention of her ex-husband. He was a mistake she was still trying to live down. "For crying out loud, I've only known Nick for two weeks."

"All right, all right." Naomi held up her hands in surrender. She knew better than to push Crystal too far. "But I'm still happy you're dating Nick."

"So am I," she said, throwing an arm around Naomi's shoulder as they returned for more boxes. "I have no idea what's going to come of it, but I've decided that it's more trouble to fight it than to go with it and see what happens."

Though Crystal hadn't intended to betray her feelings quite so much, Naomi read between the lines. Whether she wanted to admit it or not, her daughter had some pretty strong feelings for Nick Hanford. Naomi couldn't have been happier, because Crystal was going to need someone to lean on when she and Dan left for Arizona. Maybe Nick would be the one to fill the incredible void that would soon be carved into Crystal's heart.

CHAPTER NINE

THE LAKESIDE BAR AND GRILL was a long, narrow building that sat on a hilltop overlooking Indian Lake. The inside was one cavernous room divided in half by a horseshoe-shaped bar, with a dining room on one side, a band, dance floor, and postage-stamp-size tables on the other.

"You're right! The music is deafening!" Nick said, leaning close to Crystal's ear as they followed the hostess toward a circular booth in the far corner of the dining room. They slid in from opposite sides, but met in the middle. "This is a little better," he said without having to shout. "At least I can hear myself think."

Crystal grinned at him. "I was under the impression that was the reason you wanted to get out of the house tonight—so that you *couldn't* hear yourself think."

"True, but I'd rather be able to indulge in a little conversation while I'm not thinking."

"You mean you can't talk and think at the same time?" she asked slyly.

Nick shook his head. "You're not going to cut me any slack tonight, are you?"

"Do you want me to?"

"Maybe just a little." He took a long look at her. She was stunning tonight. Her hair fell loose and silky around her shoulders, and she was wearing a little more makeup than usual. Nick liked her natural look, but this was lovely, too. Mascara and a touch of eye shadow high-lighted her magnificent blue-violet eyes, making them even more vivid.

The knot of tension in his gut had started dissipating the moment he'd picked her up, and was on the verge of disappearing completely.

"Why are you looking at me that way?" Crystal asked, growing warm under his intent stare.

"What way?"

"As though I'm Little Red Riding-Hood, and you're the Big Bad Wolf."

Nick grinned. "Is that how I'm looking at you?"

Crystal pretended to study the menu, even though she knew it by heart. "Yes."

"I was just thinking how gorgeous you look tonight—and what a treat it is to see you in something other than pants—even though I can't see your legs," he said, lean-ing back so that he could glance under the table. She was wearing tan boots and a pleated, calf-length skirt made of a lightweight denim that had swirled around her as she walked. A matching, short-waisted jacket defined her narrow waist, but all in all, her outfit couldn't have been considered even remotely provocative, which made it all the more enticing in Nick's humble opinion.

Crystal adjusted the loose folds of the skirt. "Well, my legs are under there. Believe me."

"They must be, to have earned you the nickname, 'Legs,'" he said with a look of absolute innocence.

Stunned, Crystal twisted toward him and Nick ad-justed his position, too, placing his arm along the back of the booth behind her. "Where did you hear that?"

"Oh . . . I have my sources."

"Rich Patterson told you, didn't he? The little snake. Wait till I get my hands on him."

"Why do you hate that nickname so much?"

"Because it reminds me—and everyone else—that I'm too tall. Not that anyone needs a reminder," she added ruefully.

"You're not too tall, Crystal," he said, unable to resist the temptation to touch her shimmering raven hair. He wrapped one lock of it around his finger. "You're perfect."

His hand was close to her cheek, and Crystal was having a hard time ignoring it. "Look who's talking. I imagine that's what Paul Bunyan said to Babe, too."

"Now, Crystal... I can accept being compared to Paul Bunyan, but you don't look a thing like a big blue ox. Trust me on this. I know what I'm talking about."

Crystal took a deep breath. For the first time since she'd known him, Nick was being openly flirtatious, and it was playing havoc with her nervous system. "I'll bet you do."

The waitress arrived, plunking cocktail napkins in front of them, and Nick reluctantly let go of Crystal's hair. They ordered catfish dinners, and Nick asked for a beer.

"And you want a club soda, right, Crystal?" the waitress asked, scribbling on her order pad without bothering to look up.

"That's right."

She bustled off and Nick slanted a look at Crystal. "I take it you don't drink?"

"No, I've never learned to like the taste of alcohol." Crystal looked down at the table and began folding her cocktail napkin into a pleated fan, suddenly feeling like the world's biggest liar. Of course, she hadn't lied—not exactly—she just had a built-in self-defense mechanism that screamed at her, "Don't talk about it!" All children of alcoholics had it. Over the years, Crystal had learned to cope with the devastating effects of her early childhood, but there were some patterns that were harder to break than others. This was one of them.

And besides, if she told him the truth it would lead to the long, complicated, sordid story of her life—which would certainly destroy their festive mood. If she and Nick kept seeing each other, he would eventually have to know the truth, but she wasn't ready to tell him yet. Maybe it was dishonest, but she couldn't bear seeing revulsion in his eyes—not yet. His respect had come to mean too much to her.

Though her tone was casual, a warning bell sounded in Nick's head. Once upon a time, Marjorie hadn't liked the taste of alcohol, and he knew only too well what had happened to her.

Don't be ridiculous, Nick, he told himself sternly, shaking off the thought. *Crystal is nothing like Marjorie. Absolutely nothing.* If he hadn't spent so much time today tiptoeing through the past, he would never have given her comment a second thought.

Accepting her explanation at face value, he let it drop and went on to other things. "I'm really glad you came tonight, but it didn't occur to me until after we'd talked that you might have rather spent the evening with Dan and Naomi since they aren't going to be in town much longer."

"They're not home tonight," Crystal said, relieved that he had changed the subject. Releasing the abused napkin, she explained, "Mom and Dan play pinochle with friends on Saturday nights."

"You mean I rescued you from an evening of boredom?"

"You spared me an evening of moving boxes," she corrected. "You should see the house. You can hardly find a path to move from one room to another. Your place is in better shape, I hope."

Nick assured her that everything was unpacked just as the waitress returned with their drinks. Several people dropped by to chat—some to express their condolences that Crystal's promotion had fallen through, and others just wanting a closer look at the new ranger. Their dinner arrived, but the flow of visitors didn't stop. At first, Nick chalked the looks and comments they were getting up to curiosity, but by the time they had finished with dinner, one thing seemed clear: everyone in town knew Crystal Elliot, and most of them had heard that she was dating the new ranger.

"Am I wrong," Nick asked, lowering his voice and leaning close to her, "or are we receiving a lot more attention than the situation warrants?"

"Haven't you heard? We've been the hottest item in town ever since my pickup was spotted in front of your motel room last Saturday. Of course, whoever started the rumor completely overlooked the fact that your Bronco *wasn't* in the parking lot."

Nick groaned. "I'm sorry, Crystal. That's what you get for being a good samaritan."

"My reputation will survive. Next week someone else will do something scandalous, and we'll be old news."

Was she as nonchalant about the gossip as she sounded? Nick wondered. "As long as we're already the hot topic, why don't we make the most of our notoriety. Let's go dance."

He held out his hand to her, but Crystal hesitated. "Nick, I'm not much of a dancer."

"Then we'll only dance to the slow songs." There was nothing particularly suggestive about his remark, but it made Crystal's heart race, all the same. Nick stood and picked up the check. "Come on. I see a half a dozen hungry couples at the door, any one of whom would kill for this table. What do you say?"

"All right. They're your feet. You can't say you weren't warned." He offered his hand again, and this time Crystal took it, savoring that delicious feeling of being small and delicate. She slid to the end of the booth and Nick pulled her to her feet. With his hand at her waist, they threaded their way between the tables. Nick took care of the check at the cash register by the front door, and then they moved around the end of the bar toward the other room where the lights were dimmer, the people rowdier, and the music decidedly louder.

Skirting the dance floor, they dodged the outflung arms and legs of a chorus line circling the floor backward in a raucous Texas Two-Step.

"I think there's a vacant table over there!" Nick shouted.

"What?" Crystal shouted back.

"Ta-ble," he said, exaggerating the syllables so that she could read his lips. "O-ver th-ere. We—" he pointed to her, then himself, then the table "—sit."

He looked so much like an Indian scout in a corny B western that Crystal cracked up. She said something to him, but when Nick shook his head, mystified, she took hold of his arm for balance and stood on tiptoe to reach his ear. "I said, white man speak with forked tongue."

Nick laughed and bent his head to hers. "No, white man speak with sore throat. Come on." He led her to the table, and they squeezed between the two crowded tables that were on either side of the empty one. A waitress appeared almost immediately and Nick ordered his second beer and another club soda for Crystal.

It was much warmer on this side of the room, and when Nick slipped out of his casual gray sports jacket, Crystal did the same. Clapping in time with the music, they watched the dancers through one two-step number, then another, until finally the band segued into a soft, slow ballad. "That's our cue," Nick said, taking Crystal's hand.

A curious sensation of dread and anticipation filled Crystal as Nick led her toward the dance floor. She hadn't lied to him—she wasn't a very good dancer for the simple reason that she'd had so little practice. In high school, boys had been so intimidated by her height that very few had been secure enough to ask her to dance. To keep from feeling left out, Crystal had cultivated a "buddy" image that had allowed her to have male friends without putting them under the pressure the awkward girl-boy thing always seemed to generate. As a consequence, she'd never really learned to dance, and in the intervening years, she'd made it a practice to refuse all invitations.

But Nick wasn't going to let her refuse this time...and truthfully, she didn't want to. The thought of embarrassing herself by stepping on his feet was daunting, but it wasn't unpleasant enough to overcome her incredible desire to feel Nick's arms around her.

They reached the dance floor, and suddenly, Crystal felt that everything was moving in slow motion. Nick drew her toward him, sliding one arm around her waist. The distance between them closed to only a few inches, and then disappeared completely. Crystal turned her head, resting it on Nick's shoulder, and they began moving with the music.

There were no fancy steps to trip her up, just a slow, gentle shuffle, with Nick's arm, warm and secure, at her back. His cheek was pressed lightly against her hair, and the subtle fragrance of his after-shave filled Crystal's senses.

It was wonderful. Dancing with Nick was the most remarkable, sensual experience Crystal had ever had. She felt protected and utterly feminine. She felt desirable. She felt Nick's heart beat, and a warm, liquid ache form deep inside her.

Nick was experiencing his own kind of ache. Had any woman ever smelled sweeter or felt so good pressed against him? He didn't have to bend over to hold her, he didn't have to crane his neck to feel the silk of her hair against his cheek. Her head fit perfectly on his shoulder, and Nick knew instinctively that they would fit perfectly everywhere else, too. Piercing desire warred with his sense of propriety, and he was almost grateful when the music ended. He wouldn't have missed the experience for the world, and wouldn't pass up another opportunity, but for the moment, he needed to regain control of his erotic fantasies about holding Crystal a lot closer than he could on a crowded dance floor.

Hand in hand, they returned to the table as another upbeat number started. There was no way they could talk, so they simply sat and enjoyed the music. Nick's arm was draped casually across the back of Crystal's chair, and despite the noise and the crowd, she felt at times as though they were the only people in the room. They danced two more slow numbers before the band took a break. A jukebox that was much easier on the ears began wailing a soulful ballad.

"The band is great," Nick said, relieved that he no longer needed to shout. "Are they local?"

"Yeah. As a matter of fact, I went to school with most of them." She started to tell him how the group had formed, but just then a perky little peroxide blonde wearing a skimpy tank top and jeans that were much too tight caught Crystal's attention with a wave. Dragging a scruffy-looking young man along behind her, she barreled through the crowd.

"An old friend?" Nick asked, wondering about the strange, unreadable look that had passed over Crystal's face the moment she saw the girl.

Crystal shook her head. "A former in-law," she replied softly, then plastered on a welcoming smile. "Hi, Lyla." She stood long enough to give the girl a hug, then sat and invited Lyla and her friend to join them. They purloined two chairs from a nearby table, and when they were all seated, Crystal performed the introductions. "Nick Hanford, this is Lyla Bass and..." The young man with Lyla looked familiar, but Crystal couldn't remember his name.

Fortunately Lyla came to her rescue. "Jeff Zelinski. You remember Jeff's dad, don't you? He runs the feed store over in Cotton."

Of course. One of Tommy J.'s old drinking buddies. Crystal swallowed a surge of resentment. She tried not to think of the number of times her brother had tried to stop drinking, only to succumb to the lure of the peer pressure that had been placed on him by "friends" like Jeff Zelinski. But those friends had never actually *forced* Tommy J. to drink. That had been his responsibility, and Crystal tried not to hold it against Jeff. "Sure. I knew I'd seen you somewhere. Hi, Jeff." They said their howdy-do's all around, and Nick noted that though Crystal was friendly and polite, she wasn't particularly comfortable.

"So, how've you been, Crystal? I hadn't seen you in forever."

"I'm doing fine, Lyla," she replied. "How about you?"

Lyla's eyes brightened as she pulled Jeff's hand into her lap and leaned against him. "Oh, just great. In fact, that's kinda why I was glad to see you tonight. I been plannin' to call you 'cause I wanted to tell you the good news before you heard it from somebody else."

"Good news?"

"Jeff and me are gettin' married next month."

She said it with a touch of defiance, as though she half expected Crystal to disapprove, but Crystal wasn't at all surprised. Actually the only thing that did surprise her was that Tommy J.'s young widow had waited nearly a full year before deciding to remarry. Lyla was a sweet girl, and in many ways she had deserved better than she'd gotten from Crystal's late brother; most of all, she deserved not to have been made a widow at the age of twenty-three.

"That's great, Lyla. I'm really happy for you." She smiled at Jeff. "Both of you."

Jeff mumbled a thanks, then drained the beer he'd brought to the table with him, and Crystal couldn't ignore the horrible premonition that poor little Lyla was jumping out of the frying pan into the fire. But that wasn't a fair assessment and she knew it. Just because Jeff drank didn't mean he had a problem. For Lyla's sake, she prayed that he could handle liquor better than Tommy J. had.

Lyla talked enthusiastically about the wedding, and Crystal responded with equal enthusiasm, but Nick got the impression that Lyla was just using inane prattle to cover her fear that Crystal might not approve.

"Come on, Ly, I need another brewski," Jeff said, dumping his empty mug on the table. "Let's hit the bar. Nice seein' you again, Crystal." He acknowledged Nick with a nod of his head and stood, pulling Lyla up with him.

"Gotta go," she said with a sheepish grin. Apparently she considered Jeff's manners macho. Crystal considered them rude. "Good seein' you, Crystal. I'll be sure to send you an invitation to the wedding."

"Thanks, Lyla. I'll try to be there." She watched them go, and her plastered-on smile faded as a flood of unpleasant memories assaulted her.

"Are you okay?" Nick asked gently, leaning toward her.

She glanced at him sharply, as though she'd momentarily forgotten he was there. "Oh, sure. I'm sorry about all that—I didn't mean to leave you out of the conversation."

"That's all right. You said Lyla was a former in-law?"

Crystal nodded. "She was married to my brother, Tommy J."

"They're divorced?" he asked, though somewhere inside he knew better. The haunted look on Crystal's face answered his question long before her words confirmed his suspicion.

"No, Lyla's a widow. Tommy J. was killed in a car wreck last year."

Nick's arm was still resting on the back of her chair, and he couldn't resist brushing his hand against her hair. "I'm sorry, Crystal."

"So am I," she replied sadly. "Tommy J. wasn't perfect, but he was a very sweet person."

"You loved him a lot," Nick said, noting the obvious.

"Yes, I did. But that wasn't enough to save his life."

"It never is, Crystal."

"I know." She smiled at him, a sweet, sad smile that touched Nick deeply and made him want to wrap her in his arms so that he could shelter her from life's painful realities. The protective instinct was so strong and startling that Nick was grateful when Crystal gave him a playful poke and lightened their mood. "Hey, I thought we were supposed to be having fun tonight."

"That was our agreement, wasn't it?" When Crystal nodded, Nick decreed, "All right. No more depressing thoughts. Let's dance."

The band had just returned for their next set, and as soon as they started to play, Nick led her to the dance floor. Again, he held her close and the world ceased to exist. They danced every slow dance until finally Crystal thought she might fly apart unless she was soon allowed to experience a more intimate, less public contact with Nick.

And he felt exactly the same way. They listened to the music and danced through one more set, but when the band took another break, Nick leaned close to Crystal and suggested they leave.

Her heart pounding much too hard, Crystal nodded and collected her jacket. They slipped outside to the parking lot. The weather was mild, and there was a magnificent full moon. "Are you ready to call it a night?" she asked.

"Not really. I was just hoping to get you alone for a few minutes."

His voice was as warm and thrilling as the emotion swirling around inside Crystal. She stared up at him and found that his eyes were dark with tenderness and longing. "Would you like to take a walk down to the lake?"

He didn't take his eyes off hers. "That sounds romantic."

Crystal could hardly find the breath to answer him. "I suppose it could be."

"Taking a romantic walk by a moonlit lake is the kind of thing people do on a *real* date, Crystal," he said softly, brushing one hand lightly against her cheek. "Have we crossed that line?"

Crystal moistened her lips tentatively. "Not yet."

He edged closer to her. "Are you ready to cross it?"

"I guess that depends on how big a step we're talking about.... I'm not quite ready to throw myself headlong across it, but I could feel comfortable sliding one foot to the other side."

Nick grinned. "In that case, why don't we just take a *short* walk."

"All right." She pointed toward the end of the building. "The path starts just around the corner."

As they moved along the front of the building, Nick slipped one arm around her waist and Crystal reciprocated the gesture as though it was the most natural thing in the world. When they came to the steep path, Nick reluctantly released her, but somehow they always managed to retain some form of contact. He held her hand, guiding her down the hill, or she placed her hand on his arm or his shoulder for balance.

The full moon and lights from the marina below lighted their way, and eventually they emerged onto a road that led to the docks. Even though there was little activity in that direction, Crystal led them away from the marina to another dirt path that followed the shoreline until they reached a deserted outcropping of rocks at the water's edge. They found a moderately comfortable, flat-topped rock, and sat facing the lake. The water shimmered in the moonlight, and soft night sounds enveloped them. Vaguely in the distance they could hear the music from the Lakeside Bar and Grill.

"This is nice," Nick said, drawing Crystal close.

She snuggled against him. "Yes, it is."

They sat there, listening to the night, watching the lake . . . holding each other and wondering what it would be like to do more. Nick brushed his lips against Crystal's hair and his arms tightened around her waist.

Crystal wondered why all the oxygen had suddenly left the atmosphere. "You know . . . this is actually a man-made lake. There's a dam down at the other end that controls—"

"Crystal."

"What?"

Nick gently angled her head toward his. "Stop playing tour guide. There's something else I'd much rather learn tonight."

Crystal thought she might become lost in the depths of his dark eyes. "What's that?" she barely managed to whisper.

"I want to know if kissing you is as wonderful as I remember it." His mouth lowered to hers, and Crystal draped her arm around his shoulder, letting her hand stroke his hair as he took possession of her senses.

The kiss was somehow both gentle and insistent. It demanded that Crystal be an active participant, not a passive spectator, and she eagerly complied. When his tongue stroked hers, she reciprocated the gesture. When he teased her by withdrawing, she chased after him, letting him know by deed how much she had enjoyed the intimate invasion. Nick groaned, enthralled by her eager response and he kissed her again and again, each time pressing deeper and deeper into the welcoming recesses of her mouth, until finally a kiss was no longer enough.

Slipping his hand under her open jacket, he slowly brushed against her waist and then upward until he came in contact with the lush underside of her breast. The teasing movement was enough to make Crystal arch her back, and Nick accepted the invitation to fill his hand with the globe of her breast. He kneaded it gently while his mouth slanted across hers and his tongue impatiently wooed hers into his mouth once again. Through the soft fabric of her blouse and lacy underwear, his thumb found her hardening nipple and teased it with slow, deliberate circles. Crystal whimpered, and it was such a soft, sexy sound that Nick's control nearly shattered into a thousand pieces.

Burning to get closer, he shifted her onto his lap, nestling her against the hard ridge of his manhood. Crystal moved sensuously against him, knowing that she was inflaming him, but not caring about the consequences. She'd never wanted anyone this much. She'd never experienced a need this demanding. Nick's every touch, gentle or insistent, left her feeling as though she was on fire, and the pleasure-pain of it was almost more than she could bear. He rotated his hips, letting his hardness tell Crystal what he wanted, and she moaned again.

"Oh Lord, I want to make love with you," he whispered raggedly as his lips nipped and caressed her throat. "If I can't touch you without all these clothes between us, I think I'll go crazy." Impatiently he unbuttoned her blouse and peeled it to one side. With sweet, shocking sensuality, he kissed the breast he had so thoroughly aroused, and then insistently took it into his mouth, lathing the hard crest with his tongue.

It was the most erotic sensation Crystal had ever felt. "I...oh, Nick..." His teeth gently nipped at her, and she bit her lower lip to keep from crying out.

"Come home with me, Crystal. Please."

One instinct was telling Crystal to say no. She shouldn't do this. They hadn't known each other long enough...Nick's life was complicated...her life was full.... She was already on the verge of falling in love, and going home with him, completing the act they were both aching for, just might send her tumbling head over heels over the edge.

There were a lot of good reasons to say no, but the fire in her breasts and between her thighs was screaming that she say yes. She wanted to touch Nick, too. He was hot and hard against her, and she wanted to know the full measure of his masculine strength. She was burning up, and only Nick could put out the fire that had started smoldering almost from the moment she'd first seen him.

Need warred with logic. "I want to make love with you, too, Nick," she whispered between ragged breaths. She pulled away ever so slightly and the sight of his dark, passion-filled eyes was almost her undoing. "But I don't..."

Nick looked into her eyes. They were glazed with desire, but he also saw confusion there.

"Hush...it's all right..." he whispered, gathering her against him, brushing his lips lightly against hers. "You're not ready for this, are you?"

"No." She sighed regretfully. "It feels so...*right*, but I don't think it is."

"Because we work together? Because I'm your boss?"

Crystal shook her head. "No. It has nothing to do with work." She looked into his dark eyes. On her own, she might never have had the courage to admit the real reason, but the tenderness in his gaze gave her all the courage she needed. "I'm just not ready to feel this much for you, Nick."

Her honesty made Nick want her all the more, and made it that much more difficult to gently ease her off his lap. He kept one arm around her waist, holding her close to his side as she adjusted her clothing.

"I'm sorry," she said with unmistakable sincerity.

Nick took a shuddering breath and pressed a kiss to her temple. "Don't be. You're very special, Crystal. If we ever do make love, it isn't something that will be casual for either one of us."

It wasn't an admission of love, but it was certainly something Crystal needed to hear. "I hope not. I don't think I could live with a meaningless affair."

The pressure in Nick's loins was still so intense that he couldn't imagine where he found the ability to smile, but he did. "Oh, I think what we feel for each other means something, Crystal. In a lot of ways, we're perfectly matched—our goals, our ideals, our dreams.... And physically we're well matched, too." He couldn't resist running one hand along her thigh. "The thought of having your long legs wrapped around me has been driving me crazy...."

Crystal took a shaky breath and looked out over the lake, remembering all the sleepless nights she'd had because of Nick. "That thought has been making me crazy, too."

"Good." He tilted her face toward him and kissed her lightly. She moaned and melted against him, and Nick smiled. Obviously she wasn't any more in control of her passions than he was. He wasn't trying to pressure her into making love with him, but the knowledge she still wanted him was comforting. "Then maybe we're not too far away from making those fantasies a reality."

"I thought your life was too complicated for a relationship, Nick?" she said softly. She hated to break the spell, but she needed some clarification of what was happening.

Her comment brought Nick back to reality and he remembered what he was facing in the days ahead. "My life is complicated, Crystal. I have no idea what's going to happen when I bring Trisha home, but I do know that denying my feelings for you won't help my daughter one bit." He grinned sheepishly. "I wasn't worth a damn last week because I spent so much time trying to pretend I wasn't attracted to you."

Crystal blushed. "Is that what you were doing?"

Nick raised one eyebrow. "Weren't you?"

"Yes." She looked at the lake, but Nick gently cupped her cheek and urged her to meet his tender gaze.

"It didn't work for either of us, did it?"

"No, it didn't," she whispered. Nick kissed her lightly. Her breath hissed into his mouth, and he reluctantly withdrew.

"Then we're in agreement?" he asked huskily. "We're past the point of pretending?"

"Way past," she answered breathlessly.

"Then why don't we take this thing one day at a time and see where it leads us?"

"I'd like that, Nick."

"Good." He kissed her again, intimately this time, and Crystal responded with a kind of abandon that robbed Nick of thought. What little progress he'd made toward controlling his hunger vanished as though it had never existed. "Lord, how I want you," he moaned against her mouth, then abruptly pulled away. "Have you ever made love on a rock, Crystal?"

The devilish gleam in his eyes told her that he wasn't serious. "No," she said shakily, and then, because she couldn't resist, she placed her hand on Nick's thigh. "Is it hard?" she asked coquettishly.

Her touch almost shredded Nick's control, but he grinned wolfishly at her double entendre. "Unless you want to find out just how hard, we'd better get out of here. Immediately."

He stood and held out his hand. Crystal accepted it and they left the moonlit lake behind.

CHAPTER TEN

NICK WASN'T SURE HOW he managed it, but he actually slept that night. By some miracle his evening with Crystal had brought him a strange sort of peace. He was still worried about Trisha, of course, but instead of being frightened he was now eager to face what lay ahead. He felt as though he was standing on the threshold of a new life—a life that included the most remarkable woman he'd ever met.

He'd gone to sleep thinking of Crystal, and a sweet, erotic dream in which she'd been a principal player woke him on Sunday morning. Thoughts of her carried him through his shower, then breakfast, and not even the dread of the long drive to Kentucky was enough to mar his good mood.

What Nick was feeling felt suspiciously like love, but it had been so many years since he'd experienced the delights of this giddy, emotional roller coaster that he was afraid to label the emotion. *One day at a time,* he reminded himself. That was what he and Crystal had agreed to. It seemed like an excellent plan.

His bags were already packed, so it didn't take long for him to get on the road—or at least it wouldn't have if he'd been able to find the manila envelope filled with papers his lawyer had sent him. He tore the apartment apart looking for the documents that had to go back to Kentucky, but they simply weren't there. The only other place they could have been was at the office, so he finally gave up, locked the house, and headed for the station. He pulled his car in by the sidewalk and hurried into the deserted building.

Sure enough, the folder was lying on the corner of his desk where he'd left it. He snatched it up, then froze at the sound of a man's voice coming from the outer office.

"Hello? Is somebody out there?"

"Rich?" Nick stepped out of his office and found Rich Patterson, all decked out in a trendy jogging suit, peeking around the corner. "What are you doing here?"

"Nick! Hi. I couldn't imagine who was out here." He moved into the reception area. "I just came by to catch up on a little work and get some papers I needed for tomorrow morning. I thought you were going to be out of town for a few days."

"I'm on my way right now." He waved the folder and grinned. "I had to pick up some papers, too."

"As long as you're here, have you got a minute?" Rich asked. "That new logging contractor called me at home yesterday with a whole slew of questions I couldn't give him definite answers on."

Nick glanced at his watch. He'd promised Trisha he'd pick her up about five and take her to supper tonight, but he still had a few minutes he could spare without making him late. "Sure. Come on in."

"Just let me get the papers, and I'll be right with you." Rich dashed back to his desk, then joined Nick in his office. He outlined the concerns of the contractor, who wasn't happy with the proposed route of the logging road that would lead to the stand of timber he'd been contracted to cut. They discussed alternate routes, and Nick made a concession or two, but overall, the route that had been chosen was the best one, and Nick wasn't inclined to make drastic changes.

"See if that pacifies him," Nick said finally. "And if it doesn't, tell him to wait until I get back. In the meantime, if you have any other problems, just ask Crystal. She can handle anything that crops up."

"Oh, I know she can," Rich said a little too quickly, then grew distinctly uncomfortable.

Nick looked at him reassuringly. "Rich, I know that Crystal had been promised this job. I also know that she's more than qualified to handle it. You don't have to be embarrassed about feeling that way, too."

Rich smiled, grateful that Nick hadn't taken offense. "Thanks. I feel guilty about everything that happened, but I've tried not to be sensitive about the subject. I know Crystal doesn't resent your being here, so I certainly have no right to."

Nick cocked his head to one side. "Why on earth would you feel guilty, Rich?"

The young forester rolled his eyes to the heavens and slumped into his chair. "I helped talk her into believing that she had the job." When Nick still looked puzzled, Rich continued. "I guess you know that Dan Gatlin announced Crystal's promotion at his retirement party."

"Yes."

"Well, Crystal was a little upset about the announcement because she didn't want to count on getting the job until she actually had written confirmation. She kept saying '*if* I get the job,' but we kept telling her it was already hers and that she was just being silly for doubting." He shook his head sadly. "If we hadn't insisted she accept the district supervisor's verbal assurance, she might not have been in for such a big disappointment. In all the time I've known Crystal, her one and only goal has been becoming a district ranger. It was the most important thing in her life.''

Nick hadn't thought it was possible for him to feel worse about the mix-up that had cost Crystal this job. He'd known this promotion was important to her, but he'd had no idea it was the most important in her life. ''I really hate that this happened, Rich. Getting this district was important to me, but I really wish that the paperwork on Crystal's promotion had gone through quicker. It would have spared her a lot of disappointment.''

But if that had happened, I never would have met her, he reminded himself. It was terribly selfish of him, but despite what he'd just told Rich, he couldn't bring himself to truly regret the mix-up. What he did regret was that as long as they both stayed in Oak Ridge, Crystal could never achieve her lifelong dream of being a ranger. The thought that she might someday leave in order to reach her career goal left Nick with a very hollow feeling in the vicinity of his heart.

''I wouldn't worry about it, Nick,'' Rich tried to reassure him. ''As near as I can tell, Crystal's already gotten over the disappointment. She's a pretty incredible lady—she's as sweet as pie on the outside, but inside, she is one tough cookie. A real survivor.'' He shrugged his shoulders expressively. ''Of course, with her upbringing, I guess she had to be.''

That captured Nick's undivided attention. ''You mean because she was orphaned so young?''

Rich's eyebrows went up in surprise. ''Orphaned? Where'd you hear that?''

Nick frowned. He hadn't actually *heard* it anywhere. ''I guess it was just an assumption I made because she was raised by foster parents,'' he confessed.

The young man shook his head. Crystal's life story was such common knowledge that it never occurred to him that she might not approve of him enlightening their boss—who also happened to be the man she was dating. "No, that's not it at all. Crystal's dad was an alcoholic. He died a year or two before I came to Oak Ridge, but from what I've heard, he was a real derelict. Her mom got tired of living on welfare and took off for parts unknown when Crystal was about seven years old. The poor kid was left with taking care of her father and brother all by herself."

Nick did a pretty good job of hiding his shock, but inside he was reeling. Crystal was raised in an alcoholic home? Why hadn't she told him? Was that why she didn't drink?

Of course it was, he thought, remembering how he'd asked her that question last night—and how she'd lied to him. "She took care of her brother?" he asked, stalling for time to digest this information and also looking for a way to keep Rich talking. "Why on earth did the county social workers allow that?"

"Who knows? I guess they thought one parent was better than no parent at all. They probably didn't know how bad it was."

"How bad was it?" Nick asked, trying to keep his voice even.

"It got pretty bad toward the end," Rich replied. "Crystal's dad started bringing home some of his drinking buddies, and a couple of them tried to molest her. I never heard the whole story, but apparently it happened several times. The last time they came after her, she and Tommy J. slipped out a window and ran to a neighbor's house. That's when she was sent to live with the Gatlins."

Nick felt sick. It hurt him physically to think of Crystal suffering the kind of degradation Rich was describing. How could anyone live through something like that and still turn out to be a happy, compassionate, loving woman like Crystal? Or was she really what she seemed to be? he wondered. She'd taken great pains to hide her sordid past from him; what other secrets was she keeping?

And what "secrets" have you been keeping? Nick's conscience asked him. *You haven't exactly been forthcoming in explaining why you're suing for custody of Trisha. You're hardly in a position to criticize.*

A hundred questions were buzzing through Nick's mind, clashing violently with emotions he couldn't even identify. Earlier this morning, he'd actually fancied himself falling in love with a woman he knew absolutely nothing about. His pity for the life Crystal had been born into warred with the vague but disturbing feeling that she had somehow betrayed him.

Nick needed answers to his questions and time to sort through his conflicting emotions. Unfortunately the answers were going to have to wait. He glanced at his watch and realized that if he didn't leave for Kentucky immediately, he'd be late. He couldn't go out to the farm to talk to Crystal because Trisha had to come first. He'd known that all along, but he'd let his feelings for Crystal cloud his judgment.

It's a pity I didn't concentrate more on Trisha instead of getting involved with Crystal in the first place, he thought with disgust at himself that carried over into the way he felt about Crystal, too.

After he'd left the station, Nick couldn't recall exactly what he'd said to Rich when he abruptly got up from his desk and hurried out to his Bronco; something about having lost track of the time and needing to get on the road, probably.

He kept his speed to the posted limits, but the six-hour drive to Kentucky flew by in the blink of an eye. His mind painted horrifying images of the kind of life Crystal must have led as a child, and his sense of betrayal quickly vanished. He couldn't blame Crystal for not wanting to talk about her past. As soon as the shock wore off, he realized that she probably would have told him herself before their relationship progressed much further. She was essentially an honest person; at least that was what Nick wanted to believe. Unfortunately he wasn't entirely sure what he *should* believe.

Part of him yearned to reach out to her. He wanted to comfort and protect her, to shield her from ever experiencing that kind of ugliness again. Crystal had overcome incredible odds to become a woman of integrity and compassion.

In one way, Nick's respect for her multiplied a hundredfold, but that wasn't enough to repress the part of him that wanted to stay as far away from her as possible. He was ashamed of the sentiment, but it was true and he couldn't deny it.

Alcoholism had destroyed his marriage. He knew better than anyone what it did to people's lives. It wasn't possible that Crystal could be unaffected by what she'd suffered; on the contrary, she probably had deep wounds that would never heal. Nick had already observed how hard she worked at hiding painful emotions; Trisha was the same way. They probably even had some of the same scars, and that was what worried Nick the most.

Trisha had to come first, and Nick couldn't envision entangling his life with that of a woman who probably had as many or more problems as his own daughter. He still didn't know how he was going to help Trisha; he certainly couldn't take on the job of helping Crystal, too.

Nick argued with himself all the way to Kentucky, trying to sort through his emotions. By the time he arrived, he had reached two inescapable conclusions: he'd been wrong to become involved with Crystal in the first place, and though it wasn't going to be easy, he was going to end their relationship before it went any further. It was the only logical thing to do.

But if that were the case, why did the thought leave him feeling as though someone had just torn out his heart?

Trying to ignore the emptiness, he put Crystal out of his mind and concentrated on the grueling ordeal ahead of him. The optimism he'd felt this morning had disappeared like a will-o'-the-wisp, and he somehow managed to convince himself that what he felt for Crystal had been nothing more than illusion.

It was a deception that didn't work for very long.

CHAPTER ELEVEN

NICK WAS SO TENSE that every muscle in his body felt as though it had been abused by overexertion, yet outwardly he appeared quite calm. His hands were folded on the table, and as the judge looked up from the papers he was perusing, Nick realized that he had been holding his breath. Across the aisle from him, Marjorie's tension showed in her face and in the trembling hands she clasped and unclasped nervously in her lap.

Of course, Nick realized that part of her trembling could have been the result of not having had a drink for the four hours it had taken their lawyers to present their respective cases. He could still remember a time when Marjorie had been beautiful, but her drinking had stolen that beauty. Her face was puffy and sallow, and her body had gone from voluptuous to something resembling an unstuffed scarecrow. She was only a shadow of her former self. At one time Nick had felt sorry for her. Today, he had no room for pity.

Judge Henry Bristol cleared his throat and looked at Nick, then Marjorie. "Mr. Hanford...Mrs. Hanford... After weighing all the evidence that has been presented this afternoon, I am now ready to render a decision in the matter of custody of your minor child, Patricia Louise Hanford. Frankly I'm from the old school that still believes a child is better off in the care of his or her mother."

The judge paused to clear his throat again, and Nick's heart tripped in alarm. This couldn't be happening. How in the name of God could any man listen to what Judge Bristol had heard this afternoon and still make a statement like that?

"However," he continued, "in this particular situation, I find that I must put my own prejudices aside. While I'm not completely convinced that Mr. Hanford's charges of abuse and alcoholism have been proven beyond a shadow of a doubt, I cannot ignore the testimony of Patricia Hanford. Though it was clear that this was an extraordinarily painful decision for her, she has stated in no uncertain terms that she would prefer to live with her father. Miss Hanford is not a child. She is a young lady. I believe she is old enough to know what is in her best interests, and I cannot bring myself to ignore what might or might not be a plea for help.

"Therefore, it is the determination of this court that guardianship of the minor child, Patricia Louise Hanford, be passed from her mother, Marjorie Hanford, to her father, Nicholas Hanford. I will expect both parties to work out equitable visitation privileges for Mrs. Hanford, and once those have been agreed upon, I will render this verdict final."

He banged his gavel. "This court is now adjourned." He stood and looked from one attorney to the other. "Gentlemen, I hope you can get that visitation agreement on my desk first thing tomorrow morning. I don't want to have to adjudicate the matter."

Nick barely heard the sternly worded admonition. It was over. Trisha was safe. Smiling with relief, he turned and looked at his daughter, who was sitting in the first row of the gallery. Her feathery mane of auburn hair made her pale face look as white as a sheet. She tried to return his smile, but Nick could tell that she didn't consider this quite the victory that he did. Having to testify against her mother had nearly torn her in half.

Praying that eventually he would be able to soothe some of her pain, he went to her and gathered her into his arms. "It's over, sweetheart. I know it was hard, but the worst is over now."

She looked up at her father with ill-concealed distress. "Why did he make it sound like it was all my fault?"

Nick was confused. "Who, honey?"

"The judge. If I hadn't said what I did, he might not have taken me away from Mom."

Nick placed his hands on her shoulders. "Trisha, don't you want to live with me?"

"Of course I do," she whispered with a hint of desperation. "But why did he have to make it my fault?"

Nick felt sick inside. Why hadn't he anticipated the effect the wording of the judge's ruling was going to have on her? "Trisha, it's not your—"

"Trisha? Trisha, honey?" Pale and tearful, Marjorie slipped away from her lawyer and her parents, heading straight for her daughter. "Trisha, how could you do that? How could you say what you did about me?"

"Marjorie, don't," Nick commanded sternly. "Don't blame this on Trish."

"Don't tell me what to do, Nick," she said, throwing him a hateful glare. "Don't even talk to me. I'll get her back somehow, I promise. I'm not going to let you do this to me."

"You did this to yourself, Marjorie. When are you going to face up to that and take responsibility for your own actions?"

Marjorie straightened her shoulders and whisked a strand of auburn hair off her forehead. "When I have something to feel responsible for, that's when!'' She looked at Trisha, but there was no softening of her voice or her face. ''This is all your fault. If you had just called your father last Christmas and canceled your vacation the way I told you to, none of this would have happened!''

The tears Trisha was trying so hard to hold back finally escaped her control. ''I'm sorry, Mama.''

''No, you're not, but you will be, as soon as you see what living with him is really like!''

''Marjorie, shut up,'' Nick growled, pulling Trisha into his arms. He dropped a kiss on the top of her head. ''Come on, sweetheart. Let's get out of here.''

''You can't walk out on me!'' Marjorie shouted as Nick ushered Trisha toward the door. ''I have a right to talk to my daughter!''

Charles Keating grabbed hold of his daughter when she started to follow Nick. ''Marjorie, stop it. You're not doing anyone any good.''

''God, I need a drink,'' she muttered, allowing her father to lead her back to the table where the two lawyers were conferring.

Knowing he couldn't leave the courthouse until the issue of visitation was settled, Nick took Trisha down a long hall and around a corner where they could have a modicum of privacy. ''Trisha. Trisha, look at me.'' Gently he raised her tearstained face so that he could look into her eyes. He had never felt so helpless in his life. What could he say? What *should* he say? ''I know you love your mother, Trisha, but she's wrong. This is not your fault. Please believe that, sweetheart. If anyone is to blame, it's me, because I didn't see what she was doing to you.''

''No!'' she protested tearfully.

"Yes, Trisha. I'm so sorry I let her hurt you. I love you, sweetheart. I want you to believe that with all your heart."

Her sob wrenched Nick's heart. "I do, Daddy. I love you, too."

He gathered her into his arms and let her cry. Tears stung his own eyes, but he held them back. Giving in to his own guilt and anguish wasn't going to help his precious daughter.

CRYSTAL FOLDED the dish towel and placed it on the empty draining rack. The little cuckoo clock in the dining room announced that it was seven-thirty, and Crystal wondered what she was going to do with herself for the rest of the evening. She'd insisted on fixing dinner and doing the dishes herself, but now those chores were finished. Normally she spent Tuesday evenings in an advanced aerobics class. She had opted to skip it tonight, explaining to Dan and Naomi that since their evenings together were dwindling to a precious few, she wanted to stay home with them.

That was true enough, but it had only been half the truth. The other reason she had stayed home was that she was praying Nick would call with the results of the custody hearing. Saturday night when he'd walked her to the door, he'd promised to let her know how the hearing turned out and when he would be returning. He just hadn't said *when* he might call her with that information.

Since he had not yet told her why he was suing for custody, Crystal had little reason to hope that he might feel the need to share the news with her. Nonetheless, she was clinging to that grain of hope with all her might.

Feeling at loose ends, she wandered into the living room, but Dan and Naomi were deeply involved in their favorite TV show. She sat for a few minutes and tried to get interested, but when she realized it was pointless, she put on a light jacket and told Dan and Naomi that she was going outside the check on her birds.

The barn owl, Hercules, and the kestrel, Jezebel, had both been faring quite well over the last few weeks. In fact, Crystal was convinced that the owl would soon be ready for release. Last week she had transferred him from his ten-by-ten-foot cage to a long, covered dog run where he had plenty of room to exercise his damaged wing. As a result, he was growing stronger every day.

Though the kestrel had carved a soft spot in Crystal's heart, it was the cantankerous owl she chose for company as she came around the house into the moonlit yard. Sitting on a stump near the dog run, she watched Hercules, and Hercules watched her, but instead of finding a sense of peace, Crystal found only a deep well of confusion and a renewed sense of impending doom.

Dan and Naomi would be leaving in less than two weeks. Every time Crystal thought about it she wanted to cry, but tears seemed like such an inadequate way of expressing her grief. The pain was too deep to touch, and so she continually shied away from it, refusing to acknowledge it.

It was far easier to think about Nick. He had brought something special into her life, and though she had no idea where it was going to lead her, she was looking forward to the journey. It was time she stopped shying away from relationships with men.

At one time, every fiber of her being had ached for the kind of relationship her foster parents shared. She had wanted a husband who would be her partner, her lover, and her friend. She had desperately wanted a house full of children, because she needed to be able to give back some of the love and nurturing Dan and Naomi had given her.

But after her disastrous, short-lived marriage to Roger Elliot, Crystal had decided that she was incapable of loving someone and sustaining a relationship as all-encompassing as marriage. She had changed her priorities. Her career became the only thing that mattered. She had filled her life with work and community service in order to drown the aching need for a partner to share her life with. She had denied her longing for children, convincing herself that she really didn't want the responsibility for shaping the life of a child. Instead, she would settle for shaping the future of one of the nation's forests. It had never really seemed like a fair trade, but she had convinced herself it was what she wanted more than anything in the world.

Crystal couldn't have said exactly when all those old longings for a home and family had resurfaced, but she acknowledged that they were still fully intact, no longer dormant.

Had Nick Hanford brought those feelings back to life? she wondered. Or had they started surfacing after her brother's death last year, and she just hadn't recognized them for what they were? Tommy J. had been more like her own child than a sibling; her earliest memories were of taking care of him after their mother had deserted them, leaving them in the hands of a man who cared about nothing except where his next drink was coming from. Maybe Tommy J.'s death had been the catalyst for the reemergence of her need to have a family of her own.

"Or maybe I'm just hearing the steady tick-tick-tick of my biological clock," she said with a short laugh. "What do you think, Hercules? Am I falling in love because there's a wonderful new man in my life, or because it may soon be too late for me to have kids?''

In answer, the owl tilted his head drunkenly from side to side, then swooped off his stump perch and flew the length of his cage, landing on the stump at the other end near Crystal. He screeched at her, spreading his wings in attack display, and Crystal laughed. "Is that your way of telling me you couldn't care less?" Hercules screeched again, and Crystal stood. "All right, all right, I'm going. You have absolutely no romance in your soul, old man. See if I ever ask for your opinion again!''

She returned to the house feeling a little better than when she'd left. A movie was just starting and she quickly popped a huge batch of popcorn before settling into her favorite chair. Pippin immediately made her way clumsily to the back of Crystal's chair and settled in to watch the movie, too. On one side of her, Dan was stretched out on the sofa, and on the other, Naomi was curled up in her recliner. A sense of contentment spread through Crystal. She was with the two people she loved most in the world, and she decided to stop worrying about her feelings for Nick.

Though she vowed that she wouldn't give another thought to whether or not he would call, by the time the movie ended her heart was somewhere in the vicinity of her toes. He hadn't called, and he wasn't going to. She tried to convince herself that it really didn't matter, but the effort wasn't successful.

Dan and Naomi turned in for the night, and Crystal was just about to do the same when the phone finally rang. Her heartbeat skipped into overdrive, and she warned herself not to be silly. It probably wasn't even Nick. If she expected too much, she was bound to be disappointed. There was no reason to get her hopes up.... And there was also no reason to let the phone ring more than once.

Diving across the room, she snatched up the receiver and said a little prayer. "Gatlin residence."

"Crystal? It's Nick. I hope I'm not calling too late."

Crystal released the breath she'd been holding. "Of course it's not too late. I'm just glad you called."

"I promised I would, but this is the first chance I've had."

He sounded incredibly tired, and a little stab of fear pierced Crystal. Had he lost the case? "How did it go today?"

There was a long pause. "I won."

"Oh, Nick, that's wonderful! I know how important this was."

"More important than you can possibly imagine, Crystal," he said, leaning against the headboard of his motel room bed. Nick still wasn't sure why he'd picked up the phone and dialed Crystal's number. He'd told himself it was only because he'd promised her that he'd call, and as his second in command, Crystal needed to know when he'd be returning to work. The excuse had been terribly hollow. He'd had a grueling day, and whether he wanted to admit it or not, he'd desperately needed to hear the sound of Crystal's voice. It didn't make sense, considering the fact that he had resolved not to pursue a relationship with her, but at that moment, Nick was too miserable to care.

Crystal couldn't help but wonder why he didn't sound happier about the outcome of the hearing. "But it's all over now, isn't it?" she asked.

"No, Crystal. I'm afraid this is only the beginning."

The sadness in his voice wrenched at her heart. "Nick, what's wrong?"

He wiped a weary hand over his face. "My daughter is in the next room crying herself to sleep, that's what's wrong. That damned judge gave a ruling today that made it sound as though this is all Trisha's fault, and then Marjorie dumped a whole truck load of guilt on her.... What am I going to do, Crystal? How do I make my little girl stop hurting?"

"Oh, Nick..." Crystal was at a complete loss, but she felt his pain as sharply as if it had been her own. "I don't know what to say. You never told me why you were suing for custody, so I don't have a clue about what's going on. How could any of it be Trisha's fault?"

Nick cursed his emotional outburst. "I'm sorry, Crystal. I shouldn't have said anything."

"I want to be able to understand, Nick. I'd like to help you if I can—even if it's nothing more than listening." She paused a second, then took a big chance by admitting. "I care about what you're feeling."

"I know," he said with a sigh. "I think that's why I needed to talk to you. All day long I have felt so inadequate and inept and...and so damned alone that I just needed to hear a friendly voice. *Your* voice," he amended.

Crystal felt a strange, wonderful warmth envelop her heart. "Well, my voice is at your disposal, Nick. Do you want to talk, or should I just recite the Gettysburg Address?" she asked wistfully, and was rewarded by Nick's deep-throated laugh.

"Thank you, Crystal."

"For what? I didn't do anything."

"You made me laugh. Believe me, that's something I haven't done in days. It's a miracle I even remember how."

Crystal curled her legs under her and snuggled into the corner of the sofa. "Tell me what's happening, Nick. Why did you sue for custody of Trisha?"

"All right, I'll tell you," he said, growing wary again. "If you'll tell me why you never explained how you ended up living with the Gatlins. Why didn't you tell me about your father, Crystal?"

A stab of panic pierced her. It was the same feeling that always overcame her when she was forced to come face-to-face with her wretched childhood. Over the years, she'd learned to control the panic rather than allowing it to control her, but she knew she'd never be completely rid of it. "How did you hear about my father?"

"I ran into Rich Patterson Sunday morning at the office when I dropped by to pick up some papers. We got to talking, and the story sort of... came out." If it was possible, Nick was even more confused now than he'd been on Sunday. He'd thought he had a workable plan—cut Crystal out of his life and avoid potential problems. Tonight, when he'd been desperate to hear her voice, that plan no longer seemed viable. There had to be another alternative. "Why did I have to hear it from Rich? Why didn't you tell me?"

Crystal had the horrifying feeling that the entire future of her relationship with Nick rested on these next few minutes. "I didn't tell you at first, Nick, because frankly, my past wasn't any of your business. I don't know how much Rich told you, but I didn't exactly have a childhood worth bragging about."

"That much I gathered," he replied. "I'm truly sorry about what you must have gone through."

"I survived it, Nick."

"But not without scars."

"No, not without scars," she said sadly. "But I have made peace with what my father and that life did to me, Nick. I've learned how to rise above it, and I've even managed to alter some of the patterns that could have made my life very different from what it is today."

Nick wanted to believe that. "If that's true, why did you feel it was necessary to lie to me Saturday night, Crystal?"

"Lie?" She was genuinely confused.

"When you told me you didn't drink because you never learned to like the taste of alcohol," he reminded her, unable to keep a hint of bitterness out of his voice. "That *was* a lie, wasn't it?"

"I'm not an alcoholic, recovering or otherwise, if that's what you're getting at, Nick," she said carefully.

Her statement shocked him, and his first instinct was to adamantly deny that the thought had ever crossed his mind, but that was only partially true. He had never allowed the idea to take substance, but subconsciously that was what he'd really been afraid of the moment he'd heard that her father was an alcoholic. Alcoholism was a disease that tended to transfer itself from one generation to the next.

Nick felt a palpable relief until he remembered that Marjorie wouldn't admit that she was an alcoholic, either.

"Nick? Are you still there?" Crystal asked when the silence on the line became more than she could bear.

"Yes."

She felt a rush of tears welling up, and stiffened her jaw against them. "We have a problem, don't we?"

Nick heard the pain in her voice, and it was nearly his undoing. "My ex-wife is an alcoholic, Crystal," he admitted reluctantly. "That's why we got divorced. It's also why I sued for custody of Trisha. Her drinking is totally out of hand."

"And the last thing in the world you want is to become involved with someone else who might have a drinking problem," she said, hating herself for not having told Nick the truth Saturday night when she'd had the chance. She'd not only escaped her past, but she had also made peace with it; but by not telling Nick, she had made it seem as though she was keeping some deep, dark secret.

Nick hated admitting that she was right, but he had no choice. "I have to think about what's best for my daughter, Crystal. But I can't seem to forget that you are one of the most wonderful women I've ever met. In a very short time, you've become something important in my life." Nick would have given anything to be able to reach through the telephone lines and take Crystal into his arms. "When I heard about your childhood, my first instinct was to run away from you. But the moment I heard your voice tonight, I realized it may be too late for that."

Relief flooded Crystal. He wasn't ending a relationship that had just barely begun. "Nick, I didn't lie to you because I was trying to hide something. In fact, it wasn't really a lie at all. I never learned to like the taste of alcohol. In high school, I experimented with liquor the way most kids do, but every time I took a drink, I'd think of my father stumbling home dead drunk in the middle of the night. I'd remember peeling him out of filthy clothes and putting him to bed. I'd remember cleaning up after him when he was sick, and trying to coax food down him so he wouldn't die of malnutrition.

"To me, drinking meant poverty, shame, embarrassment, and a fear so overwhelming that sometimes I couldn't even function normally," she explained, trying not to feel those emotions as she named them off. "Fortunately I had Dan and Naomi Gatlin to help me recognize what I was feeling when I was a kid, and later, I got professional help."

"But you still couldn't explain all that to me last Saturday night," he reminded her, aching to hold her.

Crystal laughed weakly at the irony. "Nick, I didn't want to tell you about my father for the same reason you didn't tell me about your ex-wife. The first rule in an alcoholic home is *Don't Talk About It*. It's imprinted on our brains in big, bold letters, and it doesn't go away. We don't want anyone to know that someone we love is an alcoholic, because deep down, we're afraid it's our fault. We're afraid other people will judge us and find us lacking. And we're afraid to examine ourselves too closely for exactly the same reason."

Nick looked inside himself and discovered that what Crystal was saying was absolutely true. He hadn't realized it before, but the reason he'd been so reluctant to tell Crystal about Marjorie was that he'd been afraid she would think less of him for having been married to an alcoholic. He was also afraid she would think he was a terrible father because he hadn't taken Trisha out of that environment sooner. That fear was still very real to him.

"You're right," he replied. "I had any number of opportunities to tell you about Marjorie and Trisha. I guess I was just afraid of what you'd think."

"It sounds to me as though we have a lot of talking to do, Nick," she said, then added hastily, "If you think it's worth the trouble."

Nick found himself at a crossroads once again. This time, there was no hesitation because he realized with absolute clarity that he wasn't just *falling* in love with Crystal Elliot, he'd already hit bottom. "Crystal, I think that having you in my life is worth *whatever* it takes to get you there. But I haven't been exactly fair to you, you know. I should have warned you that becoming involved with me means taking on the problems of my daughter, too. Doesn't that scare you away?"

"No," she replied softly. Despite the miles that separated them, she felt closer to Nick than she'd ever dreamed was possible. "We just have to take things one day at a time, as you suggested the other night. If what we feel for each other is meant to be something wonderful, it'll happen with just a little nurturing and care on our parts. But in the meantime, you have to let Trisha be first in your life."

"I'm glad you recognize that, Crystal."

"Believe me, I do, Nick. She needs all the love and security you can possibly give her."

"She's in a lot of pain, Crystal." He told her what had happened in court, and also explained what had happened at Christmas when he'd made the horrible discovery that Marjorie was abusing their daughter. Crystal listened, offering support when it was needed, and advice when it seemed appropriate.

They talked for hours about Nick's marriage and Crystal's father. They examined what alcoholism had done to their lives, and discussed what Nick was going to have to do to help his daughter when he brought her to Oak Ridge.

"When do you think you'll be back?" she asked. Stretched out on the sofa, thrilled and comforted by the sound of Nick's voice, Crystal had completely lost track of how long they had been talking.

"Probably not until late Thursday night." Nick yawned. He was bone tired, but that wonderful feeling of being on the threshold of a new life had returned. "Tomorrow Trisha and I are going to pack her belongings, and Thursday morning we have one final court appearance. Marjorie and I haven't been able to agree on her visitation rights, so the judge is going to have to settle it. We'll start for home right after court."

"Then I guess I'll see you Friday morning at work."

"I wish it was going to be sooner," he said, his voice filled with longing. "I want you in my arms right now."

His throaty whisper sent a chill racing down Crystal's spine. "There's no place I'd rather be."

"Thank you for everything."

"You won't be thanking me when it comes time to pay this phone bill," she teased.

"It's been worth every penny—and more." He paused, not wanting to say good-night. "Well, you ought to get some sleep."

This time it was Crystal who yawned. "I know. So should you."

"Right. Good night . . . sweet dreams."

"Good night, Nick." She waited until she heard the telltale click of the phone on his end of the line, then returned her own receiver to the cradle. "I love you," she whispered, just trying the phrase on for size.

It fit like a glove.

THE APARTMENT STILL SMELLED vaguely of fresh paint and new carpets as Nick turned on the lights and ush-

ered Trisha inside. They dropped their armload of suitcases just inside the door and looked around.

"Well, what do you think, sweetheart?" he asked.

"It's great, Daddy!" Trisha answered with an enthusiasm Nick suspected was entirely false. "It smells so
new. I like that."

"That's good. This furniture is the same old stuff I had
in Washington, but your room is going to be entirely new.
After I get off from work tomorrow, we'll head for the
mall and go shopping." Nick felt like an idiot. They'd
already discussed this yesterday, and again today on the
long ride from Kentucky. It seemed that whenever he became uncomfortable, he started babbling about plans for
their future. Probably it was because neither one of them
were comfortable talking about the past.

"I can hardly wait. Is my bedroom through here?" She
started for the hall and Nick followed her. "Oh, this is
nice, Daddy. It's so big," she said with what seemed like
genuine enthusiasm this time.

Nick glanced from the empty room to Trisha's smiling
face and mentally thanked Crystal for her advice. "Do
you have any ideas about decorating it yet?"

Trisha nodded and admitted almost reluctantly, "I've
always wanted to be an interior decorator. I guess this will
prove whether or not I'm going to be any good at it."

Nick was surprised. "I thought you wanted to be an
archaeologist."

She turned away, embarrassed. "That was ages ago,
Daddy."

Nick hid a smile. If he remembered correctly, "ages
ago" was just last summer when he'd taken her on a tour
of the Smithsonian. "Well, I promise you, sweetheart,
whatever you decide to do, you'll be good at it." He
moved up behind her and placed his hands on her shoul-

ders. "And as long as you're practicing to be a decorator, why don't you see what you can do with the living room? I just threw the furniture in there wherever it seemed to fit."

Trisha looked up over her shoulder at him, almost afraid to believe he meant what he'd said. Her mother had never let her move a single stick of furniture in their house—not even in her own room. "Really? Could I really do that?"

"Of course. We'll work on it this weekend. You just tell me what to move, and I'll move it."

Trisha glanced away and stiffened her chin against the flood of tears that wanted to rush into her eyes. "That'll be fun. I'll do my best, and if you don't like it, you can always change it back."

Gently Nick turned his daughter to face him. "This is our home, Trisha. It's as much yours as it is mine, and I just want us to be happy in it."

His daughter swallowed hard. "I'll try."

"Oh, Trisha." He gathered her into his arms. "Happiness isn't an obligation. It's something that comes from inside you. I hope you learn that someday, because you deserve to be happy."

"Are you happy, Daddy?" she asked quietly.

"I'm happy you're here with me," he told her truthfully, and then he remembered her reaction Tuesday when the judge had seemingly placed all the responsibility for what had happened on Trisha's shoulders. He didn't want to do that to her, too; it would be wrong to allow her to believe that she was solely responsible for his happiness. "I'm also happy with my new job and with this new town and the new friends I've made.... And I'm very happy about having made one friend, in particular," he said, praying that he was doing the right thing.

Tuesday night he and Crystal had discussed whether or not he should tell Trisha about their friendship, and Crystal had left that decision strictly up to him. His decision had been to tell her if the proper occasion arose. He didn't think there would be a better time.

Trisha pulled away and looked at him, her expression guarded. "A woman friend?"

"Yes. Does that bother you?"

She shrugged. "Why should it? I don't even know her."

"I think you'll like her, Trisha. You two have a lot in common. Do you remember the farm I told you about? The one where we're going to stable Morning Glory?"

"Yes. It's where you rode the black gelding, Goliath."

Nick grinned. Trisha never forgot anything about a horse. "That's right. Crystal lives on that farm and she also works at the station with me."

"Is she the one who takes care of the birds?"

"Yes."

"Oh." Trisha nodded as though that explained everything. "I guess you're really serious about her."

"It's a friendship that might someday become serious," he explained. "Actually we've only had a couple of dates, but I'd like to keep seeing her. She's a terrific person."

Trisha forced a smile. "I'm sure I'll like her."

It was obvious that Trisha wasn't sure about that at all, but Nick tried not to let it worry him. Rather than anticipating a problem, he knew he'd be much better off waiting to see what happened when Crystal and Trisha met. "I hope so, sweetheart. Well, I think I'm going to get a shower and unpack, then what do you say we have a snack before bed?"

"Sounds good to me. But—" she paused and grew very uncomfortable.

"What, Trisha?"

She looked down at the floor. "Do you think it would be okay if I called Mother and let her know we got here okay?" she asked tentatively.

"Of course. You can call her anytime you want, Trish."

"You really don't mind?" she asked hopefully.

"Of course I don't mind." This time Nick knew for a fact that he was telling a lie, but this one was strictly for Trisha's benefit. "I know that despite everything that has happened, you still love your mother very much. You don't have to be embarrassed about that."

"I hurt her a lot, Daddy. She thinks that means I don't love her anymore."

"In time she'll realize she's wrong," he said, feeling absolutely powerless to ease his daughter's distress. He'd already told her a dozen times at least that she wasn't to blame for what had happened, but he had no idea how to convince her that her mother's problems weren't her fault. Not knowing what else to say, he told her, "The phone's in the living room, but there's an outlet in here if you'd like a little privacy."

"Thanks, Daddy."

"You're welcome. I'm going to go hop into the shower now." He moved to the door, then stopped and grinned at her. "And you be sure to put a telephone on your shopping list, okay? We'll find one to match your new room. Something in pink, maybe?" he asked hopefully.

Trisha rolled her eyes. "Daddy! Pink is so uncouth."

Uncouth? Nick filed the word for future reference. He wasn't quite up to speed on the current state of the teenage slang. "Sorry. We'll worry about color coordinated phones tomorrow."

He disappeared down the hall, and Trisha stared after him for a long moment. Her father had always been funny and kind and very loving, but for the last four years, he hadn't been around enough to make much of a difference in her life. She had tried not to blame him for that, because she knew better than anyone how hard her mother was to live with. Always in the back of her mind, though, had been a resentment she didn't quite know how to cope with—and still didn't.

She'd never doubted that he loved her, but she was afraid to believe that he really wanted her here with him. Somewhere inside her was a deep and terrible fear that he would leave her now just the way he'd left her four years ago. One of these days, if she wasn't very, very good, he'd get tired of her and send her away.

The fact that her father had a girlfriend didn't decrease Trisha's anxiety, but she truly didn't begrudge him a little companionship. She knew that he had dated from time to time in Washington, but none of those women had been important enough to introduce to his daughter.

Or maybe it was the other way around. Maybe his daughter hadn't been important enough to be introduced to his lady friends.

No. Trisha rejected that idea almost immediately. She knew she was important to him. It would be silly of her to try to convince herself that she wasn't. But whether or not he loved her enough to keep her with him forever— that was another issue altogether.

Trying to pretend that her fear of abandonment didn't exist, Trisha retrieved the telephone from the living room, placed it in her bedroom, and quietly closed her door.

She didn't really want to call Kentucky, yet she felt compelled to. No matter how many times her father told her she wasn't responsible for her mother, Trisha couldn't bring herself to believe it. Guilt ate away at her, and she wondered if she would ever find a way to escape it.

And would she ever find a way to be happy the way her father wanted her to be?

Somehow, she didn't think so.

CHAPTER TWELVE

"ARE YOU SURE you're going to be okay here by yourself today?" Nick asked Trisha as he finished the last of his coffee.

"I'll be fine, Daddy. You go on to work and don't worry about me. I'll watch some TV and make some sketches for my new room."

"All right. First thing Monday morning, we'll get you enrolled in school." He stood and started collecting their breakfast dishes, but Trisha took the plates out of his hands.

"I'll do the dishes."

Nick smiled at her. "But you cooked breakfast, too. That hardly seems fair."

"I'm used to it." She dumped the dishes in the sink and returned for a second load. "Were the eggs okay?"

"Everything was perfect, sweetheart. Thank you," he said as he returned the butter and jam to the refrigerator. He hadn't intended for Trisha to prepare breakfast, but she'd surprised him by starting the meal while he was getting dressed for work. He didn't want to discourage her from helping out around the house, but he didn't want her to feel like a maid, either, so they cleared the table together, despite Trisha's warnings that he was going to be late for work if he didn't leave soon. He promised to call her if he could get away for lunch, and finally he left for work feeling as though he was deserting her.

He arrived at the office to find that everything was in absolute chaos. An environmental organization that had been trying to stop timber cutting in a section of the Ozark National Forest near Hot Springs had shifted its attention to the Osage. A group of protesters were camped out in the station ready to do battle, and Nick spent most of the morning trying to convince them that he wasn't a money-grubbing bureaucrat who was going to single-handedly strip the earth of all its trees.

"You're good at this," Crystal told him appreciatively when the group finally left. Nick had wanted her on hand to field any questions he couldn't answer, but he was getting to know the Osage so well that he hadn't needed much help.

"I've had practice dealing with environmentalists on a national level. It was good experience." He smiled at her. The long talk they'd had Tuesday night had been good for them. They hadn't had a chance to say two words of a personal nature today, but even their working relationship seemed better than before. "And you did a good job, too. There's nothing you can't handle around here, is there?"

Crystal shrugged. "Dan was a good teacher. And so are you. I'm not sure I could have done as well as you did with those environmentalists." Since it seemed that their business had been completed, Crystal decided it was time to ask the question she'd been aching to ask all day. "How's Trisha doing? Did you get in late last night?"

Nick's smile faded a little. "Yeah. She's doing fairly well under the circumstances. It's been a rough week for both of us."

"I thought about you a lot," Crystal said quietly, wishing they were anyplace but at the station, because the look on Nick's face told her he would dearly love to take her into his arms. Unfortunately the desk between them seemed a mile wide.

"I thought about you, too. Our talk did me a world of good, Crystal. My only regret is that we didn't have it sooner."

"I regret it, too."

A filament of longing stretched between them. "I wish I could tell you when we'll have some time together, just the two of us, but I don't—"

Crystal leaned forward in her chair. She reached for his hand, intending to cover it with her own, but an attack of shyness overcame her. Regretting the impulsive gesture, she started to withdraw her hand, but Nick wouldn't allow it. He sandwiched her hand between both of his, and Crystal wondered how something so simple could feel so good. "Nick, please don't worry about me— about us. One of the things I've always respected most about you is your concern for your daughter. I'm sure you can imagine why I think that's so remarkable."

"Yes." With gentle fingertips, Nick traced delicate lines on the back of her hand. "Crystal . . . I told Trisha about us. I thought she deserved to know that there was someone special in my life."

Crystal was delighted that Nick felt his relationship with his daughter was strong enough to withstand that kind of honesty. "I'm glad. What did she say? What did *you* say?"

Nick grinned. "Only that we'd dated a few times and that I planned to continue dating you. I also told her I thought you two would have a lot in common, considering your mutual love of horses." He released her hand abruptly as a thought occurred to him. "Damn. That reminds me, I've got to call Lonnie at the stable. I need to let him know that Morning Glory is being delivered tomorrow."

"Tomorrow? That's great. I can pass the message along, if you'd like," she offered. "I have to go down and exercise Cinnamon after work."

"Thanks. Do you think he'd mind if I brought Trisha out sometime tomorrow? She'd really like to see the stable and be there when her horse arrives." He reached for her hand again. "And it would also give you and Trisha a chance to meet."

Crystal smiled at the prospect. "That would be great. You're both welcome at the farm anytime. Do you know about when Morning Glory is arriving?"

Nick shook his head. "Just some time tomorrow afternoon. Trisha's grandfather offered to have one of his hands bring her over. Under the circumstances, it was a generous offer, and I didn't have the heart to pin him down to a more exact time."

"Don't worry about it. We'll be at the house all day, so come out whenever you feel like it. I'll give Trisha the grand tour."

"Thanks," he said with a smile. "Oh, by the way, Trisha's really excited about the prospect of decorating her own room. We're going shopping tonight, and probably tomorrow morning, too. Thanks for the good advice."

"Anytime."

Nick's grin faded slowly and he stood. He came around to the front of the desk and sat on the edge. He glanced from the closed door of his office to the open window that overlooked the front of the building. Then he looked at Crystal with enough intensity to melt steel.

"I have a thoroughly unprofessional desire to kiss you," he told her quietly.

Crystal's breath hitched in her throat. "Shame on you." She stood and found herself much too close to him. "I think I'd better go back to my office before we do something we might regret."

"I seriously doubt that I could ever regret kissing you. If I remember correctly, there's nothing in the world quite like it." He grinned devilishly. "And I'm pretty sure I remember correctly."

Crystal raised her head haughtily. "You're incorrigible, sir. I'm going back to work." She flounced toward the door, and Nick laughed.

"All right, but just remember that you can't escape me, lady."

With her hand on the doorknob, Crystal turned and gave him a saucy wink. "That's what I'm counting on, fellah."

He laughed again, and Crystal made a hasty exit. As she returned to her office, though, some of her bubbly mood evaporated. Tomorrow she would be meeting Nick's daughter for the first time. Did Nick realize, as she did, that the fate of their budding relationship rested firmly in the hands of an emotionally distraught teenager? It wasn't unreasonable to expect that Trisha might be threatened by her father's girlfriend.

If she couldn't win Trisha over, Crystal knew that she could kiss Nick Hanford goodbye. She worried about it the rest of the day, all evening, and most of the night. The next morning, she tried to block it from her mind as she helped Dan and Naomi clean out the garage—one more of the chores on Naomi's seemingly endless list of things that had to be done before she and Dan left for Arizona next week.

The physical labor was good for Crystal, but by noon she was drenched with sweat, and moreover, her emotions had somehow managed to tangle themselves into a knot. Anxiety about meeting Trisha mixed and mingled with her dread of Dan and Naomi's imminent departure. Her concern and empathy for Trisha warred with a selfish, unconscionable desire to spend some time alone with Nick. Her intellectual need to take her relationship with him slowly did fierce battle with a purely physical need to make love with him.

Crystal had never imagined that she would ever find any part of her life ruled by sex, but as she threw herself with vigor into cleaning the garage, she felt like a cranky, frustrated old maid. The cold shower she indulged in after the garage chore was finished helped only a little.

"Crystal, you're as nervous as a long-tailed cat in a room full of rocking chairs," Naomi observed as they worked around each other trying to clean up the kitchen after lunch. Dan and Lonnie were outside loading another truckload of Rescue Mission donations into the pickup.

"Sorry, Mom." At the sink, Crystal turned on the tap and began stacking dishes in the basin. "I'm a little anxious about meeting Nick's daughter this afternoon." She stopped what she was doing and turned to her mother. "That trip Nick took last week..."

Naomi looked at her expectantly. "Yes?"

"It was a custody hearing. Nick's ex-wife is an alcoholic."

"Oh, my." Naomi put down the dish towel she'd just removed from a drawer. "Has his daughter been living with her long?"

"Since the divorce four years ago. From what Nick has told me, Trisha has had a pretty rough time."

"Well, that certainly explains why you're so jumpy today."

Crystal nodded. "I feel as though I'm sitting on pins and needles. What if Trisha hates me, Mom? That's entirely possible, you know," she said quickly. "Right now she's drowning in insecurity and guilt. It would be the most natural thing in the world for her to cling to her father and to consider any outsider a threat. What do I do? How do I handle this?"

Crystal's distress was obvious, but Naomi couldn't suppress a little laugh. "Oh, honey, don't do this to yourself. When you meet Trisha, you'll know exactly what to do. You have wonderful instincts when it comes to dealing with children—particularly ones from alcoholic homes. I've known that for years. Dan and I have brought a lot of kids into this house, and you've given something special to every one of them."

"That's because I know how they feel."

"Then just put yourself in Trisha's place and deal with the problems as they arise." Naomi cocked her head to one side. "You're in love with Nick, aren't you, honey?"

"No!" Crystal said much too quickly. "Of course not. I told you last week that I like him a lot, but I haven't known him long enough to really love him."

"Yes, you have," Naomi said with a wise, ageless smile. "You still have a lot to learn about him, but that doesn't mean you can't already be in love. The human heart doesn't always wait until all its questions are answered. If it did, people would make fewer mistakes."

"Do you think I'm making a mistake, Mom?" Crystal asked apprehensively.

"I don't know," she answered honestly. "My sixth sense tells me that you're not. Frankly I've been very worried about the emotional vacuum you've been wan-

dering around in all these years. Your life is bursting at
the seams with work, hobbies, classes, community service.... You're so busy it's sometimes hard to tell whether
you're coming or going, but all that activity has just been
a convenient way of avoiding the truth.''

"What truth?"

"That your career isn't really the most important thing
in your life—it's just something you settled for because
you were so devastated by your divorce from Roger Elliot."

A niggling voice of feminism forced Crystal to ask,
"Are you suggesting that a woman can't be fulfilled by
a career?"

"You know better than that," she said with mild re-
proof. "But I know *you*, Crystal. I know how good you
are with children, and how much you've wanted a family of your own. I know what you think of the wonderful bond Dan and I have, and how much you used to
want that for yourself. I think Nick Hanford has made
you want all those things again. Am I wrong?"

Crystal knew better than to try to lie to her mother.
"No. You're not wrong. I want this relationship with
Nick to work more than I've ever wanted anything in my
life." She sighed deeply. "And that scares me to death."

"Don't be scared, honey, be grateful. Fear is only
going to make you want to run from happiness. What
you have to do is embrace the possibilities."

"That's what I'm trying to do."

"Then don't be intimidated by the thought of meeting
Nick's daughter. Just be yourself."

Naomi's advice was excellent, but Crystal found it
hard to follow. She tried to keep busy while Dan and
Naomi drove into town with the Rescue Mission dona-
tion. By the time she saw Nick's car coming up the lane,

she had created an image of Trisha Hanford that was a composite of all the negative characteristics of every troubled child she had ever known. The result was a horrifying cross between Lizzie Borden and Lady Macbeth.

That image vanished like a morning mist the moment she met Trisha. Nick's daughter was a sweet, shy, achingly polite young lady who was clearly terrified of meeting her father's girlfriend. She was also an uncommonly pretty girl. Her auburn hair was pleated into a French braid down the back of her head, and she had huge brown eyes very similar to Nick's. She had also inherited his height. At fourteen, she was already over five-feet-nine inches tall, and it was obvious from her gangly frame that she hadn't stopped growing yet. It was also obvious from her stooped shoulders that she hated her height.

That alone was enough to make Crystal empathize with her, but there was something else that drew her to the child. It was the guarded look in her eyes. Crystal had seen that same look in the faces of many of the other foster children the Gatlins had taken in; and she had seen it in her own face, too. Trisha Hanford was not a child who considered the world a fun, friendly place. On the contrary, for Nick's daughter, the world was a most frightening place filled with insecurity and uncertainty.

Crystal's first impulse was to cuddle the girl in her arms and promise her that everything was going to be all right.

Instead, she settled for giving her a warm, cheery welcome on the Gatlins' front porch. "It's nice to meet you, Trisha," she said after Nick had completed the introductions.

"It's very nice to meet you, too, Ms. Elliot."

"Please call me Crystal."

Trisha laced her hands behind her back. "Thank you."

"Your dad has told me a lot about you." It was an innocent pleasantry, but Crystal realized her mistake the moment the words were out of her mouth. A look of panic flashed in Trisha's eyes before she could effectively hide it and her gaze darted to her father as she tried to figure out how much he had told this stranger. Crystal understood exactly what she was feeling and casually continued as though she hadn't noticed the look at all. "Until I heard about you, I thought there was no one in the world who loved horses more than I do. Nick convinced me I was dead wrong. Your horse's name is Morning Glory, isn't it?"

Trisha's relief was palpable. "Yes, ma'am—I mean, Crystal. She's a thoroughbred from my grandfather's stable—he breeds and trains racehorses," she explained. "Is she here yet?"

"I'm afraid not. Would you like to take a tour of the stable to see where she'll be boarding?"

"Yes, thank you." Trisha looked up at her father. "Is it okay, Daddy?"

Nick placed his arm around her shoulder. "Of course. That's what we came for."

"Come on, I'll walk you down." They slipped off the porch and started toward the stable. "You know, Trisha, we've never had a thoroughbred on the farm. Do you think there's a chance the other horses will become jealous?"

Trisha actually giggled, and Crystal breathed a sigh of relief. "Could be. Morning Glory is awfully pretty."

A few strategically placed questions had Trisha talking freely about her horse and her grandfather's stable. Her knowledge of horses and the business of raising them was quite impressive. When they reached the stable,

Crystal introduced her to Lonnie, and Trisha proceeded to ask him a series of pertinent questions about the operating procedure of the stable. She inspected the place from top to bottom. She talked to Lonnie about feed and exercise, and was apparently delighted to learn that there were no restrictions on when she could come out to the farm to ride her horse.

The only thing about the stable that seemed to displease her was its distance from town. She was accustomed to riding Morning Glory every day, but that was going to be difficult now. Nick promised that he would bring her out as often as possible and Trisha accepted his promise with gratitude, but it was clear that she was going to miss her daily workouts.

When she showed an active interest in the other horses, Lonnie, who was more than a little impressed with her knowledge and her professional attitude, offered to introduce her to all the animals in the stable. Armed with apple slices and sugar lumps, Trisha was soon oblivious to everything but the horses.

Knowing they'd never be missed, Crystal and Nick wandered outside and sat on one of the bales of hay near the door.

"Your daughter is absolutely charming, Nick," Crystal said quietly.

"I know," he said, keeping one eye on the door, waiting for Trisha to emerge. "But sometimes she's a little too charming. I'm so proud that she's respectful and well mannered, but is her behavior normal? I mean, how many kids do you know who'd come through here and ask the kind of questions she's been asking?"

Crystal understood his concern. "None," she admitted. "But on the other hand, how many kids do you know whose grandfathers own race horses? Trisha has obviously spent a lot of time with professionals, and she's taken what she's learned and put it to practical use."

Nick looked at her, a frown furrowing his brow. "But she's so serious about everything. Sometimes I wonder if she knows how to have fun. She views everything as a task to be accomplished." He shook his head in amazement. "Yesterday I had promised her that we'd go shopping for her bedroom stuff after work. When I got home, she had a list prepared, with everything categorized according to the type of store we'd be likely to find it in. When we got to the mall, she addressed one category at a time. She didn't make a single impulsive purchase or deviate from her list one iota. We marched through the mall with the single-mindedness of Sherman marching to the sea."

Crystal couldn't keep from chuckling at his analogy, and Nick's scowl deepened. "You think I'm wrong to be worried, don't you?"

"No, Nick. You have every right to be worried, but Trisha isn't going to change overnight." Crystal paused a moment, trying to find the words to explain his daughter's behavior. "You see, Nick, children need structure in their lives. They need stability. They need a set of rules and the knowledge that those rules are going to be enforced. But an alcoholic home is chaotic. A child never knows what to expect from one minute to the next. The rules change constantly, so Trisha has had to create her own rules. She's had to find some way to exercise control over an uncontrollable situation. She can't control whether or not her mother takes a drink, so she focuses on tiny details that most people would be more than happy to leave to chance."

"So what do I do, Crystal?" Nick asked, desperate for anything that would help him understand and help his daughter.

"You give her rules, you stand by them, and gradually you add spontaneity to her routine. Once she knows that her life isn't going to be turned upside down every time she least expects it, she'll probably loosen up some."

"You make it sound so simple," Nick said in a tone that suggested he knew otherwise.

"It's not. You'll make a lot of mistakes. Whether she realizes what she's doing or not, Trisha will come up with a hundred and one tests for you, and you'll fail some of them."

"But I don't want to make mistakes, Crystal. I've already made too many. I should have gotten her away from Marjorie long ago."

Crystal shook her head. "That's in the past, Nick. You can't change it. All you can do is go on from here. It's not going to do Trisha any good to have her father consumed with guilt."

"Daddy? Are you out here?" Trisha called as she hurried out of the stable.

"Right here, honey." Nick rose to meet her. "What did you think of the horses?"

"Mr. Gatlin has some excellent breeding stock," she commented, then gave Crystal a shy smile. "Cinnamon is a real sweetheart. She's really built for speed, isn't she?"

Crystal stood and dusted the seat of her jeans. "I'll say. She has the heart of a true racehorse."

"We'll have to try her out against Morning Glory sometime. That would be quite a race."

"You're on. Cinnamon could use some good stiff competition to keep her from getting too uppity."

Trisha giggled again, and Nick smiled. "It sounds like the race of the century is shaping up here. I may sell tickets for this," he teased.

"Oh, Daddy."

Nick laughed and gave his daughter a playful hug. The sound of a vehicle coming down the lane had them all turning expectantly in the hope of seeing a Keating Farms trailer arrive, but it was only Dan and Naomi returning from town. The pickup took the right fork, heading toward the house, and Crystal invited Trisha to come up and meet the Gatlins.

Though it was clear she hated leaving the stable, Trisha agreed, and sandwiched herself in loosely between her father and Crystal as they returned to the house.

"Daddy told me about the birds you take care of," Trish commented. "It sounds fascinating."

"Would you like to see them? Pippin, my little saw-whet owl is inside, and the others are in cages on the other side of the house."

"I'd like that, but—" She hesitated, and Nick came to her rescue.

"But you want to be down at the stable when Morning Glory arrives," he guessed. Trisha nodded. "I tell you what, why don't I keep watch on the porch while Crystal shows you her birds? I'll holler if I see the trailer coming. It may be another hour or two before they get here."

"All right."

Dan and Naomi were waiting for them as they approached the house. Nick once again performed the introductions, and Trisha was once again impeccably polite. What little shyness she had shed in the stable returned as she greeted a new set of strangers.

"You're going to have to have a long talk with Trisha, Dan," Crystal told him as they all stood milling by the porch steps. "She's quite an expert on horses." She looked at Trisha and explained, "Dan is leaving next week for Arizona where he and his son are going to raise and train quarter horses for rodeo riders. You two have a lot in common."

Trish nodded politely, but looked a little intimidated by the prospect of conversing with Dan.

"Oh, goodness, if you get Dan talking about horses, we could be standing here for days," Naomi said jokingly. "We're going to need a pitcher of lemonade."

"Why don't you bring it out here on the porch, Mom?" Crystal suggested. "I'm going to introduce Trisha to Jezebel and Hercules while Nick keeps an eye out for Morning Glory. We'll be back in a few minutes. Ready, Trish?"

"Yes, ma'am."

As they circled the house, Crystal explained how the kestrel and the barn owl had come into her keeping.

"What do you feed them?" Trisha asked.

"Live mice are best, but I also have a vitamin-rich feed mixture that I get from the zoo up in Springfield. I feed them twice a day, morning and evening."

Trisha asked more questions—all of them extremely perceptive and intelligent—but when Crystal finally stopped in front of the kestrel's enormous wooden cage, Trisha fell silent, studying the placid little falcon through the narrowly spaced doweling that comprised the door of the cage.

"What do you think?" Crystal finally prompted.

"She's so pretty," Trisha whispered, as though she feared disturbing the brightly colored little bird. "And she's watching me."

"She's suspicious of all strangers, which is good. If she gets too dependent on humans, it will inhibit her ability to survive in the wild."

"How can you stand the thought of releasing her?" Trisha asked.

"It's not easy sometimes," Crystal admitted. "But I know that she'll be much happier living as she was meant to. Would you want to live the rest of your life in a cage, or tethered on a leash in someone's yard?"

"I guess not."

"Here, watch this. She loves to get a bath." Crystal hurried to the side of the house and returned a moment later with a garden hose. Jezebel saw her coming and began dancing from side to side on the stump she was using for a perch. Trisha giggled, then laughed outright at the bird's antics as Crystal trained a light spray of water on her. Wings flapping, she jumped from one stump perch to another, turning in circles and whistling happily.

"You want to try it?" Crystal asked, offering the hose to Trish. She accepted it eagerly, and Crystal stood back as Trisha showered the kestrel.

After another minute or two, Jezebel stopped performing and Trisha looked at Crystal. "Does that mean she's had enough?"

Crystal nodded, and Trisha released the trigger on the nozzle of the hose. "Now the real show begins. She'll preen her feathers until every single one is perfect. That's why I call her Jezebel—because she's so meticulous about her appearance."

Sure enough, the kestrel settled onto her perch and began preening her rust-colored feathers. They watched for a while, then Crystal guided Trisha to the dog run and introduced her to Hercules, who was considerably less charming, but no less fascinating to watch. Trisha had a seemingly endless stream of questions, and Crystal answered them all patiently.

"I'm going to be releasing him at dusk tonight," she finally told her. "Would you like to stay and help me?"

"Could I?" Trisha asked, almost jumping up and down with excitement. Gone was the perfect little lady who had arrived over an hour ago; in her place was an exuberant, wide-eyed little girl. Crystal wished that Nick was here to see her excitement. It might have eased his mind to know that all the childlike wonder had not been squeezed out of his daughter.

"Of course you can stay," Crystal assured her. "If your dad approves, of course."

Trish's eyes danced with expectation. "May I go ask? Right now?"

"Sure. Let's go."

They hurried around the house, and Crystal thought that Nick might get to witness Trisha's exuberance after all. Unfortunately the minute the girl rounded the corner and saw Dan and Naomi sitting in the porch swing with Nick resting in one of the wicker lawn chairs nearby, she slowed her pace. Her shyness returned, and she approached Nick in an entirely decorous manner.

"What did you think of the birds, sweetie?" he asked as she climbed the steps.

"They were wonderful. I've never seen anything like them—not even in a zoo. Crystal even let me give Jezebel a bath." She shot a glance at Crystal that almost seemed like a plea for help, and Crystal was only too happy to give it.

"I'm going to release Hercules at dusk and I've invited Trisha to stay and help me, if it's okay with you."

"Yes, stay," Naomi said as she poured glasses of lemonade for Crystal and Trisha. "And stay for supper, too. We're having hunter's stew, so there's plenty to go around."

"Thank you, Naomi, but I don't want to impose," Nick replied.

"Who's imposing?" Dan asked. "You have to hang around until Morning Glory arrives anyway. You might as well make a day of it. There's always room for two more at the Gatlin table."

Nick looked at his daughter. "What do you think, kiddo? Want to stay for supper, too?"

"I'd like that very much," Trisha replied politely, but Nick could see that her eyes were sparkling unreservedly. Obviously Crystal—or at least her birds—had won Trisha over completely. It was an excellent beginning.

His warm smile flashed from his daughter to Crystal and lingered on her face a moment as he silently tried to convey his gratitude. "I guess we're staying."

"Wonderful," Crystal said as the warmth of his approval washed over her.

It was, indeed, an excellent beginning.

CHAPTER THIRTEEN

NICK AND TRISHA spent the remainder of that Saturday afternoon and evening at the farm, and were also invited to join the family for the Gatlins' final Sunday afternoon in Arkansas. Saturday became a little hectic after Morning Glory arrived; the horse had not made the long trip well, and Trisha spent a considerable amount of time trying to calm the thoroughbred. When Crystal was ready to release Hercules, though, she was more than ready to give the event the full attention she felt it deserved.

Crystal enlisted her help in putting food onto the hacking platform in the event that Hercules had trouble making his first kill after his weeks in captivity; then, together, they opened the door of the dog run and slowly backed toward the house where everyone else was waiting and watching.

It didn't take the owl long to see its avenue of escape. Crystal and Trisha were barely out of the way when Hercules flew the length of the pen, stopped on his perch for a quick inspection of the area, then spread his wings again and left the cage. Trisha gasped when it appeared that the huge owl was flying toward them, but Hercules had no such intention. He banked sharply to the right and flew into the trees. From one of the highest branches of an ancient oak, he paused for a moment to look down at the humans, then silently disappeared into the gathering darkness.

The show was brief, but impressive.

Everyone milled around in the yard for a while, hoping for another glimpse of him, but when it became obvious that he was gone for good, Naomi herded her family and guests into the house, where supper was waiting.

It wasn't until they were all gathered around the table that Nick began to notice there was a forced gaiety about the occasion, which carried over into Sunday's festivities. It seemed no one could forget that Dan and Naomi would be leaving for Arizona in just a week.

Crystal was as effervescent as champagne, determined not to let one moment of the day become maudlin, but more than once Nick wanted to take her into his arms and tell her everything was going to be all right. He settled for an occasional touch on her hand or her shoulder that could have meant anything or nothing.

What surprised Nick most about the day was that Lonnie accepted his presence, albeit grudgingly, and even tried to be polite. He wasn't always successful at it, but Nick appreciated the effort. He also appreciated the effort everyone made to make Trisha feel at home. She never really came out of her shy shell, but Nick could tell that she was having fun.

They picknicked in the backyard and played a rousing game of horseshoes. Naomi made a freezer of homemade ice cream, which everyone ate with abandon, and they settled onto the porch for a lazy afternoon. Several times during the day, Nick noticed Trisha and Crystal behaving strangely, as though they had a secret they weren't willing to share just yet. When they disappeared around three o'clock, he wondered what was going on, but decided not to launch a search for them. It pleased him immensely that Trisha seemed so comfortable with

Crystal, and he didn't want to intrude on anything that might bring them closer together.

The "secret" turned out to be the race between Morning Glory and Cinnamon that had been suggested the day before, and everyone gathered at the "finish line" by the meadow fence while Crystal and Trisha walked their horses around the course. When they were finally ready, Dan used a handkerchief to start the race, and Lonnie had everyone in stitches with his raucous imitation of a track announcer.

Morning Glory and Cinnamon stayed neck and neck through the first turn, but on the back stretch, the thoroughbred began edging ahead. Crystal managed to keep the race close, but by the time they hit the finish line, Morning Glory was a good two lengths ahead. The crowd of four spectators went wild with excitement, and Nick particularly was ecstatic when he saw the look of unadulterated pleasure on his daughter's face.

"That's a magnificent horse, Trisha," Dan complimented as the "jockeys" brought their animals to the fence. "Why isn't she racing for real?"

"She suffered some tendon damage when she was a colt, and no one expected her to fully recover," Trisha explained, patting her horse's neck. "It still flares up from time to time. She has good speed, but she doesn't have the stamina to hold up under a hard racing schedule." She slipped out of the saddle. "Excuse me, please. I need to walk her now."

"Me, too," Crystal said as she dismounted and stroked Cinnamon's lathered neck. "You gave it your best shot, girl," she crooned to the horse. "You deserve a good rubdown."

"I'll get your stuff ready." Lonnie, who'd been sitting on the fence, jumped down and hurried off to the stable.

"That's quite a young lady you've got there, Nick," Dan said quietly.

"I could say the same thing about your daughter, Dan," Nick replied, watching Trisha and Crystal as they led their horses down the fence row. "She's very special."

Dan looked at Nick archly. "How special?"

"Dan!" Naomi exclaimed softly, brushing his arm reproachfully.

Nick turned to the former ranger and found himself being closely scrutinized. "Are you asking whether my intentions are honorable, sir?" he asked with only a hint of amusement twinkling in his eyes.

"That's exactly what I'm asking."

"The answer is yes. My intentions are honorable. Crystal is the most remarkable woman I've ever met."

"Are you in love with her?"

"Dan!" Naomi chided again, but her husband ignored her.

"Well?"

Nick didn't flinch. "No offense, Dan, but that's between Crystal and me. We have a long way to go, but we're off to a promising start."

Dan nodded, but his expression was still a little on the stern side. "I expect you to treat her right, Nick."

Naomi sighed with exasperation. "Oh, for crying out loud. I'm not going to stand here and listen to any more of this Victorian nonsense." She looked beseechingly at Nick. "Please forgive him. My husband doesn't always have the sense God gave a goose." She sighed. "I'll be up at the house if you need me."

Both men laughed as she marched away, but they sobered quickly. Dan levered himself onto the fence, and Nick joined him. "You're worried about what's going to happen to Crystal after you leave, aren't you?" Nick asked.

"Real worried," Dan admitted. "I guess she told you about her first husband."

"No," he answered, realizing that there were still serious gaps in his knowledge about Crystal. "We've talked a little about her father, but we've never really spoken about her marriage."

"I guess that's not surprising. It was very brief, and very traumatic. Crystal was away from home for the first time, working in the Shawnee National Forest over in Illinois. I never really got all the details, but I've always felt that she jumped into that marriage just because she was homesick."

"That's not uncommon," Nick commented.

"No, but I'd hate to see something like that happen to her again," Dan said, piercing Nick with the intensity of his gaze. "Don't get me wrong, Crystal's a lot stronger now than she was ten years ago when she married Roger Elliot. She's older and wiser, but in a lot of ways she's still as vulnerable. I'd hate to see any man take advantage of that."

"So would I," Nick replied, meeting the older man's gaze steadily. "I'm not some randy young buck out for a few cheap thrills, Dan. I'm nearly forty years old, with a half-grown daughter. I'm a survivor of a wretched marriage, and four moderately lonely years of bachelorhood." He smiled and shook his head wryly. "Believe me, Dan, when I came to Oak Ridge, getting involved with a woman—*any* woman—was the last thing on my mind. I just hadn't counted on meeting someone as incredible as Crystal. But if you're asking for my personal guarantee that our relationship is going to become something permanent—''

"No, no," Dan said with a wave of his hand. "There are no guarantees in this life, son. I know that. I just needed to be sure that you realize what a sweet, vulnerable girl Crystal really is. She keeps her vulnerability well guarded, though, so sometimes, all men see is that she's strong and independent. But when Naomi and I leave, her guard's going to be down, and my girl is going to be wide open for the kind of heartbreak that could destroy her."

Nick frowned, wondering if perhaps Dan was over-stating the situation a little out of fatherly concern. "Are you asking me to back away from her, Dan?"

"Good Lord, no," he said, straightening in surprise. "I don't think Crystal would ever forgive me if I did something like that. I'm just asking you to be careful."

"I'm always careful, Dan."

"Good. Now come on, let's go up to the house and wait on our girls. I want to see if there's any more of that ice cream left."

WORKING IN SIDE-BY-SIDE STALLS, Crystal and Trisha put the finishing touches on their well-groomed horses. They had already discussed their race at length, and had eventually fallen into a companionable silence.

"May I ask you a real personal question, Crystal?" Trisha asked suddenly, as though she'd been trying for sometime to get up the nerve to ask.

"Of course," Crystal replied, wondering with dread what constituted "real personal." Was Trisha about to question the nature of her relationship with Nick?

The teenager grinned shyly. "How do you do it?"

Crystal gathered up her grooming equipment and slipped out of Cinnamon's stall. "Do what?"

"How do you hold your shoulders up so straight? Don't you hate being tall?"

Crystal almost sagged with relief. "Sometimes I do. When I was your age I hated it more than most people could possibly imagine. Kids called me the Jolly Green Giant." She rolled her eyes to the heavens. "Boy, I really hated that."

"Me, too," Trisha said in a small voice. "So why do you stand up so straight?"

"Because there's nothing I can do about being tall. That's simply the way I was meant to be, and I have to live with it. But I'll tell you a little secret. The real reason I keep my shoulders back is that I don't want anyone to know that I hate being tall. That's how I got all those kids to stop teasing me when I was young."

Trisha frowned. "I don't understand."

"Well…it's like this." Crystal leaned against the post that supported Morning Glory's stall. "If people know they can get under your skin by teasing you, they'll keep doing it. Most of the time they don't even realize that they're being hurtful—it's just something to do. But if you pretend to be proud of being tall, and can make believe it doesn't bother you, they'll leave you alone. And eventually, you even start believing it yourself."

"I don't know if I could do that or not."

"You do it when you ride Morning Glory. You sit a horse as beautifully as anyone I've ever seen."

Trisha gathered her equipment and left the stall, closing the door behind her. "That's because I'm proud of Morning Glory, and I want her to be proud of me." She darted a small, self-conscious glance at Crystal. "Does that sound weird?"

"Not at all." She reassured her with a smile. "But I think that what you're really saying is that the only time you're proud of yourself is when you're with Morning Glory. You're an excellent horsewoman."

Trisha scuffed the ground with the toe of her boot. "I'm not all that good."

"Yes, you are," Crystal said firmly as she headed for the tack room to put the grooming equipment away. "And what's more, you know it. The minute you walk into a stable or get on that horse, your face absolutely glows with confidence."

"Is that wrong?" she asked, following her.

"Wrong? Of course not! It's absolutely wonderful!" Crystal stopped abruptly and looked at her. "Trisha, everyone needs something to feel good about. In fact, we need lots of things to feel good about. You're very pretty, and you're smart. You're wonderful with horses, and you're a very sweet, likable person. You have a lot to feel proud of. Even being tall. Be proud of that, too, and say the heck with the rest of the world. Short people don't know what they're missing . . . you and I will never have to stand in the front row to see a parade pass by."

Trish giggled. "You make it sound easy."

"It's not, sweetie. I wish it was," she said a little sadly. "Being proud of yourself is one of those horrible things in life that takes practice, but it's worth it. Sometimes it helps just knowing that someone else is proud of you, though."

A shadow passed over Trisha's face. "I'd like to make Daddy proud of me."

"Oh, he is, Trisha. Believe me, he is. Didn't you hear how he was cheering you on when we were racing? When you won, he was so proud I was afraid he was going to pop a button on his shirt."

"Your dad was cheering you on, too," Trisha said with a laugh.

"Dan's my head cheerleader. He's had a lot of practice rooting for me."

Trisha looked at Crystal and hesitated for a moment before asking, "Why do you call him Dan instead of Dad?"

Time for a little straight talk, Crystal decided. "Because Dan and Naomi Gatlin aren't my real parents. I came to live with them when I was twelve."

"Why? Did your real folks die?"

"No. My mother ran away when I was seven. I have no idea what happened to her. I stayed with my dad for a few years after that, but finally a social worker took me and my brother away from him."

"Why?" Trisha asked, thinking about the way she'd had to leave her mother.

This was the opening Crystal had been hoping for—the perfect opportunity to let Trisha know that she had a friend who understood much of what she had been going through. Keeping her tone even and unemotional, she replied, "Because my father was an alcoholic."

"Oh." There was a long pause as Trisha slipped into the tack room and put her gear away. "That's too bad."

"Yes, it is. Alcoholism is a very sad disease because it hurts so many people."

Trisha refused to look at Crystal, but asked with false casualness, "Why do they call it a disease?"

"Because that's what it is. No one really understands it, but for an alcoholic, taking even one drink is like taking poison. You know, it's really strange, Trisha," Crystal said reflectively. "I loved my father very much, but I also hated him, too. And I was so ashamed of hating him that sometimes it actually hurt. Physically hurt."

Trisha left the tack room and retrieved her saddle from the bench where she'd left it earlier. "Did you ever stop hating him?"

"Eventually. When I realized that he was sick and he couldn't help himself. But you know what helped me more than anything?"

Trisha still refused to look at her. "What?" she asked suspiciously, but Crystal didn't hear the new, tense edge that had crept into her voice.

"It was when I realized that no matter what I had done—no matter how much I had loved him or how good I had been—it wouldn't have made him stop drinking. I really used to think that it was my fault, but it wasn't. When I realized that, it became easier not to hate him."

Trisha turned to Crystal, her eyes narrowed with suspicion—and a touch of raw, unadulterated anger. "Daddy told you, didn't he?"

Crystal's heart sank. She'd gone too far, said too much. "About your mother, you mean?"

"Yes."

She nodded. "I know why he sued for custody, Trisha."

Trisha's hands balled into angry fists. "He shouldn't have told you that! He shouldn't have told you! I didn't want you to know!" she shouted, then turned and ran from the stable as though the hounds of hell were on her heels.

"Oh, God," Crystal whispered, sinking onto the bench by the tack room door. "What have I done?"

"I'M SO SORRY, Nick," Crystal said, switching the telephone receiver from her right hand to her left. Only minutes after Trisha ran out of the stable, Crystal had returned to the house to find that the girl had already convinced Nick it was time to go home. She'd claimed that she wanted to spend some time putting her newly furnished bedroom in order.

Nick had known that something was wrong, but he hadn't wanted to question her in front of the Gatlins, so he had acquiesced to her request. They had already been headed for his car when Crystal approached, and all he could do was exchange helpless, puzzled looks with her as he thanked her for her hospitality and drove away.

It wasn't until later that night after Trisha was in bed that Nick finally had a chance to call Crystal to find out what had happened in the stable. "Sorry for what, Crystal? Trisha insists that nothing is wrong, but I know otherwise," he said, keeping his voice low. "What happened? You two were getting along so well."

"It's all my fault, Nick," she said, misery squeezing her heart. She recited as much of her conversation with Trisha as she could remember. "I was only trying to give her something to think about, but she's so damned bright I should have realized she'd figure out what I was doing. I should have known how she'd react."

"How could you know that, Crystal?"

"Because I've been where she is right now. I know how ashamed she feels. I pushed too hard."

"Stop blaming yourself. It'll be okay," Nick reassured her, a little surprised at how panicked she sounded. "I'll talk to her. Who knows, maybe this is what Trisha and I needed in order to get some of our feelings into the open."

"Talking is good, Nick. I hope you can. But you don't need an outsider meddling where she doesn't belong, making things worse."

"What outsider?" he asked, confused.

"Me! I'm an outsider. I didn't have any right to say what I did to Trisha."

"Crystal, calm down," he said, realizing that she was taking this much too seriously, as though she'd done some irreparable damage to his daughter. "I asked for your help, remember? And I also dumped Trisha's problems into your lap when I asked you to give us a chance to have a relationship. That makes you anything *but* an outsider."

Amazed and concerned by her attitude, Nick kept talking until she was calmer. It occurred to him that not only was she blaming herself, but she was also afraid that he was going to blame her. He tried to assure her that wasn't the case, but when they ended their call he still wasn't certain he'd gotten through to her.

Hoping he'd have better luck with Trisha, he went to her room and rapped lightly on the door. As he'd suspected, she wasn't asleep yet.

"Just a minute, Daddy," she answered. He heard a rustling sound as she turned on the light and donned her housecoat.

"Can we talk a minute, honey?" he asked when she finally opened the door.

"I have school tomorrow," she reminded him, shifting uncomfortably from one foot to the other.

"This won't take long, and I think it'll make us both sleep better."

Trisha stepped back and sat on the edge of her bed. Nick pulled out the chair to her new desk and moved it toward the bed. "I just talked to Crystal. She told me what happened today."

Trisha looked down at her white eyelet comforter and traced the lacy pattern with her forefinger.

Nick waited for her to comment, but when it became obvious that she wasn't going to, he continued. "Are you mad at me for telling Crystal about your mother?"

"No," she said without looking up.

"I'm sorry, Trisha, but I don't believe you."

Her gaze flew to his. "I couldn't be mad at you, Daddy! I love you."

"Trisha, honey, you can love me and still be mad at me. One thing doesn't have anything to do with the other," he explained patiently. "If you're angry, tell me and we can talk about it. That's the only way to make it better."

There was a long pause as Trisha returned to tracing patterns on her comforter, but this time Nick refused to fill the silence. Finally she asked very quietly, "Why did you tell her about Mom?"

Nick breathed a sigh of relief. At least they were talking now. "I told her because I thought she had a right to know. People who care about each other share things, Trisha. I talked to Crystal the way I want you to be able to talk to me."

"But now she knows that Mom was sick," she protested.

"That's right, she does. And she understands a little bit about how you feel because she's been through some of what you've been through."

Trisha looked surprised. "You mean it was true—what she told me about her dad?"

"Yes, Trisha," Nick replied, amazed that she would even ask such a question. "Did you think Crystal had lied to you?".

She shrugged. "I don't know. I thought maybe she was making it up to trick me into talking."

Her statement might have been funny if it hadn't been so pathetic. Crystal was right—the first rule in an alcoholic home really was Don't Talk About It. The rule had obviously been so deeply ingrained in Trisha that she viewed any attempt at a meaningful dialogue as a "trick."

"Crystal didn't make any of that up, honey," he assured her. "From the time she was seven years old, she took care of her little brother, she kept house, she cooked, she took care of her father when he was drunk.... She had it pretty rough until she came to live with the Gatlins, and even then she had to deal with the guilt of leaving her father."

"Like me?" Trisha asked in a small voice.

"Yes. Like you in a lot of ways." Nick reached out and captured his daughter's hand. "Crystal just wants to be your friend, honey. I guess she said what she did today because she wanted you to know that she understands some of the things you're probably feeling. Please don't hold that against her."

"I won't," she promised.

"And I hope you won't stay mad at me too long because I told her."

"I'm not mad anymore, Daddy. I swear."

He accepted her word for it. "Okay. Will you promise me one thing?"

"What?"

"Next time you get mad, please tell me. I can't explain or apologize if I don't know what I've done wrong."

She promised that she would, but Nick doubted that it would be that simple. He returned the chair to her desk and gave Trisha a big hug and a kiss on her brow. It was a ritual he had missed very much these past four years.

He murmured good-night and started toward the door, but Trisha stopped him.

"Daddy, should I apologize to Crystal?"

"That's up to you, Trish."

"Okay. Good night, Daddy. I love you."

"I love you, too, sweetheart. Good night." He closed the door, and a few seconds later the light went off.

Crisis number one averted, he thought with only a small sense of relief, because instinct told him there were hundreds more to come.

TUESDAY AFTERNOON, Crystal looked up from her computer to find Trisha standing at the door of her office, looking terribly awkward. Nick had told her she might be receiving an apology from Trisha, but based on how uncomfortable the girl looked, Crystal was afraid that what little progress they had made toward becoming friends had been shattered by the debacle in the stable Sunday afternoon. An apology made out of obligation was worse than no apology at all.

"Hi, Trisha, come on in."

"Am I bothering you? Daddy said I could come see if you weren't busy."

Crystal gave her a reassuring smile, though it was difficult. She still felt terrible about what had happened, and no amount of reassurance from Nick seemed to help. "I'm never too busy to chat. Come on in and shut the door. Did you ride the bus here from school?"

Trisha nodded as she closed the door. "The same one that goes to our street comes by here. I just got off a little early."

"That's convenient. How was your second day at school?"

She sat in the chair opposite Crystal's desk. "Okay, I guess. Most of my teachers seem nice, and nobody's called me Jolly Green Giant yet."

Crystal laughed lightly. Maybe their friendship hadn't been damaged quite as much as she'd thought. "That sounds like an excellent beginning to me."

Trisha nodded. She hesitated a moment, then plunged ahead. "I'm sorry about Sunday."

"So am I, Trisha," Crystal said sincerely.

"You were only trying to be nice."

"I wanted to be honest with you, but I guess I wasn't honest enough. I certainly didn't want to make you angry with your dad."

"We talked, and I'm not mad anymore." She gave Crystal a crooked smile. "Can we still be friends? I don't have any here in Oak Ridge yet."

Crystal felt tears sting her eyes and she smiled brightly to fight them back. "I'd be very proud to be your first, Trisha."

"Thanks." She stood and moved toward the door. "Then I guess I'll see you at the farm sometime. Daddy's taking me out for a ride this afternoon."

"I'll see you later."

"Bye," she said brightly and disappeared down the corridor.

Crystal leaned back in her chair and wondered if maybe everything was going to be all right, after all, but another part of her was trembling like a scared rabbit. She'd spent the last three days thinking that it had been a huge mistake to become involved with Nick Hanford. She wasn't qualified to handle children. She wasn't even qualified to give Nick the kind of relationship he deserved.

Her fear of failure was overpowering.

I should tell Nick I don't want to see him anymore, she thought bleakly, knowing she wouldn't do it. She was in love with him. And even though love was something at which she had never excelled, she couldn't bear the thought of losing him.

CHAPTER FOURTEEN

ON THURSDAY, a moving van pulled up to the Gatlins' front porch. A few of Naomi's favorite pieces of furniture and all the boxes that had been labeled Arizona were loaded into the van.

On Friday, Dan and Lonnie put the camper shell over the bed of Dan's pickup. They loaded their luggage and a few items Naomi hadn't wanted to entrust to the movers.

On Saturday, the family rose at dawn. Crystal made breakfast while Naomi checked the house over to make sure she hadn't forgotten anything. Dan consulted his road map one last time. They ate breakfast at the table in the kitchen because the dining-room set had been taken away on Thursday. Naomi made sandwiches for the trip. Crystal prepared a huge thermos of coffee.

At 7:05, they went out to the truck and said their goodbyes. Naomi cried as she hugged her daughter, and Crystal did everything in her power not to. The effort was pointless.

"Give Casey a big hug for me," she instructed, dashing at the tears streaming down her face.

"I will," Naomi promised. She turned to Lonnie. "You take good care of Crystal now, you hear?"

"Don't worry about anything, Mom," he said, giving her a quick bear hug. "I'll be seein' you as soon as we find a buyer for the farm. You just make sure Casey keeps a bed open for me in the bunkhouse."

Dan gathered Crystal into his arms. "There'll always be a place there for you, too, honey."

"I know that." With a sob, Crystal touched the face of the man who had given her the love, guidance and support that had been beyond the comprehension of her real father. "I love you, Dad."

The knot of emotion in Dan's throat broke loose, and tears blurred his vision. He'd never for a moment begrudged the fact that Crystal had never addressed him as Dad, but it meant the world to him that she did so now. "I love you, too, honey." He cleared his throat and stepped back. "Now, you're coming out to the ranch for your vacation this year, right?"

Crystal nodded and finally gave up trying to dry her tears. "Wild horses couldn't keep me away."

They said a round of goodbyes and everyone promised to keep in touch. There were more hugs and more tears. Naomi stood for a moment, looking up at the drafty old house where she had spent thirty wonderful years, but finally she allowed Dan to herd her into the pickup. Crystal stepped back, waving and trying to smile. The truck rattled up the lane for the last time, and the moment it passed over the crest of the hill, Crystal sank to the porch steps. Lowering her head to her knees, she sobbed as though her heart was breaking...because it was.

"CRYSTAL? Are you in there?" The screen door squealed as Nick opened it and stepped into the entry hall. All the doors and windows were wide open, but the house appeared deserted. "Crystal?"

"Nick? I'm upstairs. Come on up."

Following the sound of Crystal's disembodied voice, he jogged up the stairs and found her in the first room on the left. Dressed in jeans and an old T-shirt, with her hair pulled back into a ponytail, she was perched precariously on a ladder by the window. The room was devoid of furniture, the closets were empty, and the tall, narrow windows were bare. This was the bedroom the Gatlins had vacated that morning.

"Your timing is perfect because I just ran out of hands," Crystal said, trying to balance a curtain rod in one hand while the other attempted to unsnag the lacy white curtain that had gotten caught on the rough wood of the old ladder.

"Here, let me get that." Nick came to her rescue, freeing the curtain so that she could finally secure the rod to the brackets.

"Thank you." She turned on the ladder to give him a bright, cheerful smile, but Nick noticed immediately that her eyes were puffy and swollen from crying.

"Are you all right?"

She nodded. "I will be as soon as I get these curtains hung. Mom took the ones that were here, and I just couldn't stand how bare the windows looked from the outside." She reached up and adjusted the gathered fabric on the rod. "Of course, these things are so old they'll probably fall apart before the day is over. I should have bought some new ones, but these windows are so hard to fit. They just don't make—"

"Crystal . . ."

She stopped and looked down at him. "What?"

"You're babbling."

Crystal swallowed hard as a new batch of barely suppressed tears brimmed in her eyes. "That's because I'm tired of crying."

"Come here." Smiling gently, Nick placed his hands at her waist and plucked her off the ladder as though she weighed no more than a feather. Her arms wrapped around him and he snuggled her body against the long planes of his own. "It's okay to cry, Crystal. This is a rough day."

She sniffled and hugged him tight, but for some reason, she no longer felt like crying. Just the comfort of having Nick's arms around her was enough to make her feel as though everything was going to be all right. "I thought men were afraid of a woman's tears."

"There's nothing about you that scares me, love," he whispered, brushing his lips against her hair. "What time did Dan and Naomi leave?"

"A little after seven."

"Are you going to be all right?"

"I don't know," she said wistfully. "I had more or less planned to fall apart today and get it over with. I cried for an hour, then went down to the stable and exercised Cinnamon. Then I cried a little more while I did the laundry, and I ironed these curtains, sprinkling them liberally with tears...." She looked up at him with a sweet, sad grin. "Believe me, there's not a dry tissue left in this house."

"Sounds as though you've accomplished your mission, and managed to get a little work done at the same time," he said wryly. "Come on, let's hang this other set of curtains and move on to the next chore."

"And if I fall apart again?" she asked, feeling herself becoming lost in the warmth of Nick's dark eyes.

"I'll be here to glue you back together."

Stretching up, Crystal pressed a soft kiss to his mouth. "I like the sound of that," she whispered.

"So do I." He chased her lips and gave her a long, slow kiss that drove away all her gloomy thoughts—for a moment, at least. "Have you ever made love in the middle of the morning?" he asked huskily.

"No," she replied breathlessly.

"Then we'd better hang those curtains immediately." With great reluctance he released her and moved the ladder to the other side of the room while Crystal threaded the curtains onto the rod.

"Where's Trisha?"

Nick glanced out the window that overlooked the stable and a large part of the meadow behind it. "Right there." He pointed toward two figures on horseback who were just about to disappear into a grove of trees. "I think she made a friend down at the stable this morning."

Crystal looked out the window. "Oh, good. That's Brandy McPherson. Her family has been boarding their horses here for years. I was hoping she and Trisha would hit it off. They're about the same age."

He nodded. "Apparently they have a couple of classes together at school."

"She's a nice kid, Nick," Crystal assured him, handing him one end of the curtain rod as she climbed the ladder.

"That was my impression, too." It stretched the limits of his reach, but Nick managed to secure his end of the rod to the bracket. "Trisha's been worried because she says she doesn't make friends easily. She's really excited about joining that riding club you told her about the other day, though. I'm sure she'll find some friends there."

"Brandy is in that club," Crystal told him. "Considering their mutual love of horses, I'm sure they'll get along fine."

"I hope so." When the curtain was up, Nick looked around the room. "Now what?"

Crystal grinned. "Well . . . As long as you're here, and the ladder's here, this room could use a coat of paint."

He pinned her with a hard stare. "You're joking, right?"

She nodded. "Yes."

Nick breathed a sigh of relief. "Good. I hate painting. And besides, there's something I'd much rather do."

"What's that?"

Crystal stifled a shriek of surprise as Nick plucked her off the ladder again, one arm under her knees and the other at her back. "I'm going to kiss you again," he told her.

"You're going to break your back if you don't put me down!" she warned him, throwing her arms around his neck.

"I'll take that chance," he murmured as his lips found hers. He kissed her long and hard, until she was breathless and aching, then he abruptly put her down and dusted off his hands as though he'd just completed a difficult but particularly satisfying task. "Okay, what's next?"

"Why, you—you—" Crystal sputtered. He seemed completely unmoved by their kiss, while she felt as though she was about to explode. With mock anger, she advanced on him, swearing that she was going to get even, and Nick backed away from her. She lunged toward him, and Nick ducked out the door with Crystal in hot pursuit. He dashed down the hall and around a corner, then stopped abruptly when he came to the stairs that led down to the kitchen. Crystal stopped, too, then began advancing slowly, like a tiger stalking its prey. Nick backed down the stairs about halfway, then turned and started running again.

Laughing like frolicking children, they played a game of tag through the maze of downstairs rooms until Nick finally turned the tables on Crystal and became the hunter instead of the hunted. "We're acting like a couple of idiots. You know that, don't you?'' Crystal said, cautiously keeping a rocking chair between her and Nick, ready to run if he should lunge at her.

"Ah, but it's been a long time since I've acted like an idiot,'' he replied with a Cheshire-cat grin. "I like it.''

"What are you going to do if you catch me?'' she asked suspiciously.

Nick threw back his head and laughed like the villain in a bad melodrama. "I'm going to torture you with kisses, my pretty.''

"Oh, no! Not that!''

He twisted an imaginary moustache. "Yes, my beauty. That!''

Crystal put the back of her hand to her brow. "A fate worse than death! Can no one save me?''

"No one, my beauty. No one.'' He feinted to the left, and when Crystal dodged to the right, he grabbed her. "I have you now! You'll never escape me!''

"Help! Help!'' she called in a squeaky falsetto voice as Nick carried her to the sofa and lowered her into the soft cushions.

"You are beyond help,'' he growled.

"Oh, goody.'' Wrapping her arms around his neck, she pulled him off balance and he collapsed on top of her. "Now who's beyond help?'' she whispered.

"I surrender,'' he replied, and proceeded to kiss Crystal senseless. Not surprisingly, in the process he lost more than a few of his own senses, too.

"This is crazy,'' Crystal gasped, not wanting the pleasure to end. His lips and tongue were doing wonderful things to her earlobe, and she had never felt anything as intoxicating as the pressure of Nick's body on top of hers. "The doors are wide open—Trisha could come looking for you at any moment.''

"I know," he murmured against her throat. "She should be gone at least an hour, but kids are unpredictable."

"So we should stop."

"Yes." But he didn't. He kissed her deeply and she answered him with equal ardor, until Nick finally groaned and slipped away from her. Lowering himself to the floor, he stretched his legs out and leaned back against the sofa. Crystal wove her fingers through his hair and Nick groaned again. "Do you want to make love as much as I do?" he asked without looking back at her.

"Possibly even more."

"Not possible," he told her. "When are we going to have the time?"

Crystal sat up and began massaging the knotted muscles in his shoulders. "It's not a question of time, Nick. We have all the time in the world. The problem is privacy. And propriety. You have an impressionable teenage daughter to set an example for."

"Right." He thought for a moment. "We could go to a motel on our lunch hour Monday."

Crystal could tell by his tone that he was only joking. "And by Monday night the whole town would know about it."

"There's always my apartment."

"For a lunch hour quickie? That sounds romantic," she said dryly.

Nick nodded. "Yeah. Candlelight just doesn't have the same impact during the day."

She brought her lips close to his ear. "I'm going to get candlelight?" she asked with delight.

"And champagne."

"Sounds nice, but I don't drink, remember?"

"Oh, right. How about grape juice in fancy glasses?"

"That sounds even more romantic."

"Wonderful. Now all we have to plan is the time and place."

"That's what I like about you, Nick. You're so spontaneous," she said with just the right hint of sarcasm.

Laughing, he turned to face her. "You're a fine one to criticize. Not two minutes ago I was ready to ravish you right here on the sofa, and you had to go and get practical on me."

"As I recall," she said coquettishly, "you were the one who was *on me*."

"How well I remember," he said huskily. "We're going to have to find a way to be together soon, Crystal."

"I know. But until an opportunity presents itself, we'll just have to be patient."

Nick started to tell Crystal how difficult that was going to be, but the clatter of boots on the porch stopped him. "Daddy, are you in here?"

"Come on in, Trisha!" Crystal called as she and Nick scrambled to their feet.

"Daddy, guess what?" Trisha asked as she hurried into the living room with her new friend right behind her. "Brandy says that her riding club is going on an overnight trail ride three weeks from today. She thinks that if I join the club now, I'll be able to go with them. Isn't that great?"

Nick and Crystal looked at each other, and it was everything they could do to keep from bursting into laughter.

"That is great, sweetheart." The frustrated lover in Nick was overjoyed at the prospect, but the cautious father in him won out. "I'll have a talk with the sponsors this week so I can find out more about it."

"There'll be lots of grown-ups along," Brandy promised him. "My mom and dad are two of the chaperons."

"It doesn't cost a whole lot, Daddy," Trisha told him. "They're going to a place called Trapper's Creek."

"Oh, that's a great place for a trail ride. They have excellent camping facilities," Crystal told Nick.

Trisha shot Crystal a grateful look. "Can you call the sponsors now and ask them if I can sign up? Please, Daddy, please?" Trish begged.

Since Crystal was the one who had recommended the club in the first place, Nick looked to her for advice. "What do you think?"

"This is a great group of people, Nick," she assured him. "I've gone with them several times on overnight camp outs to Silver Springs. The kids are always well supervised, and they have a great time. I wouldn't have suggested that Trish join, otherwise."

"Okay," he said. Brandy provided him with the name and phone number of the club sponsors, and thirty minutes later he had all the details he needed and an appointment to meet with the sponsors on Monday evening to sign the parental consent forms. When he informed Trisha that it was all set, she gave him a huge hug.

"Thank you, Daddy!" She released him and turned to Crystal. For a moment it almost appeared that she was going to hug her, as well, but she seemed to visibly restrain herself. "Thank you, too, Crystal."

"You're welcome," she replied, swallowing her disappointment at Trisha's restraint.

"Come on, Trish," Brandy said, tugging at her new friend's arm. "You promised me I could ride Morning Glory." The girls trooped out, and suddenly the house was quiet again.

Nick looked at Crystal and grinned. "I haven't seen Trisha that excited about anything in years."

"I'm glad it worked out."

"So am I. But I feel guilty," he confessed.

Crystal frowned. "Why?"

"Because I can't help but be delighted that you and I are going to have some time together." He narrowed his eyes into an exaggerated look of suspicion. "Did you know about this trail ride when you suggested Trisha join that club?"

Crystal's mouth fell open in genuine surprise. "Nick! Of course not. How could you even think such a thing?"

Laughing, he pulled her into his arms. "Well, you have to admit, I have a right to wonder, after the way you chased me around the house and threw me down on the sofa earlier.... Why, I barely escaped with my virtue intact."

Crystal snuggled against him. "I have a riddle for you."

"What?"

"How many cold showers can two adults take in three weeks?" she asked innocently.

Nick chuckled as he kissed her lightly. "I don't know, but we'll compare notes in twenty-one days and find out."

IT WAS THE MOST indescribable experience in the world; Crystal had nothing with which to compare it. Nick's body was perfect—as perfect as it had appeared that first day in the forest when he'd removed his shirt and taken Crystal's breath away. But that one tantalizing glimpse had been nothing compared with the thrill of seeing him gloriously naked, the smooth contours of his body highlighted in the flickering glow of a dozen candles. It was nothing compared to the feel of his flesh against hers, and there was nothing that could ever describe the glory of the moment when Crystal felt him enter her body. He filled her so completely, kissed her so tenderly, stroked her so masterfully, that she lost all contact with reality. She cried out again and again, until her voice was hoarse. Nick's fevered cries joined hers as they became one in spirit as well as in body. . . .

Crystal awoke from the dream breathless and drenched with perspiration. A sense of loss and emptiness swept over her like a tidal wave, until suddenly she became aware of the heavy, masculine leg draped across hers and the arm that encircled her waist. Nick's head was nestled close to hers, and his warm breath caressed her cheek.

The dream had been a memory, not an empty fantasy. The ecstasy had been real. She was in Nick's apartment. Trisha was on the trail ride she'd been so enthused about. Three weeks of cold showers and frustration were a thing of the past . . . and the wait had been worth every torturous minute.

Crystal had always assumed that men like Nick Hanford existed only in fairy tales. She had never dreamed it was possible for a man to be so strong, and yet so gentle. Nor had she ever imagined she was capable of feeling all the stunning sensations that had coursed through her as they were making love.

Though she hated to make the comparison, she thought about what sex had been like with her ex-husband. Roger Elliot had fancied himself the world's greatest lover, but in truth, he had been selfish and inept. Crystal realized that now. He had taught her all the things that brought him pleasure, but he had never taken the time to learn what made Crystal gasp with delight or moan with ecstasy. Nick had been just the opposite. Crystal's pleasure had been more important to him than his own, and the result had been something too powerful for words.

Crystal relaxed and let contentment carry her away. *This is the way it's supposed to be when two people love each other,* she thought drowsily. *But does Nick really love me?* she couldn't help but wonder. He had never actually said the words. They'd spent a lot of time together these past few weeks, not just at work, but at the farm, too. Last weekend they'd taken Trisha up to Silver Springs for a picnic, and the weekend before that, the three of them had had dinner together and gone to the movies. Crystal and Trisha had gone shopping one afternoon, and they'd taken several long rides at the farm— just the two of them.

We're becoming a family, Crystal thought, then chastised herself for romanticizing the situation. Trisha seemed to have accepted Crystal as a fixture in Nick's life, but they were a long way from anything that even resembled a mother-daughter relationship—not that Crystal ever expected Trisha to look upon her as a mother. No, what she was hoping for was a gradual building of trust and friendship. At the moment, Trisha seemed to like Crystal and accept her, but there was very little open, honest communication between them.

Crystal worried constantly about her relationship with Trisha. They had a great deal of fun together, but Crystal wanted to be able to help the girl cope with all the confused emotions that were tangled up inside her. Trisha seemed determined to pretend that her life was perfect. Crystal knew better, but after the horrible mistake she'd made in the stable, she had never mentioned the subject of alcoholism again. She had decided that all she could do was make herself available if Trisha ever became ready to admit her need for help and guidance.

And in the meantime, while she was working at her relationship with Trisha, there was Nick to worry about, too. Only "worry" didn't seem quite the right word. Whether they were working or socializing, Nick was a constant source of delight. His commitment to Trisha touched her deeply. His smile made her heartbeat quicken. His dedication to his job made her proud of the opportunity to work with him. His warmth, his humor, and his compassion made her love him more every day.

But the more deeply she fell in love, the more frightened she became of losing him. Sometimes, when she wasn't with him, the panic reached outrageous proportions. Logically she knew that her fear was all part of a pattern that had been formed in her childhood, but understanding and coping were two different things. The simple fact was, she was afraid to want anything too much. She was afraid to believe that she deserved happiness. Life had proven to her that nothing good ever lasted long; and most times, life snatched the rug out from under her just when she least expected it.

So Crystal was afraid to love Nick too much. She was afraid to dream of a life with him. And after tonight, the fear would grow even worse, she realized. Tonight Nick had touched something inside her that no man had ever reached. It was the part of Crystal's heart that was feminine and utterly sensual...and it now belonged to Nick. When their relationship failed, as it inevitably would, she didn't know if she would be able to reclaim what he had taken from her tonight.

No, he didn't take it. I gave it to him, she corrected herself.

Nick stirred and his arm around her waist tightened. Crystal turned her face toward his. The candles had all gone out, but there was enough moonlight streaming in through the window to allow her to see his features clearly. Funny, she'd never noticed how long his lashes were. He was so handsome, and he was hers...for tonight, at least.

When she was with him, her fears went away, and at that moment they seemed like only a vague, silly memory. Closing her eyes, Crystal let sleep claim her, and the dream came again. Her breathing grew shallow as Nick's hands caressed her body in places she had never considered erotic; his moist lips kissed her with an intimacy that made her moan. He whispered words she couldn't quite grasp. The weight of his body pressed her deeper into the mattress, and the liquid ache between her thighs made her cry out to be possessed. The feelings were so strong and so real that they threatened to rouse Crystal from her dream, but she resisted, clinging to sleep so that the dream could reach its glorious conclusion.

But Nick's hoarse, husky voice wouldn't allow her sleep. Like Prince Charming kissing Sleeping Beauty to wakefulness, his lips plied at hers until the fog lifted from Crystal's mind and she realized that none of this was a dream. Nick's weight on top of her was real; his hands woven into her hair were real. His kisses were intoxicatingly real.

No longer a passive spectator in a dream, Crystal responded to his kiss. Her eyes fluttered open and Nick raised his head.

"Good morning, sleepyhead," he murmured as slowly—very slowly—he joined his body with hers. Crystal moaned as he filled her and Nick gasped as her body closed around him like a silken glove. He rocked against her gently, then more insistently, applying each stroke as lovingly as an artist applying brush to canvas, until the painting took on a life of its own. In a tangle of limbs and breathless cries, Nick and Crystal completed the portrait, then let it go, each knowing that it had been burned so deeply into their hearts, they could never forget the masterpiece they had created.

"I've never been awakened in quite that way before," Crystal said, her voice hushed with awe. For the first time, she became conscious of the daylight streaming in through the window.

Still poised above her, with his weight resting on his elbows, Nick chuckled. "I thought it was going to take dynamite to blast you awake. You slept right through some of my best moves."

He pressed a kiss to her throat, and Crystal sighed. It took considerable effort to tell him, "Ah, but I didn't want to wake up. I was having this incredibly sexy dream about Prince Charming and Sleeping Beauty. He was using more persuasive techniques than just kisses to wake her."

"And I suppose in this dream, *you* were Sleeping Beauty."

"Mmm-hmm." Nick was nibbling on her earlobe, and it was too much of an effort to speak.

"And who, pray tell, was the lucky Prince?"

"Hmm...that's a very good question," she said thoughtfully. "Who was that handsome stranger?"

Nick stopped what he was doing and frowned at her. "You were making love with a stranger?"

Crystal's eyes widened innocently. "I'm sorry, Nick, but it was dark."

"Well, that's a fine how-do-you-do." He slipped away from her, and Crystal followed, pinning him to the mattress.

"He smelled like you," she offered helpfully. "I think he even tasted like you." She kissed him deeply, as though she needed to prove her point. "Yes, he definitely tasted like you."

He regarded her with feigned suspicion. "But you don't know what he looked like?"

She shrugged. "He was big...and he was very good at what he was doing.... I guess it's *possible* that you were the Prince Charming in my dream."

"Gee thanks," he said dryly.

"Don't mention it," Crystal said, wrapping the sheet around her as she scrambled off the bed.

Nick sat up, not making any effort to cover himself. "Where do you think you're going?"

"To take a shower."

"May I come, too?" he asked suggestively.

Crystal stopped at the door and looked at him coquettishly. "If you think you're up to it."

Amazingly enough, he was.

THE PORCH SWING CREAKED rhythmically as Nick and Crystal rocked to and fro. A late afternoon shower had bathed the farm, making everything smell fresh and clean. The fragrant aroma of lilacs wafted around the lovers, and a sliver of rainbow peeked at them from between the scattered clouds overhead.

"This has been the most perfect day I could ever have imagined," Nick murmured, resting his cheek on Crystal's head.

"I know. I feel lazy, and terribly wicked." She thought back over the glorious day. "Sleeping late..."

"Making love..."

Crystal smiled at the memory. "Brunch instead of breakfast..."

"Making love..."

"A drive in the country and a walk through the McPhersons' meadow..."

"Making love..."

Crystal twisted to look at him. "We did not make love in the McPhersons' meadow!"

Nick grinned devilishly. "No, but I wanted to. That ought to count for something."

She chuckled and returned her head to his shoulder. "Frankly, Nick, I stopped counting after our shower this morning. Omigod!'' She straightened abruptly and whirled toward him as a horrifying thought struck her.

"What's wrong?"

"Oh, Nick! You have to go back to your apartment immediately." She jumped up and pulled on his hand, but he refused to budge.

"What are you talking about? Trisha will be here shortly," he reminded her. The McPhersons had graciously offered to transport Morning Glory along with their own horses, and were going to drop Trisha off at the farm when they returned from the trail ride.

"I know. That's why you have to go home. Now!"

"Why?"

"Because there's a *thing* in the bathroom—we left it there this morning. I saw it and was going to pick it up, but you distracted me, and I forgot all about it!"

"Crystal, what are you talking about?" Nick said, laughing at her almost comical panic.

"A thing—a *wrapper*. If Trisha sees it, she'll know!"

Nick finally caught on. "You mean the condom wrapper?"

Crystal blushed scarlet. "Yes."

With one good jerk, he pulled her down beside him again. "I picked it up, Crystal. Don't worry. All evidence of our illicit liaison has been removed from the apartment. I policed the bedroom and bathroom while you were doing the dishes this morning."

Crystal sagged with relief. "Thank God."

"Relax," he said, pulling her close. "But I appreciate your being worried. I'd rather not have Trisha learn quite so graphically that her daddy practices safe sex."

"Or how *often* he practices it. Or how well," she added smugly.

Nick chuckled. "You're very good for my ego, Ms. Elliot."

"I believe in giving credit where credit is due."

Gently he tilted her face toward his, and Crystal discovered that all humor had vanished from his eyes, replaced by a sweet intensity that robbed her of thought. "I love you, Crystal," he whispered.

"Really?" she asked, searching his face.

"Yes."

She lowered her head to his shoulder, trying to absorb the wonder of being loved. "I love you, too, Nick," she said quietly, and felt his chest fall as though he'd been holding his breath, waiting for her response.

No other words could compare with the power of the ones they had just exchanged, so they fell silent, holding each other, smelling the lilacs, listening to the creak of the swing. Crystal glanced up at the sky, looking for the rainbow. It was gone now, but it didn't matter.

The wish she'd made on it had come true.

CHAPTER FIFTEEN

"ALL RIGHT, GIRLS, Crystal and I will pick you up in front of the theater at nine-thirty on the dot," Nick told Trisha and Brandy as he navigated the treacherous Saturday-night traffic on the mall parking lot. Earlier this week, school had adjourned for the summer, and the kids were still celebrating. Every teenager in town who owned a car was cruising the lot, and those who didn't have a car were being dropped off at the theater entrance by their parents. A torrential June thunderstorm was complicating matters, and Nick was having a hard time reaching his objective. "If it's still raining when the movie ends, I want you to stay inside the lobby and watch for us, okay?"

"Oh, Daddy," Trisha whined. "We have umbrellas. Can't we walk over to the Dairy Hut? All the kids will go there after the movie."

Nick edged the car forward another few feet. "No, Trish. If you want ice cream before we go home, Crystal and I will take you by the Hut."

Crystal turned toward the back seat and saw Trish and Brandy exchange glum looks. "And we'll try not to make ourselves too conspicuous," she promised, earning a grateful smile from Trisha. She had received a lot of those in the past four weeks since Trisha had returned from the trail ride, but at times Crystal felt she was slipping farther away from the girl instead of closer to her. It was almost as though Trisha had built an invisible wall around herself. She never touched Crystal unless it was absolutely necessary, and on the few occasions when Crystal had forgotten herself and placed a casual, encouraging hand on Trisha's arm or shoulder, the child always pulled away.

It was frustrating, but Crystal was trying to be patient because it was so important to Nick that she and Trisha get along. He had become the center of her life, and every day a little of her panic about losing him subsided. His love and respect meant everything to her, and their growing closeness made her feel as though the dreams she had suppressed for so long were about to come true.

But Crystal knew that the success or failure of their relationship still hinged on the gangly fourteen-year-old in the back seat.

The car crept forward at a snail's pace, and Nick was getting frustrated. "Are you two sure you want to see this movie again? We saw it just last weekend. Why don't we rent a video and go home?"

"Daddy, everybody I know has seen *Firestorm* at least twice. Brandy and I have to catch up."

"All right, all right," he said, just as a path to the entrance cleared. Calling out a hasty "See you later," the girls scrambled from the back seat of the Bronco grappling with their umbrellas, and dashed toward the building.

Nick chuckled and edged the car forward, but traffic seemed to have stalled again. "Tell me, Crystal, is it my imagination, or is Trisha displaying signs of rebellion? She's started arguing with nearly everything I say."

"It's not your imagination," she assured him. "She's becoming secure enough to finally start acting like a normal teenager. And she's testing your rules a little." She glanced toward the mall entrance and waved to the girls, who were standing just inside the door, apparently waiting for some of their friends.

"That's good, I guess. I've seen such a big change in her in these past two months, and most of it's for the better. I can't tell you how excited I was that she finally asked Brandy to come to our house and spend the night."

Crystal and Nick had talked about that particular problem a number of times. Trisha had made several friends in Brandy McPherson's crowd, but until today she had never asked any of them over to her house, despite Nick's constant assurance that he wanted her to feel free to do so. When he'd told Crystal about it, she had explained that it was just one more symptom of being raised in an alcoholic home. Inviting a friend home if Mom or Dad was drinking was tantamount to pulling the pin on a live grenade. But the fact that Trisha had invited Brandy to spend the night was a vote of confidence in her father that Nick found very encouraging.

Thanks to a minor fender bender somewhere ahead of them, the traffic came to a complete standstill again, and Nick drummed his fingers on the steering wheel. "If we ever get out of this parking lot, we'll have two whole hours to kill, Crystal." He shot her a wicked grin. "What do you think we should do with them?"

"I don't know," she said with feigned innocence. "I guess we could rent a video as you suggested to Trisha."

"Crystal, you're leaving tomorrow for a seminar in Little Rock and this is our first night alone since that bunking party Brandy had two weeks ago. Surely you can come up with a more imaginative way to say goodbye."

She shrugged. "I figured if you had to ask, you weren't thinking the same lewd, lascivious thoughts I've been thinking."

Nick reached over and took Crystal's hand. "I've had nothing but lascivious thoughts for two weeks, lady. In fact, I'm—" Nick stopped as two boys dashed by the car, headed for the mall. "Aren't they our old friends, the Whipley boys?"

Crystal turned and looked. "That's them. Did I tell you I ran into Tony Manguson the other day? There have been a rash of burglaries these past few weeks, and he's pretty sure the Whipleys are responsible."

Nick shook his head in bewilderment. "Lewis was in a couple of Trisha's classes. She mentioned something funny he'd done to disrupt class one day, and I made it clear that she's to stay as far away from Lewis Whipley and his brother as she possible can."

Crystal nodded in understanding and glanced back toward the mall but Bobby and Lewis had already disappeared inside, and Trisha and Brandy were no longer waiting by the door. "I wouldn't worry about that, Nick. I can't imagine what Trisha would have in common with the Whipleys." Someone behind them laid down on his car horn, and Crystal turned automatically to look out the rear window. "Hold your horses. We're doing the best we can," she said, knowing, of course, that the driver couldn't possibly hear her. She started to turn back, but a flash of white on the back seat caught her attention.

"Oh, Nick. Trisha forgot her purse. I know she put all her money in it, because I saw her counting it earlier."

"Damn," he muttered.

Crystal grabbed her umbrella off the floorboard. "I'll dash in and give it to her—she's probably figured out it's gone by now, and is worried sick."

"I'll circle the lot if I have to," he told her as she jumped out and slammed the door.

The umbrella was virtually useless in the slanting downpour, and Crystal was drenched by the time she made it to the mall entrance. Her tennis shoes squished and slipped on the smooth floor, but she hurried as quickly as she could down the crowded corridor leading to the theater. Kids of every size, age, and description were knotted in the rotunda outside the ticket booth, and Crystal searched the crowd until she finally spotted Trisha's yellow windbreaker. She was in the ticket line with Brandy at her side—and the girls weren't alone. Flanking them were Bobby and Lewis Whipley.

A chance encounter?

Of course it is, Crystal thought, trying to discount the fact that earlier, the girls appeared to have been waiting for someone.

Someone in the crowd called Brandy's name, and when both girls turned simultaneously to see who had hailed them, Trisha's eyes connected with Crystal's. The guilty flush on her face was all it took to disprove Crystal's chance encounter theory. This was an arranged meeting, and Trisha knew that her father would never approve.

Standing her ground, Crystal raised Trisha's purse into the air. The girl said something to Brandy, then rushed across the room to claim her bag. "I didn't know you and Brandy had dates," Crystal said evenly, trying not to sound like the wicked witch of the West, or worse, Cinderella's evil stepmother.

"We don't!" Trisha exclaimed guiltily.

"But you arranged to meet Bobby and Lewis here, didn't you?"

"'Course not!"

"I want to believe that, Trisha, but I don't. You have guilt written all over your face."

The guilt melted into contrition. "Don't tell Daddy. Please, Crystal, please."

"I have to tell him, Trish. You know your father has said you're too young to date. And not only that, he just a minute ago told me that he'd warned you to steer clear of the Whipley brothers. You know that what you're doing is wrong.''

"But it won't happen again, Crystal, I swear. We won't even sit with them tonight. Brandy and I were at the Dairy Hut this afternoon and we just happened to run into Lewis. He said he was coming to the movie tonight, and we said we were, too, and it just sort of happened. It's not really a date or anything.''

"That may be, but I still have to tell your father,'' Crystal said carefully.

A look of panic washed over her face. "But he'll be mad at me. Oh, Crystal, please don't make him mad at me. Please.''

An image of what had happened in the stable two months ago flashed through Crystal's mind, and suddenly she felt as though she was on very shaky ground. She didn't want to make a mistake in handling this situation, too. "He won't be mad at you if you tell him the truth, and promise not to let anything like this happen again.''

"You'll let me tell him?'' she asked hopefully.

That wasn't what Crystal had meant, exactly. She'd meant that if Trish explained how the "date" had come about, Nick probably wouldn't come down on her too hard. But now, Trisha was looking at her with such pathetic expectancy that she didn't have the heart to correct her. "Do you promise that you'll tell him about arranging to meet Bobby and Lewis?''

Trisha's head bobbed up and down. "I promise. I'll tell him first thing after Brandy leaves tomorrow afternoon.''

"All right, Trish. But if you don't tell him, I will.''

"I'll tell him, I promise.''

"And you won't sit with the boys during the movie tonight?''

Trisha shook her head adamantly. "We'll find some way to ditch them. Brandy doesn't like them any more than I do."

"Okay. I'm trusting you to keep your word, Trisha. Please don't let me down."

"I won't," she promised. "And thank you. You're so neat."

Before Crystal could comprehend what was happening, Trisha threw her arms around her in a quick, clumsy, wonderful hug that made Crystal want to cry with happiness. It was the first show of unrestrained affection the girl had displayed toward her, and it meant the world to Crystal. Maybe trust was what had been needed to bring the invisible wall between them tumbling down.

Nick's daughter dashed off, and Crystal retraced the route to the car. It was still raining cats and dogs, but she didn't mind. Trisha had taken an important step toward really accepting Crystal as part of her small family....

At least, that's what Crystal foolishly believed.

"YOU'RE ABSOLUTELY SURE this is what you want to do, Nick?" Dan Gatlin asked, trying to ignore the static that crackled on the long-distance connection.

"I'm positive, Dan," Nick replied. "Trisha and I had a long talk about it yesterday afternoon, and she's ready to move in immediately. The prospect of having Morning Glory in her own backyard is almost more than she can handle. Plus, she likes the fact that Brandy McPherson is only a mile or so down the road. I know in my gut that buying the farm is the right thing to do."

"Well, I certainly can't think of anyone I'd rather sell it to," Dan said, then paused hesitantly. "Tell me, how does Crystal feel about it?"

"She doesn't know yet," Nick confessed. "And I'd appreciate it if you didn't tell her for a while. I'd like to do that myself."

Dan frowned at the phone. "Nick, I can't keep something like this from her."

"I know how you feel, Dan, but this is important to me. Can you give me a week, at least? I think she'll take the news better if it comes from me."

"Why not tell her now?" he asked bluntly.

"For one thing, she left yesterday for a wildlife management seminar in Little Rock, and won't be back until Wednesday night. After I got Trisha's approval I was going to wait and talk to Crystal before I called you, but . . . well, I've decided that I'd like this to be a surprise for her. I'm—" he hesitated "—I'm planning something special for her next weekend, and this is part of it."

"I see," Dan said thoughtfully. "I don't suppose it would do any good to ask what kind of surprise you're planning, would it?"

Nick grinned. Dan Gatlin knew very well what the surprise was. "No, sir, it wouldn't."

"Hmm. Tell me, *son*," he said, putting a little extra punch on that last word, "what are you going to do if Crystal doesn't like your surprise?"

"That's not a possibility I'm prepared to accept, Dan," he said frankly. "I love your daughter."

Dan sighed happily. "All right, Nick. I'll get the paperwork started on this end, and you get in touch with the bank tomorrow. But remember, Oak Ridge is a small town and word that you're buying the farm is going to spread pretty fast. If you want to tell Crystal yourself, don't wait too long before popping the . . . surprise."

"Yes, sir," Nick said with a grin.

"I DON'T KNOW what to say, Mr. Chapman. I'm stunned." Crystal sank back in her chair and tried to absorb the "good news" her district supervisor had just given her. She'd been surprised this afternoon when he'd invited her to dinner, and had more or less assumed that it was just his way of apologizing for the fact that she had lost the Oak Ridge ranger position because he had been tardy in putting her paperwork through. She certainly hadn't expected the announcement he had made moments after the waiter served their entrée.

Clyde Chapman was beaming at her. "I was sure you'd be pleased, Crystal. It took a little doing, believe me, but I felt so bad about that mix-up when Dan retired.... Well, let's just say that I felt I owed you one. When I heard that there was going to be an opening in the Cherokee National Forest in the Great Smoky Mountains, I knew that job had to go to you."

Crystal gave him a smile that was forced at best. "I appreciate that, Mr. Chapman, but—"

He waved one hand in the air. "Don't think anything about it. The regional supervisor owed me a favor, so I called it in. Not that you're not qualified for the job—" he added quickly.

"Thank you," she said, cutting him off before he had a chance to bluster on. "Your confidence in me is very gratifying, but . . . I'm going to need some time to think this over."

Chapman's mouth flapped open in surprise, then closed abruptly, like a large-mouth bass snapping at a baited hook. "I thought this was what you wanted, Crystal," he said after a moment. "When I called you right after Dan retired, you told me to find you another district."

So much had happened during the past few months that Crystal had completely forgotten about that conversation, but as she recalled it now, her memory of it seemed quite different from Chapman's. "I asked you to let me know when another district became available, so that I could consider it," she said as tactfully as possible. "Believe me, sir, I appreciate the effort you've put into this, but I had no idea that you would actively lobby to get me a new assignment. I'm terribly sorry that I didn't communicate my feelings to you more completely."

Chapman scowled. "Crystal, it sounds to me as though you're refusing this job."

"No, sir. I only asked for time to consider it."

"I know it was a disappointment when you didn't get the Oak Ridge District, but Nick Hanford seems to have settled into the job nicely. If you want to be a ranger, you're going to have to move. You do realize that, don't you?"

"Yes, sir," she replied, searching for words to make him understand without having to explain every detail of her personal life. Her first instinct was to refuse his offer outright, but for some reason she couldn't do that. Chapman had gone to a great deal of trouble on her account, and if she refused him flatly it might seriously affect her chances of getting a promotion in the future. And besides, she'd wanted her own ranger district for too long to simply let the dream go without giving it the thought it deserved.

But there was no denying that Clyde Chapman had just tied a big, complicated knot in Crystal's life. He was forcing her into making a decision between the man she loved and a job she would have accepted without a second thought if it had been offered to her the day before she met Nick Hanford.

In her heart, Crystal knew that she would never be able to give up her relationship with Nick, but she wanted to make a logical decision, not an emotional one. "I'm sorry to be so indefinite about this, Mr. Chapman, but my life has changed a little in the past few months. I just need time to think it over."

He wasn't pleased at all. "Crystal, only you can decide where your priorities lie, but I have always been under the impression that your career was quite important to you."

"It is," she assured him. "But sometimes our choices in life aren't quite as cut-and-dried as we'd like them to be. Even though Dan and Naomi Gatlin have moved to Arizona, Oak Ridge is still my home. Frankly I have to weigh what I'd be leaving behind against what I would gain by being in charge of my own district." She gave him what she hoped was an encouraging smile. "When I figure that out, you'll be the first to know."

"All right," he said reluctantly. "You can have until next Monday to make your decision."

"Thank you, sir." They finished dinner in strained silence. Chapman was clearly worried about what the regional supervisor was going to think if he had to tell him that the candidate he'd lobbied for didn't want the job after all. Crystal's thoughts had nothing to do with having egg on her face, though. She was remembering the joy she'd found in Nick's arms and the richness he had brought to her life. But she was also remembering how many times in the past she'd lost the things she loved the most, and how many of her dreams had failed to come true.

Chapman's job offer was a reality. A life with Nick was a dream that could shatter at any moment.

Crystal had never felt so confused in her life. And she had only one week to decide on the course her future would take.

NICK HAD LOST COUNT of the number of times he had glanced at his watch. Crystal had called yesterday to tell him that she'd be dropping by the apartment as soon as she got into town tonight, and he could hardly wait. He had missed her terribly this week. Of course, he'd known that he would, but what had thoroughly delighted him was that Trisha seemed to have missed her, as well. Over the past four days she had asked when Crystal would be back more times than Nick had looked at his watch this evening.

The two most important women in his life were becoming good friends, and Nick couldn't have been happier about it. That was one of the reasons he had decided to buy the Gatlin farm. Nick had known since the first night he and Crystal had spent together that he was never going to love anyone more than he loved her, nor would he ever find a woman who understood him as completely as she did. For weeks he'd thought about asking her to marry him, but for Trisha's sake, he had waited. It wouldn't be fair to her to rush into something that might throw her off balance.

But now, he was convinced that Trisha would be happy to have Crystal as a stepmother. Several times this week, he'd considered telling her what he was planning, but he'd stopped himself on every occasion. As soon as Trisha knew, she would probably share the news with Brandy, who would no doubt share it with her parents. Nick felt it was only fair that Crystal hear about his marriage proposal from him, rather than the community grapevine.

And besides, he had a very special weekend planned for them. He'd already arranged for Trisha to stay at the McPhersons' while he and Crystal spent the night at Silver Springs. It seemed like the perfect place to ask her to marry him. She deserved a romantic setting. She deserved all the right words, spoken with all the love he felt in his heart.

Wandering into the kitchen, Nick pulled a can of soda from the refrigerator and meandered out to the patio. The sun was just starting to set, and the house was quieter than usual. Trisha was at the monthly meeting of her riding club, eagerly planning her next trail ride. She would be home soon, though, and Nick was fervently hoping that Crystal arrived before Trisha did. It would be nice to spend a few private minutes with her saying a proper "hello."

And there was something she wanted to tell me, too, he thought, remembering their brief conversation last night. She had seemed a little subdued, but when he had asked her about it, she had claimed she was just tired. He hadn't seen any reason to doubt her, and still didn't, but—

The doorbell brought Nick out of his musings, and he hurried back inside. Crystal was home, finally, and Nick felt like a lovesick schoolboy. Chuckling at himself, he threw open the door, fully prepared to sweep his lady-love into his arms.

But the visitor at the door wasn't Crystal.

"Tony!" Nick's welcoming smile faded into a slightly puzzled frown. What on earth was Crystal's former beau doing here? "This is an unexpected pleasure. Come on in," he said, trying to cover his surprise.

The storm door squeaked as the Juvenile Officer opened it and stepped in. "I hope I'm not catching you at a bad time."

"Not at all," Nick assured him. "I was just killing time until Crystal gets back from Little Rock."

"Oh, yeah. I heard that she was out of town for a convention. Are you expecting her back tonight?"

"Any time now," Nick said with a nod. He'd seen Tony around town a number of times these past few months, but they hadn't had a conversation since the day of Bobby and Lewis Whipley's hearing. "Have a seat. Can I get you something to drink?" He lifted the can he was still carrying. "A soda? Iced tea?"

"No thanks. I can't stay long." Tony settled onto the sofa and gave Nick a friendly smile. "You must be wondering why I'm here."

"The thought had crossed my mind," Nick said as he sat in the recliner opposite his unexpected guest.

Tony shook his head. "I wish I could say this was just a neighborly visit, but I'm afraid that's not the case. Frankly this is the part of my job that makes me wish I'd become a milkman instead of a juvenile officer."

Nick's heart skipped a beat and he came to the edge of his seat. It hadn't crossed his mind that this might be a professional call. "Has something happened to Trisha? Has she been in an accident? Is she in trouble?"

"No, nothing like that," Tony assured him. "At least she's not in any trouble yet. I just thought I ought to tell you what's been going on so that you can steer her clear of trouble."

Nick scowled. "I don't understand what you're getting at, Tony."

"I didn't figure you would," he replied. "Nick, did you know that your daughter's been hanging around with the Whipley brothers?"

"What?" It was everything Nick could do to keep from jumping to his feet. "That can't be."

"I'm afraid it's true. I saw them together at the Dairy Hut about a week and a half ago, and didn't think much about it. You're liable to see just about anybody there. But then last weekend I saw Trisha and Brandy Mc-Pherson sitting with Bobby and Lewis at the movies, and

I started to worry. Tonight when I saw them together, I knew I had to come—''

"Wait a minute," Nick said, rising. "You couldn't have seen them together tonight. Trisha is at a club meeting—I dropped her off at the sponsor's house a little before seven."

"Did you actually see her go in?"

He thought back. "No, I guess I didn't. She waved to me from the porch and I drove off...." This still didn't make sense to Nick. "Tony, are you sure you know what my daughter looks like? Couldn't this be somebody else?"

Tony sighed. This was exactly what he hated about this part of his job. Parents never wanted to believe that their kids were capable of being anything other than adorable little angels. "I'm positive, Nick. Crystal introduced me to her over a month ago when I ran into them at the mall. And I've seen her a dozen times since then with Brandy—and with you. I'm not mistaken about this, Nick, and I was positive you wouldn't approve if you knew about it. Bobby and Lewis are in big trouble right now. I've got just about all the evidence I need to send them off to reform school for a nice long time, and I don't want to see your daughter getting messed up because of them."

Nick sat down, trying to absorb the inescapable truth. "I heard about the burglaries," he said, dreading the answer to his next question. "Do you have any reason to think that Trisha is involved with them?"

"No," Tony said emphatically. "As of this moment, I have absolutely nothing that would tie Trisha into any of those crimes. She seems like a really good kid, but she's new in town, and even good kids can get their heads screwed on backward now and then. I just thought you ought to know."

"I appreciate that, Tony. Really, I do." Nick's frown deepened. "You said you saw her with them tonight?"

Tony nodded. "At the mall, not thirty minutes ago. They came out of the video arcade and got into Bobby's car."

"Just the three of them?"

"Yes."

Nick felt sick. His daughter was alone with two juvenile delinquents. He came to his feet again. "Do you have any idea where they were headed?"

Tony rose. "Sorry, no."

"Damn it! I've got to go find her." He extended his hand. "Thanks for coming by, Tony. I appreciate your concern, and you have my word, you won't be seeing Trisha with the Whipleys ever again."

"No problem, Nick. It's all part of my job." He started for the door. "If I were you, I'd try driving by the Dairy Hut first. If I should happen to see them on my way home, I'll nab Trisha and bring her back here."

"Thanks, Tony." He saw the juvenile officer to the door.

"Tell me, Nick, now that school's out, what kind of arrangements have you made for supervising Trisha while you're at work?"

Nick found it hard to concentrate on Tony's question. "I drive her out to the McPherson place every morning. Brandy's mother has been a lifesaver."

That eased Tony's mind considerably. "The McPhersons are great people. Trisha is in good hands with them."

"I know." He opened the door and said a hasty good-bye, then headed for the phone the moment Tony was gone. He called the sponsors of the riding club, praying that Trisha would be there and that he'd discover this was all a horrible mistake. His prayers went unanswered. One of the sponsor's children had come down with the measles, and they had canceled the meeting. Trisha had been personally notified this morning; she just hadn't seen fit to enlighten her father.

Vacillating between blind rage and fear for Trisha's safety, Nick grabbed his car keys off the kitchen counter and headed for the door. He was only halfway across the living room when the doorbell rang again. He opened the door, still scowling.

It wasn't quite the reception Crystal had hoped for. "Nick?"

"Oh, God, I'm glad to see you," he murmured, pulling her into his arms.

She wrapped her arms around him and felt the furious drumming of his heart. "Nick, what's wrong?"

"Tony Manguson was just here," he said tersely, stepping back but keeping his hands on her upper arms, as though he desperately needed to feel connected with her. "He told me that Trisha has been hanging around with Bobby and Lewis Whipley."

Crystal frowned. "*Tony* told you that? Trisha didn't tell you on Sunday after Brandy went home?"

Nick looked at Crystal as though she was from Mars. "What are you talking about? Trisha has been spending time with the Whipleys and hiding it from me. Tony has seen them together at least three times, including tonight. Trisha lied to me, Crystal. She had me drop her off at her club sponsor's house, knowing full well that the meeting had been canceled. She's out with the boys right now."

"Oh, no," Crystal murmured as overwhelming disappointment washed through her. Nick wasn't the only one Trisha had lied to. The scene with Trisha in the mall last Saturday night played through Crystal's head like a minimovie, and she wanted to cry. Trisha had deliberately lied to her, and then she had coldly manipulated her into keeping a secret from Nick. "She never had any intention of telling you," she murmured, trying to fight the sickening feeling that she had been betrayed.

Nick studied Crystal's face, trying to make sense of her reaction, and suddenly the truth fell into place. "Did you know about this?" he demanded harshly.

She nodded reluctantly. "I saw Trisha with the boys Saturday night when I took her purse in. She—"

"And you didn't tell me!" Nick roared, unconsciously digging his hands into Crystal's arms.

His reaction stunned her. "Nick, you're hurting me," she said, trying to pull out of his grasp.

"Damn you, Crystal. How could you keep something like this from me? If you knew Trisha was with those delinquents, why the hell didn't you drag her out of there by the hair of her head? Or why didn't you at least tell me so that I could go get her?"

"Because Trisha made me promise not to!" Crystal answered, pulling away from him sharply.

"Oh, and you just went along with her—as though a fourteen-year-old girl is supposed to know what's best for her! For God's sake, Crystal, you're the adult! You should know better!"

"She promised me she'd tell you as soon as Brandy went home on Sunday. She lied to me, Nick." Not doing a very good job of hiding her anger at Trisha or Nick, Crystal repeated as much as she could remember of Saturday night's conversation with Trisha. "She begged me to let her tell you so that you wouldn't be angry, and I agreed because it seemed like an important step in getting your daughter to trust me. That is what you wanted, isn't it?"

At that moment, Nick was so angry he didn't know what he wanted anymore, except to have his daughter home and know that she was safe. "You should have told me, Crystal. I don't care what you promised Trisha." He ran an impatient hand through his hair. "My God, I can't believe that you actually came back here Saturday night and made love with me, knowing that Trisha was sitting in a movie house with two juvenile delinquents I had specifically told you I didn't want her associating with! How could you do that?"

"She told me she wouldn't sit with them at the movie! She even said she was anxious to ditch them because she didn't like them! How was I supposed to know she was lying through her teeth?"

"Like I said before, you're the adult, Crystal," he ground out between gritted teeth. "You're supposed to have more sense than that. Now, I'm going to go find Trisha, and you had better pray that those boys haven't dragged her into one of their burglary schemes—or worse!" He stepped toward the door, then stopped and looked back at her. "Well? Are you coming?"

Too angry and hurt to speak, Crystal dug her fingernails into the palms of her hands and started for the door. She had only made it halfway when the storm door opened and Trisha walked in on the tense tableau she had created.

"Hi, Crystal! I'm glad you're back. Hi, Daddy." Trisha looked up at her father, who had stepped around her trying to get a look at the car that had dropped her off.

"Hi, Trisha," he said evenly. Relief had done nothing to conquer his anger, but he knew better than to pounce on her. "Did you have a good meeting?"

"Oh, yeah. We got some plans made for the next trail ride." She looked uncomfortably from Nick to Crystal, then skirted between them, heading for the kitchen. "Is there any soda?"

"Get back in here, Patricia," Nick said sternly, stopping her in her tracks. "We have some talking to do."

"I think I should leave now," Crystal said quietly. In a sense, she could understand why Nick had been so angry at her, and logically she knew that many of the harsh things he'd said were simply a gut reaction to his own fear for Trisha's safety. But knowing that didn't take away the pain of the way he'd spoken to her, and it certainly didn't assuage the sting of Trisha's betrayal. It was going to take a while to forgive what Trisha had done—and what Nick had said.

"No, I think you should stay," Nick replied, shutting the door. "This concerns all of us."

Crystal looked at him sharply. "I don't think so, Nick."

"What's going on?" Trisha asked, suddenly growing fearful.

Nick turned his full attention to his daughter. "I hear you've been seeing a lot of Bobby and Lewis Whipley."

Trisha's eyes widened and she looked at Crystal in horror. "You told him! You promised me you wouldn't tell!"

"And *you* promised me you *would* tell!" Crystal retorted.

"I was going to!"

"When?" she demanded harshly. "When were you going to tell him? You certainly didn't do it Sunday afternoon as you promised you would."

Trisha flushed guiltily. "We got to talking about other things, and I forgot."

"You don't forget a promise like that, Trisha."

"I did forget!" she insisted.

"And did you also forget that tonight's club meeting had been canceled?" Crystal asked.

"You told him about that, too!" the girl cried, too upset to wonder how Crystal had known about the canceled meeting.

"No, Trisha—"

"I hate you!" Trisha screamed. "I hate you! Now Daddy will send me away, and it's all your fault."

"Wait a minute!" Nick practically shouted, not seeing any other way to get a word in edgewise. "I am not sending you away, Trisha. And Crystal did not tell me about the meeting."

"Yes, she did!" Trisha said tearfully. "She hates me and she wants to get rid of me so she can marry you. She doesn't want me around any more than you do!"

Sobbing, Trisha ran past Nick and a second later, the door to her room slammed shut.

Crystal was trembling, fighting tears of her own, and Nick was just plain bewildered. "What just happened?"

"Hurricane Trisha," Crystal said flatly, not intending it as a joke. "I'd say that this whole thing was set up as a test. Consciously or unconsciously, she has deliberately defied you, lied to you, and manipulated you because she needs to know whether or not you're going to send her back to Marjorie."

"How could she possibly think that?"

"I don't know, Nick. Ask her." Feeling numb, Crystal stepped toward the door.

Nick frowned. "Where are you going?"

"Home."

He took a step toward her. "Crystal...please stay. We need to talk this through. As a family."

Something inside her snapped, and tears streamed down her cheeks as she looked up at him. "Trisha isn't my family, Nick," she said coldly. "And after this, I'm not sure she ever could be." She opened the door and looked back at him. "The news I came here to tell you is that Clyde Chapman has found me a job in Tennessee. I think I ought to take it."

Not waiting to see his reaction, she closed the door behind her and went home.

CHAPTER SIXTEEN

FEELING IMPOTENT, empty, and thoroughly bewildered, Nick stood on the porch, staring down the street long after Crystal's car had vanished around the corner. *What the hell is happening?* he wondered, furious with Trisha and Crystal—and with himself, too. How could Crystal calmly tell him she was leaving and then waltz off into the sunset without a backward glance? Surely their relationship wasn't so fragile that a single argument could completely shatter it. There had to be something he could say to her to make her realize what a mistake it would be to run away when they were so close to having something precious.

Or did they have something precious? Was it all just an illusion?

No, Nick decided emphatically. What he felt wasn't an illusion, and he'd just have to make Crystal realize that. But in the meantime, there was Trisha to be dealt with. How could she have been capable of such deceit? How could she have lied and manipulated everyone as she had? And why had she done it?

Nothing made sense to Nick. Thirty minutes ago his life had been neat and orderly. He'd known what he wanted and how to go about getting it. But suddenly all that had changed. He hadn't felt such a total lack of control over his life since he'd been married to Marjorie. He didn't like it one bit.

But the place to start regaining some semblance of control was with Trisha. Dreading the confrontation, Nick slipped inside and down the hall to his daughter's room. Without any idea of what he was going to say to her, he rapped on her door once and entered without waiting for an invitation.

The sight that greeted him was hardly what he had expected. Trisha's suitcases were open on the bed with clothes haphazardly thrown into them. Crossing the room with an armload of sweaters, Trisha didn't even pause when Nick entered. She tossed the sweaters in the general direction of the largest suitcase, letting them fall where they may, and returned to the bureau.

"What are you doing?" Nick demanded.

"Packing." Her voice was small, but defiance was stamped all over her tearstained face.

"Why?"

She grabbed another load of clothes. "So I'll be ready when you send me home to Mom."

After all that had happened tonight, Nick didn't have an easy time reining in his temper. "Damn it, Trisha . . . Is that what you want? To go back and live with your mother?"

"No."

"Well, that's good, because you're not going back. Like it or not, you're living with me now, and that's the way it's going to stay."

Trisha refused to look at him. "You're mad."

"Of course I am," Nick said with an exasperated sigh. "I'm mad as hell, but that doesn't mean I'm sending you back to your mother." He took a step toward her. "Trisha, I'm not playing a game here—you're my daughter, and all I want is what's best for you."

Frozen by the bed, Trisha gingerly fingered the housecoat she'd just tossed in the suitcase. "And you won't let

Crystal make you send me back?" she asked in a small voice.

"Oh, for crying out loud," Nick muttered, too irritated to be suckered in by his daughter's pitiful question. She was trying to manipulate him and he knew it, but for the life of him, he couldn't figure out why. "Trisha, what has Crystal ever done to make you think that she would want to get rid of you?"

The gangly teenager shrugged. Nick waited for an answer, but didn't get one.

"All right, let's try another question. Why did you lie to me tonight about the riding club meeting? And why have you been seeing the Whipley brothers after I expressly told you to avoid them?"

"I don't know."

"Not an acceptable answer."

Her eyes darted briefly to Nick's, then skittered away. "I really don't know!"

"Was it *because* I told you not to see them?"

Another shrug. "I guess."

"Damn it, Patricia, look at me! I want to know why you've been lying!"

"So you'd send me back and get it over with!" she said, finally coming out of her uncommunicative shell as her defiance returned in full force.

Nick paused, stunned by her answer. The sympathy she hadn't been able to manufacture in him a moment ago finally surfaced, and he moved to her very slowly. "I thought you said you didn't want to go back, Trisha."

"I don't," she said sullenly. "But you're going to do it. I know you will."

Nick could hardly believe what he was hearing. "Why would you think that?" he asked incredulously.

"Because you divorced me once before. Why would it be any different this time?"

Nick reached out to touch her, but she pulled away. "Honey, I divorced your mother, not you."

"Same difference," she replied petulantly. "You left me with her."

"I tried to get custody of you, Trisha. You know that. I wanted you to come with me then, but I lost the case."

"Then you shouldn't have left!" Tears were welling up again.

"Oh, Trish..." Again, Nick reached out to her, and again Trisha tried to pull away, but he refused to let her escape. He pulled her into his arms and somewhere inside her, a dam broke. She shuddered from the force of her tears as he crooned to her. "I'm sorry, baby. I'm so sorry. I've looked back on the divorce a thousand times trying to figure out what I could have done differently to protect you—to shield you from all the pain you've had to suffer.... I don't have any answers, honey. And even if I did, it wouldn't change anything that's happened. I can't make the past go away—I can only try to make it better for you from now on. That's all I'm trying to do, honey. I'm just trying to love you and take care of you the best way I know how."

He eased her away from him a little and gingerly tilted her face toward his. "Trisha, do you honestly believe that I'm going to send you away someday?"

Trisha swallowed hard. "Yes."

Nick sighed. "Well, I'm not. I promise you that. And Crystal doesn't want me to send you away, either. She just wants to be your friend. You can either believe that and get on with your life, or spend the next few years being miserable, waiting around for something bad that's not going to happen. And until you decide, I'm just going to keep on loving you and trying to prove that you're safe with me—and always will be."

Trisha sniffed and swiped at her tears. She didn't answer, but Nick could tell that at least she was thinking about what he had said. It was a start. "Now, I want you to put your clothes and these suitcases away," he instructed her gently. "And then I want you to come out in the living room so we can talk. You and I have a lot of things that need to be straightened out between us. All right?"

Trish gave a quick little nod. "Is Crystal still here?" she asked tentatively.

Nick felt a painful ache in the vicinity of his heart. "No, honey. She's gone." For a moment he considered telling her that Crystal might be gone for good, but he changed his mind. He wasn't ready to face that possibility yet, and despite what Trisha had done, he didn't think his daughter was ready to face it, either.

Trying to ignore his fears about losing Crystal, he kissed his daughter on the forehead and moved toward the door. "I'll be waiting in the living room." He slipped into the hall, leaving his daughter alone.

Trisha sniffed again and looked around the room. Her lies had all caught up to her as she'd known they would, but her father wasn't shipping her back to Kentucky. Not this time, anyway. Trisha wasn't sure how she felt about that. She wanted to believe that he would never abandon her again, but she just couldn't allow herself to accept his promises.

And there was something else—something deeper that Trisha couldn't even begin to comprehend. In a way, she really *had* wanted her father to send her back. That was why she had started hanging around with Bobby and Lewis—why she had done the one thing she knew would make Nick furious at her. She didn't want to go back to her mother, and yet she did want to go back. Because of Crystal, and all the things she made Trisha feel.

Unable to make sense of her jumbled emotions, Trisha pushed them aside and began cleaning up the mess she'd made. As she folded a sweater and replaced it in the drawer, something told her that straightening her wardrobe was going to be the easy part.

TOO NUMB to cry anymore, Crystal paced the living-room floor. It had been nearly two hours since she had stormed out of Nick's apartment after dropping her little bombshell. Of all the things that had happened tonight, she regretted that the most. Even after the way he had treated her, he deserved better than the verbal slap in the face she had delivered.

Crystal wished desperately that she could claim she hadn't meant what she'd said, but the sad fact was she had meant it. She'd spent the past two days in emotional turmoil, trying to decide what to do about Clyde Chapman's offer. Part of her wanted to refuse the job, and part of her wanted to take it. She had decided that her only recourse was to discuss it with Nick and make a decision based on his reaction.

Trisha's lies had changed things, though. This was the second time Crystal had made a grave error in dealing with Nick's daughter. Logically she knew that it wasn't possible to avoid mistakes, but logic didn't change the way she felt. Becoming even more deeply involved with Nick meant taking on a responsibility she obviously wasn't capable of handling.

Trisha hated her. She'd only pretended to like her because she was afraid that Nick would send her back to Marjorie if she didn't get along with her daddy's girlfriend. Those blatant facts sickened Crystal because she realized that she had grown to love Nick's daughter. In so many ways, Trisha reminded Crystal of herself at that age. She understood her so well, yet she hadn't been able to reach her or to help her.

But that wasn't my job, Crystal reminded herself sternly. *She's Nick's child, not mine. And besides, I lived through Trisha's problems once myself. Why should I have to do it again?*

The vituperative thought brought Crystal up short. Was there festering inside her a hidden well of resentment toward the girl? Crystal wanted to run away from the notion, but she couldn't. She forced herself to face it head-on.

Trisha's presence had complicated her own relationship with Nick, there was no doubt about that. Crystal was seldom alone with him, and even their most intimate moments were sometimes colored by worries about Trisha. No plans could be made for a simple date without first considering how it would affect the girl. Most of the time, Crystal felt as though she were walking on eggshells, guarding what she said and did to be sure that it wouldn't affect Trisha adversely.

Do I resent that? Crystal asked herself, and was forced to admit that yes, she did. In some small way, she resented the complications Nick's daughter had brought into her life. But there was an even larger well of resentment, too. Trisha's shyness and her vulnerability were part of what made Crystal love her, but they were also constant reminders of her own dismal past—the one she had tried so hard to escape. In a very real sense, she hated Trisha for that.

That realization shocked Crystal. It was ugly and unkind. And it was also grossly unfair to Trisha. Just knowing that she was capable of feeling something so repulsive made Crystal ill. She had thought that she was a stronger, better, kinder human being than that. She wanted to run away from this new sense of self-awareness, but she didn't.

From her perch on the antlers above the mantel, Pippin swayed her head from side to side as she followed Crystal's agitated movements through the room. The little owl caught Crystal's eye, cocked her head, and blinked twice.

"You don't understand this, either, do you, Pippin? What am I going to do?"

The shrill ring of the telephone pierced the quiet house and made Crystal jump. Is it him? she wondered. She had half expected him to call, but she wasn't ready to talk to him yet—not until she figured a few things out for herself.

Certain that it was Nick, she let the phone ring as long as her conscience would allow it, then finally relented. "Hello?"

"Crystal?"

Nick's deep, thrilling voice only made the ache in Crystal's heart worse. "Yes, Nick."

"I was afraid you weren't going to answer the phone."

"I wasn't, but I started worrying that it might be Mom or Dan," she replied.

"I see." The deadness in her tone multiplied the fear Nick had been experiencing these past two hours. "We need to talk, Crystal. Not over the phone, though. Can you come into town? I don't feel right about leaving Trisha alone, but I have to see you."

"I'm sorry, Nick. I can't. I'm not ready to talk yet. There are too many things I have to figure out first."

"Like whether or not you're leaving Oak Ridge?" he asked more sharply than he intended. "Crystal, you can't drop something like that in my lap and then walk out—it's not fair. This is something that affects both of us."

"No, it doesn't, Nick. Not really. It's my life and I have to decide what's best for me."

"And what about me? Don't I count for anything?"

Crystal sank onto the sofa, trying not to cry. "You mean everything to me, Nick," she said softly. "That's the problem."

"Then let me talk to you, Crystal," he pleaded. "I am so sorry for the things I said. I was cruel and unfair, but it was only because I was so worried about Trisha. I've spent hours talking to her and I think I understand now why you didn't tell me about what happened Saturday. And she knows that you didn't break your promise to her. I'm sure you're feeling hurt and betrayed by both of us, but—"

"Nick, *please*, stop," she begged. "I'm not ready to hear this yet. I know you're sorry and I'm sure Trisha is, too."

"Then why won't you talk to me?"

"Because I need time to think! I've been expecting too much from you and from Trisha, and maybe even from myself, too. I have to figure out what I'm feeling before I can discuss it with you. Can you understand that?"

"No," he said quietly. "I can't understand it. I said things I need to apologize for, and Trisha said things that weren't even true. She doesn't hate you."

"That doesn't really matter, Nick."

Nick was astonished. "How can you say that doesn't matter? I know that you care about Trisha, and I know that you *love* me."

"Yes, I do, but—"

"Then talk to me! I need to see you, Crystal."

"I can't, Nick. I'm sorry if this sounds cruel, but right now what matters most is that I understand what's happening inside me. I'm confused. I'm frightened. But if I see you, you'll take me into your arms and I'll forget about everything else—but nothing will have been solved!''

"What has to be solved, Crystal?" he asked, confused. "We had an argument. People who love each other have them all the time. It was our first argument, but God knows, I don't want it to be our last. I love you, Crystal."

Twin tears slipped down her cheeks. "Then let me have some time to think, Nick. When I understand how I can love you so much, and still be so afraid of a relationship with you, then we'll talk, I promise."

"This is all about Trisha, isn't it?"

"No, it's about me, Nick," she insisted, but he didn't believe her. He suddenly felt as though he was about to lose the most precious thing in his life, but he realized it was pointless to argue any further.

"All right, Crystal. We'll talk tomorrow," he said finally. "But while you're doing this thinking, I want you to promise me that you won't forget how very much I love you."

Crystal folded one arm over her stomach to hold in the pain. "I won't forget, Nick. I couldn't even if I wanted to."

"Good." He paused. "May I ask you one last question?"

She hesitated. "What?"

"Do you remember what you said before you left tonight—about Trisha testing my love?"

"Yes."

"You were absolutely right, Crystal," he said. "But have you considered that maybe she was testing you, too? Think about it before you make a decision that could destroy us all."

Before she could formulate any kind of a response, the line went dead.

THE NEXT MORNING, Nick drove Trisha to the Mc-Phersons', where she'd been spending most of her summer days. Their father-daughter talk last night had been good for them both. Trisha's admission that she resented Nick for abandoning her to Marjorie had been the catalyst for a dialogue that was probably the most honest, meaningful one they'd ever had.

But despite his repeated assurances that he would never abandon her again, Nick knew in his heart that it was going to take more than words to convince Trisha that he would never send her away. Only time, patience, and love would give his daughter the peace of mind and security she needed. Fortunately he had an abundant supply of all three.

Crystal was another story, though. He had a heart full of love for her, and was willing to exercise all the patience in the world, but he was terribly afraid that she wasn't going to give him the time he needed to prove his love. Rich Patterson had told him that what Crystal wanted more than anything was to be a ranger in charge of her own forest district. Obviously Clyde Chapman had offered to make her dream come true. Now, Nick had to know where that left him.

After he dropped Trisha off at the McPhersons', he went straight to the Gatlin farm, intending to have the talk Crystal had promised him. But she wasn't there. Assuming she had gone to the station a little earlier than usual, he headed for the office, prepared to whisk her away to someplace private.

But she wasn't at the office, either. He told Mary Alice he wanted to see Crystal the moment she arrived, and then he waited impatiently, unable to concentrate on anything but the knot of fear in his chest.

At eight o'clock, she still hadn't shown up, and a few minutes after eight, Mary Alice stepped to his door to report that Crystal had just called in to say that she was going to be a few hours late. Nick called the farm, but there was no answer. He called the stable and Lonnie Macklin told him he hadn't seen Crystal since she'd driven away early that morning.

Not knowing where else to look for her, Nick settled in for an interminable morning of waiting.

AT 8:30, Crystal pulled her pickup into the McPhersons' driveway. She'd spent an agonizing night trying to decide what course she wanted her life to take, and her decision had brought her here...to Trisha.

With her heart pounding in her throat, she knocked on the door. Brandy's mother, a sweet-tempered dynamo with the patience of a saint, answered the summons. "Crystal! Come on in."

Crystal gave her a friendly smile. "Hi, Ida. Is Trisha here?"

"Oh, yeah. Nick brought her a little early this morning. I think she and Brandy are still out back feeding the chickens. Would you like to see her?"

"Actually I thought I might take her out for a little drive," she replied. "I'll have her back in an hour or so."

"Well...sure." Ida knew Nick wouldn't mind, but she was a little surprised that Crystal would take a day off from work to spend time with Trisha. Or maybe it wasn't surprising at all, Ida decided. She knew that Crystal was very fond of Nick's daughter, and she was positive that Trisha adored her father's girlfriend. "Are you playing hooky today?"

"Something like that," Crystal said with a forced smile. "I just thought Trisha and I needed some time alone for a little girl-talk."

"Well, come on. I'll walk you outside." Ida led the way through the house. "How was your conference in Little Rock?"

"Wonderful. It was a very valuable experience."

Ida shot her a curious, sidelong glance. "Are you okay, Crystal? You seem a little rough around the edges this morning."

"I'm fine," she assured her. "I just had a little trouble sleeping last night—I was keyed up from the trip, and all."

Ida didn't buy that excuse for a minute, but she didn't challenge it. She knew from experience that it was impossible to get Crystal to open up about her problems if she didn't want to discuss them. "I guess Nick told you how delighted I am to have Trisha here," she said, making casual conversation as they slipped through the kitchen door and out to the back porch. "Summers are always so boring for Brandy—her being an only child living so far out in the country. Having Trisha here has taken a big load off of me."

Crystal nodded. "I know how grateful Nick is that you offered to watch her. It's so hard to know what to do with kids Trisha's age—they're too old to put up with a babysitter, but not quite old enough to be left to their own devices."

"Exactly. And of course, it's going to be even more convenient when Nick buys your farm. I thought Brandy was going to jump out of her skin when Trisha told her she was going to be living just down the road."

Crystal stopped in her tracks on the porch steps. "What?"

Ida's face went blank, and then she frowned. "Crystal, I'm sorry. I was just positive you knew that Nick had made Dan an offer on the farm this week."

"No, I didn't know." Crystal felt as though she'd been punched in the stomach. Why on earth hadn't Nick told her about his plans? And why hadn't Dan told her? She smiled weakly to cover her shock. "I guess he wanted to surprise me."

"And I've ruined it," Ida said with a shake of her head. "I'm really sorry."

"Don't worry about it. I'm sure he was planning to tell me today." Crystal caught sight of Trisha as she and Brandy returned from the chicken coop, and she had no more time to assimilate the news. Speculating about what Nick had in mind was useless, anyway. This was just one more of the many things she'd have to discuss with him later—after her talk with Trisha.

The girls were laughing as they wandered across the lawn, but the moment Trisha looked up and saw Crystal, her laughter died. She stopped for a moment, trying to read the expression on Crystal's face, and then continued toward the house.

"Hi, Trish."

"Hi." She glanced down at her tennis shoes.

"I'd like you to go for a drive with me, Trish," Crystal said, her voice neither friendly nor harsh. "We need to talk."

Trisha nodded. "All right."

Crystal looked at Brandy and her mother. "I'll have her back in an hour or two." She moved off the steps and started across the lawn, with Trisha right behind her. Without exchanging another word, they climbed into the truck, and Crystal backed out of the driveway, then headed west on the winding country road.

A couple of minutes later, they passed the road to the Gatlin farm without even slowing, and Trisha finally risked looking at Crystal. "Where are we going?"

"We're going to a little town called Cotton."

"I've never heard of it."

"That's not surprising," Crystal said, keeping her voice neutral. "There's not much left there anymore. I guess it's what you might call...a ghost town." *My ghosts,* she added silently.

"Oh." Trisha didn't understand, and when Crystal didn't explain any further, she fell silent. They wound along back roads that she didn't recognize, but the scenery didn't interest her much. She was trying to think of the right words to say to Crystal. She knew she had to apologize, but she wasn't sure how to go about it, and Crystal's strange, quiet behavior certainly didn't help. Finally, though, the silence became too oppressive, and the words just popped out.

"I'm sorry, Crystal."

"I know you are, Trish."

That's it? Trisha thought. *No encouraging smile? No, "It's all right, honey"? No words of forgiveness?* "I shouldn't have said those awful things to you," she added.

"We all say things we shouldn't when we're angry," Crystal replied noncommittally.

"Daddy told me you didn't break your promise and tell him what happened Saturday night."

Crystal refused to look at the girl. "No, but I would have if Tony Manguson hadn't beaten me to it. You didn't keep your promise to me, so I had no reason to keep mine."

"You're mad about that, aren't you?" Trisha said in a tiny voice.

Whether the girl knew it or not, that pitiful little whine was designed to engender sympathy, but Crystal wasn't ready to give that to her yet. They had a lot of hard, straight talking to do first. "No, Trisha. I'm mad because you lied to me. Saturday wasn't the first time you'd been with the Whipley boys, and it wasn't the last, obviously. You looked me straight in the eye and told a bald-faced lie, and then you had the nerve to give me a big hug and tell me how 'neat' I am.''

Trisha cringed and fought back tears. ''I'm sorry. Really.''

Crystal shook her head. ''Sorry isn't enough. We have some problems, Trish. Big ones. Last night, you accused me of wanting to get rid of you so that I could have Nick all to myself.''

''I didn't mean that!'' she cried. ''I swear I didn't.''

''Yes, you did,'' Crystal argued. ''You may not want to believe it, but that's one of the things you're afraid of. And there are a lot of other things you're afraid of, too, aren't there?''

''No!''

''Oh, yes there are,'' she shot back, pulling the pickup onto the side of the road in front of a collection of ramshackle houses. Slipping the gearshift into park, she turned on the seat and faced her. ''And we're going to talk about them, Trish. You and I are going to stop pussyfooting around and pretending that we like each other just because we both want to please your father.''

Trisha was so mortified and hurt, she could barely speak. ''You . . . you were just pretending to like me?''

For the first time, Crystal softened her voice to a gentle, caressing tone. ''No, Trish. I never had to pretend to like you. You're sweet and smart.... But you also remind me a little too much of myself when I was your age.''

''Because I'm so tall?'' she asked tentatively.

Crystal smiled sadly. ''No. Because we were both raised by alcoholic parents.''

''Oh.'' Trisha turned her head and looked out the window. It finally dawned on her that there were houses around them, and she looked the horrible, dilapidated structures over curiously. "Is this Cotton?" she asked. Anything was better than talking about her mother's drinking problem, and that seemed to be where Crystal was headed.

Crystal looked around, too, suppressing a shudder. How many years had it been since she'd been back here? Ten, at least. And probably closer to fifteen. "Yes, Trisha. This is Cotton."

The girl crinkled her nose in distaste. "It's awful. Do people live in these houses?"

Crystal glanced down the row of shacks, taking in the broken, boarded windows...the tiny, lopsided porches...the yards filled with junk...the stench of poverty. Even after all these years, nothing had changed much. "I'm afraid so."

"If people live here, why did you call it a ghost town?"

"Because that's how I think of it."

Trisha ventured a look at her. "Why?"

Crystal captured her gaze and held it. "Because this is where I grew up. You see that house there—" she pointed "—the one with the rusty tricycle in the yard? That's the house I lived in with my brother and my father."

Trisha could hardly comprehend what she was being told. "But it's so small, and so...so..." She left the thought incomplete, and Crystal didn't help her find the word she was looking for; no mere words could communicate the horror that house represented.

Putting the truck in gear, Crystal left her old "neighborhood" behind. She turned once, then twice, moving past one or two houses that were in considerably better shape, and finally arrived in "downtown" Cotton. Most of the stores were boarded and vacant, but there were still a few shops whose existence was supported by Cotton's only industry—the gin mill that sat on the edge of town.

There was a small grocery and the Feed and Seed Store; an old-fashioned variety store, and a greasy-spoon café . . . and of course, Verna's Tavern was still there, exactly where it had always sat. . . .

"That's where my daddy used to go to get drunk, Trisha," Crystal told the girl bluntly and watched her eyes grow as round as saucers. "He stopped there every day on his way home from the gin mill where he sometimes worked. He would drink until he was too drunk to drink anymore, and then he'd come home. My brother and I would wait, cowering in that little house I showed you. We never talked about it, but we'd look at each other and wonder whether or not Daddy would come home and yell at us or if he'd be so drunk that he'd forget we were there and stumble off to bed. We'd cry ourselves to sleep, and pray that he'd stop drinking so that we could be a real family.

"That was our dream," she continued, fighting the tearful memories. "We wanted to have a family like our friends at school had. We wanted a father who noticed us. We wanted to be more important to him than his next drink of whiskey. . . . But we never were."

Crystal saw the unshed tears that were pooling in Trisha's eyes. "Does that sound familiar to you, honey?" she asked softly.

Trisha was fighting her tears so hard that she could barely breathe. "I wanna . . . go home now," she said in a choked voice.

"Not until we talk about your mother, Trisha," Crystal replied, swallowing the knot of emotion in her own throat. "We've spent the past few months pretending that she doesn't exist. We've been playing like everything is wonderful, but it's not. I understand so much about how you feel, but I've been walking on eggshells around you because I was afraid of making a mistake. I didn't want to upset you. I didn't want to risk making you mad at me, or making you not like me.''

The dam holding Trisha's tears back finally broke. "I do like you, Crystal,'' she sobbed.

"I'm so glad,'' Crystal said, pulling the girl into her arms as she'd yearned to do since the moment she'd seen her this morning. Trisha clung to her, and Crystal rubbed her back comfortingly. "But you feel very guilty about liking me, don't you?'' she whispered.

Sobs racked Trisha's body. How had Crystal known her secret—the one she could barely even admit to herself? How had she known that every day Crystal seemed more wonderful, which only made the feeling that she was betraying her mother grow worse and worse?

"That's why you've been lying to your dad, isn't it, Trisha?'' Crystal went on. "You deliberately tried to make him angry so that he'd send you back to Marjorie because you feel so disloyal to your mother.''

"How...how did you know?'' Trisha asked with a hiccuping sob.

"Because I did the same thing when I first went to live with the Gatlins,'' she replied, resting her cheek on Trisha's head as she continued to stroke her hair. "Dan Gatlin was everything I'd ever wanted my own father to be, but when I started to care about him I felt like I was betraying my own dad. But you don't have to feel that way, Trisha. Being friends with me doesn't mean that you have to stop loving your mother.''

Trisha emitted a hoarse, strangled cry. "Why can't my mom be like you?'' she cried, venting her anger and pain in unrestrained tears. "Why, Crystal? Why?''

"Oh, baby... Your mom is sick.'' Tears were streaming down Crystal's face, too, but she made no effort to dry them. Her arms were holding Marjorie Hanford's daughter close, and whatever it took, she was determined to give this child back the things her mother had stolen from her. "I'd like to help you understand her sickness, honey. I'd like to help you forgive her, and be happy with yourself and your dad...and me. But if that's going to happen, Trish, we've got to stop playing games and start being honest. We've gotta start trusting each other, honey. Really trusting."

Crystal pulled away a little and brushed at the wispy auburn hairs plastered to Trisha's face. "That's why I brought you to Cotton, Trisha. What I showed you today I haven't even shown your daddy, because I can't bear thinking about what growing up in that house was like. I don't want people to know that I lived like that. I was so ashamed of that house that I couldn't even go back there to help my brother collect my dad's things after he died. Cotton is my secret, Trisha, but I showed it to you because someday I hope that you'll be able to share your secrets with me."

Trisha looked up at Crystal for a long time, studying her face and trying to comprehend the enormity of the gift her father's girlfriend had given her. Finally she nodded and returned her head to Crystal's shoulder. "Can I tell you a secret now?" she asked quietly.

"Of course, sweetheart."

"I love you," she said with a little hiccuping sob.

Crystal stroked her hair. "I love you, too."

NICK PARKED HIS CAR at the Indian Lake Marina and walked down the road to the dirt path that led to the outcropping of rocks where he and Crystal had once sat by the lake and contemplated making love. Her call to him twenty minutes ago had been very brief.

"As soon as you can get away from the office," she had said, "meet me at Indian Lake." She hadn't needed to tell him where she would be waiting.

He'd left the station immediately. The forest wasn't going to burn down if he took a few hours off from work, but if he didn't talk to Crystal soon, Nick was afraid that he might self-destruct.

A steady plop, plop, plop, greeted him as he rounded the bend, and he saw Crystal standing at the water's edge, skipping stones on the tranquil lake. There were sailboats and small pleasure boats on the water today, and the sounds of happy vacationers drifted on the gentle breeze. This spot, though, seemed secluded from the world.

Nick approached Crystal cautiously. He sensed that she knew he was there, but when she didn't acknowledge him, he stopped and waited, watching her, burning the sight of her into his memory.

"I saw Trisha this morning, Nick," she said without preamble. "We went for a drive and had a long talk."

Was that a good sign or a bad one? he wondered. "Did she apologize?"

Crystal smiled wistfully. "Yes."

He moved closer, joining her on the smooth rock ledge. "Are you going to let me apologize?" he asked softly.

"You already did. Last night." Crystal stepped away from the water and sat. Nick joined her without an invitation. "You were right about Trisha, Nick. What you said about her testing me ... It made me realize a lot of things I hadn't understood before."

"Such as?" he prompted, aching to hold her, but knowing it would be wrong to try. She still hadn't even looked at him yet.

"I've always been afraid of wanting too much, Nick. I guess I'm a little cynical of the way life makes you promises and then snatches away what you want most. That's why I've been so terrified of losing you."

"You're not going to lose me, Crystal."

She glanced at him, then her gaze skittered away. "You can't guarantee that, Nick."

He stared out over the lake for a moment. "There's an element of risk in loving anyone."

"I know. And part of me knows you're worth that risk."

"But the other part . . ."

"Is afraid," she confessed. "I've never once allowed myself to truly believe that you and I could have a future together."

"Crystal, look at me," Nick urged her, gently touching her face to turn it toward his. "I would gladly spend the rest of my life proving you're wrong."

She gave him a gentle, wistful smile. "I know that, Nick. Sometime late last night, I allowed myself to believe. For the first time. It was the most frightening experience of my life, but this morning I still believed it. That's why I had to talk to Trisha. I knew that you would be bringing her out to the McPhersons', and that you'd probably stop by the farm to see me, so I left early. I had to see her first, before I could explain any of this to you."

The knot of fear around Nick's heart began unraveling the moment Crystal had said she could believe in the future. She couldn't have come to that realization and also decided to run away. Or could she have? "Why did you need to see Trisha first?"

"Because I've been scared of your daughter, Nick. I was so much in love with you that I was terrified of making a mistake, saying the wrong thing. . . . I built my relationship with her solely on the need to prove to you that she and I could get along. I was hoping that if Trisha and I could be pals, you would see that it was possible for you and me to have a relationship."

"What's wrong with that?"

"Nothing, except that I forgot about what Trisha needed. I was conscious of her pain and the problems she was hiding, but I was afraid of trying to help her."

"I didn't fall in love with you so that you could be my daughter's therapist, Crystal."

"I know that. But if we're ever going to have a real chance for happiness—as a family—Trisha and I have to forge our own relationship. We have to learn to love each other because of who and what we are, not just because we're both desperate to please you."

"Is that what you've been doing?"

Crystal looked away from him and skimmed another rock across the lake. "Until today," she replied. "Today we left the surface and finally touched each other where it counts. I think Trisha and I are going to be okay, Nick."

The last of his fear vanished, leaving sweet hope and love. "Does that mean you've decided not to accept the job in Tennessee?"

"I'd like to ask you a question before I answer that," she replied, finally turning to face him. "When were you going to tell me that you'd made Dan an offer on the farm?"

Nick didn't care how she had learned that secret. The only thing that mattered was the love he saw shining in her eyes. "I was going to tell you this weekend," he answered, brushing the back of his hand across her cheek. "It was intended as part of a surprise package. I was going to take you up to Silver Springs, tell you I was buying the farm . . . and ask you to marry me."

Crystal took a deep, involuntary breath as her heart expanded with love. "Ask me now, Nick," she pleaded softly as one tear slipped down her cheek.

"Oh, Crystal," he murmured, dragging her into his arms. "Marry me, please. I love you so much."

She laid her head on his shoulder and reveled in the joy of being loved. "I won't ever stop being afraid of losing you, Nick. Sometimes I'll get scared of our dreams...." She raised her head and touched his face lovingly. "But I won't ever stop loving you. Is that enough to see us through whatever life throws at us?"

Gently, very gently, Nick dried her tears with his lips. "It's all I'll ever need, my love. Say yes."

"Yes," she murmured, losing herself in his dark, loving eyes.

"Say... I believe," he urged tenderly.

"I believe," she said without hesitation or fear in a strong, clear voice that carried across the lake to anyone who cared to listen.

Harlequin romances are now available in stores at these convenient times each month.

Harlequin Presents
Harlequin American Romance
Harlequin Historical
Harlequin Intrigue

These series will be in stores on the 4th of every month.

Harlequin Romance
Harlequin Temptation
Harlequin Superromance
Harlequin Regency Romance

New titles for these series will be in stores on the 16th of every month.

We hope this new schedule is convenient for you. With only two trips each month to your local bookseller, you will always be sure not to miss any of your favorite authors!

Happy reading!

Please note there may be slight variations in on-sale dates in your area due to differences in shipping and handling.

HARLEQUIN'S "BIG WIN"
SWEEPSTAKES RULES & REGULATIONS
NO PURCHASE NECESSARY TO ENTER OR RECEIVE A PRIZE

1. To enter and join the Reader Service, scratch off the metallic strips on all your BIG WIN tickets #1-#6. This will reveal the values for each sweepstakes entry number, the number of free book(s) you will receive and your free bonus gift as part of our Reader Service. If you do not wish to take advantage of our Reader Service but wish to enter the Sweepstakes only, scratch off the metallic strips on your BIG WIN tickets #1-#4. Return your entire sheet of tickets intact. Incomplete and/or inaccurate entries are ineligible for that section or sections of prizes. Not responsible for mutilated or unreadable entries or inadvertent printing errors. Mechanically reproduced entries are null and void.

2. Whether you take advantage of this offer or not, your Sweepstakes numbers will be compared against the list of winning numbers generated at random by the computer. In the event that all prizes are not claimed by March 31, 1992, a random drawing will be held from all qualified entries received from March 30, 1990 to March 31, 1992, to award all unclaimed prizes. All cash prizes (Grand to Sixth) will be mailed to the winners and are payable by check in U.S. funds. Seventh prize will be shipped to winners via third-class mail. These prizes are in addition to any free, surprise or mystery gifts that might be offered. Versions of this sweepstakes with different prizes of approximate equal value may appear at retail outlets or in other mailings by Torstar Corp. and its affiliates.

3. The following prizes are awarded in this sweepstakes: ★ Grand Prize (1) $1,000,000; First Prize (1) $25,000; Second Prize (1) $10,000; Third Prize (5) $5,000; Fourth Prize (10) $1,000; Fifth Prize (100) $250; Sixth Prize (2,500) $10; ★ ★ Seventh Prize (6,000) $12.95 ARV.

   ★ This presentation offers a Grand Prize of a $1,000,000 annuity. Winner will receive $33,333.33 a year for 30 years until interest totalling $1,000,000.

   ★ ★ Seventh Prize: A fully illustrated hardcover book published by Torstar Corp. Approximate retail value of the book is $12.95.

   Entrants may cancel the Reader Service at anytime without cost or obligation to buy (see details in center insert card).

4. This Sweepstakes is being conducted under the supervision of an independent judging organization. By entering this Sweepstakes, each entrant accepts and agrees to be bound by these rules and the decisions of the judges, which shall be final and binding. Odds of winning in the random drawing are dependent upon the total number of entries received. Taxes, if any, are the sole responsibility of the winners. Prizes are nontransferable. All entries must be received at the address printed on the reply card and must be postmarked no later than 12:00 MIDNIGHT on March 31, 1992. The drawing for all unclaimed sweepstakes prizes will take place May 30, 1992, at 12:00 NOON, at the offices of Marden-Kane, Inc., Lake Success, New York.

5. This offer is open to residents of the U.S., the United Kingdom, France and Canada, 18 years or older, except employees and their immediate family members of Torstar Corp., its affiliates, subsidiaries, and all other agencies and persons connected with the use, marketing or conduct of this sweepstakes. All Federal, State, Provincial and local laws apply. Void wherever prohibited or restricted by law. Any litigation within the Province of Quebec respecting the conduct and awarding of a prize in this publicity contest must be submitted to the Régie des loteries et courses du Québec.

6. Winners will be notified by mail and may be required to execute an affidavit of eligibility and release, which must be returned within 14 days after notification or an alternative winner will be selected. Canadian winners will be required to correctly answer an arithmetical skill-testing question administered by mail, which must be returned within a limited time. Winners consent to the use of their names, photographs and/or likenesses for advertising and publicity in conjunction with this and similar promotions without additional compensation. For a list of major winners, send a stamped, self-addressed envelope to: WINNERS LIST, c/o Harlequin Reader Service, 3010 Walden Ave., P.O. Box 1396, Buffalo, NY 14269-1396. Winners Lists will be fulfilled after the May 30, 1992 drawing date.

If Sweepstakes entry form is missing, please print your name and address on a 3" × 5" piece of plain paper and send to:

In the U.S.
Harlequin's "BIG WIN" Sweepstakes
3010 Walden Ave.
P.O. Box 1867
Buffalo, NY 14269-1867

In Canada
Harlequin's "BIG WIN" Sweepstakes
P.O. Box 609
Fort Erie, Ontario
L2A 5X3

Offer limited to one per household.
© 1991 Harlequin Enterprises Limited   Printed in the U.S.A.

LTY-H191R

Take 4 bestselling love stories FREE

Plus get a FREE surprise gift!